Tutoring THE PLAYER

CAMPUS Wallflowers

BOOK ONE

USA TODAY BESTSELLING AUTHOR

REBECCA JENSHAK

Rebecca Jenshak
www.rebeccajenshak.com

Cover Design by Lori Jackson Designs
Editing by Edits in Blue and My Brother's Editor
Proofreading by Sarah at All Encompassing Books

Tutoring THE PLAYER

For all the quiet girls.

I hear you.

Prologue

Daisy

"Would you come down from there?" Violet yells up from the ground. My cousin isn't the biggest fan of heights or rickety ladders. "You're going to catch pneumonia or an airborne STD."

"They won the game," I say with a quick glance down at her.

She's standing on the lowest rung, neck craning up to see over the fence into our neighbor's yard. "Who cares? Win, lose, they party just the same."

She might talk like she's immune to the fun next door, but I've caught her wistfully staring out her bedroom window a time or two in that direction.

"They look so happy."

From my spot in this old tree house, I have a perfect view of the backyard next door. A small group of girls dance in the grass to a catchy, upbeat song. In another area, guys huddle together playing cornhole. Others are in the heated pool, splashing and playing. Everyone else is hanging out on the large patio that spans the back of the sprawling house.

The alcohol is flowing, and the atmosphere is so happy and light that the air even feels different this close.

"The night is young, and they're buzzed. Of course, they're happy." Vi's tone is all indifference. "Give it a few hours, and people will be so drunk the happiness will dim."

She's wrong. At least once a week, I sit up here watching them drink and laugh, and I can attest that they leave as happy as they came.

"Come on," she whines. "You promised we'd finish *Pride and Prejudice* tonight."

I smother a groan but do remember agreeing to that plan before I realized there was a party happening next door. I'm not even cool enough to know about parties, let alone be invited.

"Five more minutes."

"Fine. I'll make popcorn." Her voice moves away from the tree house. "If you aren't inside when I hit play, you're on trash duty for the rest of the month."

"Yeah, yeah. I'll be there." The wind blows my hair around my face. I untie the flannel shirt from my waist and slip it on, then hug my knees to my chest and drop my chin to rest on my arm.

Three months ago, I moved in next door to the hottest party spot at college with Violet and two other friends, Jane and Dahlia.

The White House, as it's called, is aptly named, not only because of its size and color but because the epic parties thrown here are the college version of being asked to dine with dignitaries or royalty. Or, I'm guessing, since the closest I've come to attending a party there is watching from my favorite nook on the other side of the property line.

The starting lineup for the university's men's basketball team lives next door, but it's an all-inclusive place to be for the elite population on campus—members of Greek life, jocks of the top sports, stunningly gorgeous girls, and *him*.

Liam Price—hockey player, junior, engineering major.

We have a physics class together this semester, so I know the tilt of his shoulders as he leans back in his seat, the way he chews on the end of his pen when he's thinking, and that his friends sometimes call him Dreamboat as a way to tease him about his neatly styled blond hair and preppy clothes.

Tonight he's sitting with his teammates on the side of the patio closest to me. The guys he's with are drinking one cup of foamy beer after another, but not Liam. Like many other nights I've watched him, he holds a water bottle in one hand. He laughs and talks along with his buddies, but as they get drunk and loud, his calm and put-together presence never wavers.

My pulse races as a pretty girl approaches his circle of friends. The way she waltzes up to a group of guys with such confidence and ease is truly inspiring. He unfolds his tall frame, offering his seat to the newcomer. She smiles and places a hand on his forearm, then gushes something I can't hear over the party noise before taking his chair.

Did I mention he's a gentleman?

He drains the rest of his water and looks around the party. Sometimes I think he doesn't feel like he fits in either. Still, he's on that side of the fence.

My breath hitches when his gaze lifts to the tree house across the property line, but as soon as I think he's seen me, his stare continues on.

Invisibility is my superpower. Except I can't turn it off. For three months, he's looked in my direction without seeing me.

"Daisy!" Violet yells from the back door. I'd take the trash out every month until the end of time if I thought sitting up here and studying my popular peers would get me any closer to being one of them.

With a sigh, I take one last longing look at everything I'm

missing out on and then start down the ladder. My Saturday night plans include watching Colin Firth as Mr. Darcy for at least the third time this semester. Violet has a thing for Austen, and I have a thing for romance and optimism, so I don't mind so much. I prefer the Matthew Macfadyen version, though.

Before I moved next door, I might have even been excited to quote our favorite lines and swoon as Darcy falls for Elizabeth. Back then, it was easy to write off these parties like I wasn't missing anything, but now...

Now, as I enter the quaint and quiet stone house practically hidden next to the massive one next door, I wonder, what would it take for a campus wallflower to climb the fence and be seen?

Chapter ONE

Daisy

"I'M LATE," DAHLIA CALLS AS SHE HURRIES DOWN THE stairs with an apple in one hand and her golf bag slung over her shoulder. She puts the apple in her mouth to wave and then flings open the door. A breeze flows through the living room as she slams the door behind her and jogs across the street, joining more student athletes on their way to practice.

Our house is only a few blocks from campus, nestled between dorms on the southside and Ray Fieldhouse and the rest of the athletic facilities.

Weekday afternoons are the best for people watching.

"I haven't seen any baseball players in their cute pants," Violet says, looking over my shoulder.

"They have a day off. I heard a guy in class talking about it." Jane flips through a Cosmopolitan magazine on the couch. She looks up from the page and pulls back the curtain giving us a better view.

Basketball players jog the street, football players are heading in for weight training in cut-off T-shirts, and if I squint, I can just make out the empty baseball diamond in the distance. The hockey arena is two blocks west and out of view, but I like to picture Liam at practice in all that padding, flashing that big, bright smile underneath his helmet.

The prick of a needle on my shoulder makes me jump.

"Hold still. I'm almost done." Only Violet could sound annoyed and sympathetic at the same time.

As instructed, I stand perfectly still while she uses me as a model for her latest creation. The material falls to the floor with a small train. The bodice is a black corset that squeezes my ribs and pushes up my small boobs to an impressive, gravity-defying height. Soft, see-through lace covers my shoulders and arms, and clasps at my neck with a vintage brooch. The cropped blouse does nothing to cover my cleavage, but I'm certain that's the point.

The dress is Victorian Gothic with a sexy edge. Very Violet. She's studying fashion design, and her affinity for all things historical comes through loud and clear with everything she creates.

Violet places a pair of stilettos in front of me and then sits to do the bottom hem.

"Wouldn't it be better if you pinned it with me flat footed? That way you'll be able to wear two or three-inch heels, no problem." My cousin is a good two inches shorter than me and has a propensity for heels, whereas I prefer to keep both feet firmly planted on the ground.

She shakes her head, black hair swishing around her shoulders with the small movement. I step awkwardly into Violet's hot pink stilettos. Her feet are a half-size smaller and pinch my toes. It's a good thing the only thing I need to do in these is stand.

Violet removes a pin from the cushion around her wrist and secures the fabric at the top of my foot. I force myself not to fidget. We've been at this for the better part of an hour, and Violet isn't much company as she works. She is deep in concentration, and any words she speaks as she makes her way around me, pinning the material in place, are to instruct me or comment on the people outside. And Jane spends her entire break between classes reading through the dozen of magazines she subscribes to—physical and digital.

"Okay." Violet stands and does another circle around me. "What do you think?"

"It's gorgeous, as always. What's it for?" I step out of the heels, thankful to feel my toes again.

When Violet grins, her entire face lights up with excitement. "It's for the Wallflower Ball in January."

My shock of her creating another dress for the event (this would be number three she's designed and made for the ball) is temporarily blinded by her nickname for the masquerade party she's putting together. "Can we stop calling it that?"

In a flash, her smile falls into an annoyed frown. "Wallflowers are awesome. Own it."

Oh, I'm owning it. Not like I have a choice. That's one of many differences between Violet and me. She's friendly and outgoing. People are always quick to like her. She did the dance team in high school and, she'd kill me for telling anyone, was even the homecoming queen. Two months into our freshman year at Valley, she just gave it all up and decided she was over partying and hanging with vapid, self-loathing assholes. Those are definitely words straight from her mouth.

"What's wrong with the last two you made for the ball?" I smooth my hand down the lace skirt. I can't get over how soft it feels.

"Nothing. This one is for you." Her smile is locked back in place. She pulls out her phone and snaps a picture of me, all while I still process her words.

"I can't wear this."

"You can." She moves to stand beside me and holds out the screen of her phone to show me the photo she took. "It's perfect."

The dress *is* perfect. I hardly recognize myself from the neck down. I'm far more comfortable in my own clothes, not because I don't love this but because it's far too beautiful for me.

I glance at my stunning cousin. Our fathers are brothers, but our personalities are as different as the way we look. My hair is the color of wet sand, and my blue eyes are nothing special. I'm average height and just... well, average. Violet, on the other hand, inherited her mother's Korean genes. Her long hair is a soft black, and her eyes are a dark brown that lighten when she laughs.

I love my cousin, but she doesn't always understand what it's like to be the shy, quiet girl.

"Do you not like it?" Uncertainty tugs her brows down as she searches my face. Sometimes I forget that Violet has insecurities. It doesn't make any sense to me because she's so good at everything she does.

"Are you kidding me? I feel like a harlot."

She still stares at me with big, unsure eyes.

"That was a compliment. I've never felt more beautiful, Vi. I'm just not sure it's me."

"You could be a harlot. You'd just have to speak to your crushes instead of watching them from the tree house." This from Jane, who puts the magazine down and comes to stand in front of me. "You look beautiful, Daisy."

I appreciate their confidence in me, however unfounded. I have a pretty good idea of how it'd go if I actually spoke to Liam, and it doesn't end up with me wearing this dress on a date where he pulls me into the corner and ravishes me because he just can't wait another minute to have me. The dress is good. It isn't *that* good.

Violet's lips pull up at the corners, and she squeezes me from the side. "It's going to be great this year." She moves to unzip me. "Did I tell you that I was able to book the big ballroom in the Moreno building? And Jane's parents donated tablecloths and these gorgeous candle centerpieces." She looks at our roommate. "Thanks again for that."

"No problem." Jane sits back on the couch and picks up her magazine.

"Wow. That's quite a step up from last year's little shindig in the dorm lounge." We had flat soda in Solo cups, and the lighting was fluorescent.

Violet first had the idea for a masquerade ball when we were living in the dorms last year. Her roommate was off to some sorority formal, and we were both pining over how there weren't big social events for people like us who didn't rush Greek life or date guys popular enough to be invited to them. So, we organized one, or Violet did.

"Yes, it's gotten a little out of hand." She shrugs through an excited smile that tells me it's going to be way, way over the top.

"How can I help?" I ask.

"Could you take care of the flowers? The florist up the street already has us on her schedule, but I need to give her specifics."

"Flowers?"

"Yes, flowers." She cuts me a look. "It's the *Wallflower* Ball."

A groan slips past my lips. "You really have to stop calling it that."

"I'll text you all the details. Are you sure you can do it? The whole concept revolves around the flowers. They're doing an arch and..." She trails off when it's clear I'm only half-listening. "Don't forget."

"I will go this week."

"Thank you."

She takes the dress from me, and I pull on my far-less-stylish one and boots.

"I'm off to class." My pulse jumps because I'm going to see Liam in fifteen minutes.

My roommates grin. They know how much I look forward to this class twice a week.

"Say hi to Liam for us," Jane teases.

Not likely.

Chapter TWO

Daisy

OUR PHYSICS PROFESSOR IS A SHORT, BALD MAN WITH a booming voice and a quick smile. He spends the two-hour lab pacing the front of the room and trying with all his might to get us pumped about our work. He's great. Friendly, a little quirky, and a whole lot animated. He teaches with his whole body, hands waving wildly as he gives us instructions for today's assignment.

But despite his best efforts, my attention is pulled to the guy sitting at the table in front of me. Today Liam wears a black polo shirt with jeans. His blond hair is covered by a matching black baseball cap. Even when he's casual, he's put together. He leans on his left elbow, pen poised against his full lips, giving our boisterous professor his entire focus.

He's a direct contradiction to the guy next to him. Jordan Thatcher's messy black hair curls around a backward hat that says

I heart MILFs. His shirt is wrinkled, and his socks don't match. He's handsome if you don't mind that *I just finished practice and couldn't be bothered to find clean clothes* look.

Liam and Jordan are teammates, but they're so different I don't understand how they're friends off the ice. While Liam is known for being a good guy, Jordan's reputation is less pristine. If there's a party, he's there. Girls love his carefree, party-hard attitude. I find it… daunting. Sure, I'd love to care a little less and break out of my shell, but Jordan doesn't seem like he cares about anything.

His head is bowed over his desk, and he scribbles furiously like he's taking down every word Professor Green says. Except even from my table behind him, I can see what he's really doing is coloring in the block letters of the notebook brand on the front.

When the professor has finished and given us the go-ahead to start, I sigh and glance at the empty chair next to me. It's the third week in a row that my lab partner has been a no-show. She's either dropped or on her way to failing.

I read through the instructions that I partially missed while staring at Liam. He and Jordan always walk in at the last second, so it really isn't my fault that I need the first few minutes of class to scope him out.

I pull my hair back into a ponytail as Liam stands in front of his stool. He's tall, and his broad shoulders pull the fabric of his shirt as he leans over to scribble something on a piece of paper. His partner is less enthusiastic, sitting and watching as Liam gets them started.

Blowing out a breath, I drop my gaze back to my own desk. I like physics, but this is going to be a lot to get through on my own.

"Miss Johnson." Professor Green approaches my table as I'm re-reading the first steps of the lab. He clicks his tongue, hand on his hip as he looks at the empty space beside me. "Your partner is missing again."

I offer an awkward smile.

"These labs are really meant for two." He opens his stance and stares down his nose at the classroom. My pulse thrums quickly as he weighs his options. Every other table is paired up. It'll be just my luck that he'll decide to be my partner or stick me with a group that ignores me and continues in their happy twosome. I hate this kind of attention. It's like walking into a room full of people or being called on in class. My skin itches and I twist my hands in front of me.

It feels like everyone is avoiding looking up from their table because they know Professor Green is searching for somewhere to place me. It's irrational. I know this. Most of them probably don't even realize what's happening. It isn't like they notice me any other time, so why would now be different? Still, I hate the thought of being added to a group that doesn't want me.

"Let's put you with Mr. Price and Mr. Thatcher."

My heart drops into my stomach. Frozen, I don't speak or move while Professor Green steps closer to Liam and Jordan with a pleased smile at his problem-solving.

"Miss Johnson will be joining you until her partner returns," he tells them.

To my horror, Liam looks around, completely clueless about who Miss Johnson is.

It's me, you idiot, I scream in my head, then silently apologize because it isn't his fault I've never once worked up the courage to speak to him. Actually, that isn't true. Once, I sneezed, and he said, "Bless You," and I thanked him.

Jordan and Liam finally locate the only unpartnered person in the class. Liam's eyes widen in an observing sort of way as he stares at me. He lifts a hand in a polite wave. Jordan scoots his stool over with a loud screech against the tile floor.

I scoop up my belongings, and on rubber legs, I move the eight feet from my table to theirs.

"Hi, I'm Liam." He moves into the middle spot behind the table and offers me his chair. "This is Jordan."

He leans back slightly so I can see Jordan on the other side of him.

I nod to each of them.

"I didn't catch your first name," Liam says. "Unless you want us to call you Miss Johnson."

"Dai-sy." My voice shakes on both syllables.

His smile sets free a thousand butterflies inside of me. This close, he seems so much taller.

"Cool. Nice to meet you, Daisy. We were just about to trace the rays of the concave lens. Do you want to do the honors?"

Jordan snorts. "Honors?"

Liam ignores him and flips on the light on the projector. Rays of light stretch out onto the paper. I'm still partially frozen.

"Need a pencil?" He lifts his from the top of his notebook, and because I'm not sure where mine is at the moment, I accept it.

My hand shakes as I trace along the rays with a ruler. I'm embarrassed to admit how his presence a mere foot away from me has me unsteady on my feet and struggling to make air flow through my lungs.

The daisy charm on my necklace swings forward as I crouch over the table. Liam drums his thumbs absently on the table.

"There," I say when I'm done.

I finally get a deep breath that clears some of my nerves, but then I get a big inhale of his faint cologne, and my chest tightens. He even smells perfect.

Liam looks to Jordan. "What's next?"

Jordan stays sitting on his stool while Liam and I finish marking the paper. Every step, Liam checks with him, and then the two of us complete it. I can tell it's how they always do things, and it doesn't surprise me that Liam has been doing the brunt of the work.

While Liam reads through the next step in our assignment, I take the opportunity to stare at him up close. His brows tug together in concentration, and the tip of his tongue pushes between his teeth. He has great bone structure, high cheekbones, and a long, straight nose. He's clean-shaven, and his skin has warm undertones that make his blond hair and blue eyes contrast nicely.

I feel Jordan's gaze on me. When I meet his dark stare, a humored smile curves his lips. Blushing at being caught checking out his friend, I fidget with my necklace and look around at the other tables while Liam finishes.

"So, Daisy." Liam's voice brings me back. "What's your major?"

"Physics," I say automatically in the practiced response I've honed, and then I add, "and art. Physics and art."

A slow smile lifts the corners of his mouth. His forehead crinkles as his brows raise in surprise. "Double major?"

I wet my lips and nod. A few seconds pass before I realize the polite thing to do is ask him the same question back, even if I already know the answer.

"What about you?"

"Civil engineering." He pokes his pencil toward Jordan. "Both of us."

I refuse to look at Jordan again, but I aim a smile between them.

After thirty minutes, my anxiety finally abates enough that I find my voice.

"You play hockey, right?"

"Yeah." Liam beams at me. "How'd you know."

I point to Jordan's Valley U hockey T-shirt.

"Right. Have you been to a game?"

"No," I admit, now wishing I hadn't brought it up.

"What? Never? What year are you?"

"Sophomore."

He shakes his head and shoots me a playful smile. "You're missing out. We're pretty good."

He's being modest. They won the Frozen Four two years ago, and last year got pretty close to going back to the national tournament.

Jordan, who's stayed quiet except for reading instructions, speaks up, "Don't bother, man. It doesn't really seem like her kind of thing."

He does a quick and dismissive once-over of my dress and boots. At five foot four, I'm slightly shorter than average, and my small bone structure makes me look younger and smaller than I am. I probably won't be strapping on pads anytime soon, but violence in of itself doesn't bother me. Though admittedly, I don't completely understand why anyone thought it was a good idea to put a bunch of guys on ice skates and give them sticks and permission to ram into one another.

"It is," I protest.

"Yeah?" Jordan grins. "My mistake. Who is your favorite hockey player?"

My cheeks heat with embarrassment.

"Home games are the best," Liam ignores him, leaning forward and blocking Jordan from my view. "The roar of the crowd and excitement is like a big party. You should come sometime and see for yourself."

"Yeah, maybe."

I don't really know why I haven't gone before. It's just one more thing I've passed on for safer, quieter options. Plus, Violet has sworn off sporting events unless it's for Dahlia, and all my friends are friends with her.

The rest of the class passes with more small talk, and the three of us finish the assignment before anyone else.

"We work well together," Liam says as he hooks his backpack over one shoulder.

"Yeah," I agree a little breathlessly. My heart races like it did earlier. "Thanks for letting me join."

"Of course. Have a good day, Daisy."

I suck in a breath at my name on his lips.

"You too, Liam," I chirp back.

Jordan hangs back a second, and when I don't say anything, he chuckles. "Yeah, great. I'll have a good day too."

I speed walk to the café to meet Violet. She's already sitting with a coffee, her sketchbook in front of her. When she sees me, she looks up and breaks a smile.

"What happened? You look way too happy."

"I talked to him."

"Who?"

"Liam." I pace in front of her, waving my hands wildly. "And he talked to me. Like a lot. He was so nice, Violet. Like not just polite, but friendly. He asked me questions, and he invited me to come to a hockey game." Or maybe he just said I should go to a game. Whatever. It's as close to an invite as I'm ever getting.

"Whoa. Seriously?"

I nod my head quickly like a bobblehead.

"Oh my gosh. I can't believe it. What spurred you to do it? Was it all the *Pride and Prejudice*? Women knew how to speak to dudes back then—cut them with words without even trying." Her eyes widen. "Ooooh, or was it the dress?"

"My lab partner was absent again, and I got moved to their group."

"Their?"

"Liam and Jordan," I grumble the second name a little. It would have been a perfect two hours if it weren't for him.

"Ah, the bad boy to your good guy crush." She takes a bite of her sandwich. "One of them is faking."

"I don't think it's Jordan."

"Then maybe Liam isn't really that nice."

"He is, Vi." I finally sit and remember dreamily how considerate he was. No one else would have welcomed me into their group like that. He was everything I hoped he would be. No, even more.

"All right, if you say so." Violet leans her elbows on the table. "You finally talked to him. Now what?"

Now what, indeed.

Chapter THREE

Jordan

THE MOOD IN THE LOCKER ROOM IS THICK WITH frustration. My shoulder blades rest against the back of the wooden stall, and my breathing still comes in quick, ragged gulps. Sweat pours down my face. I haven't moved yet, but I can already feel the burn of my muscles in my quads.

"Fuck me. That was brutal." Even talking is painful.

Liam grunts beside me. He hunches over, elbows on his knees and a towel draped over his head. A glance around at the rest of the team tells me everyone is hurting as bad as we are.

It's a month into the season, and we look like shit. We only lost two guys to graduation and transfers at the end of last year, but our conference champ record is taunting us as we struggle to put the puck in the net. Coach decided we needed a little motivation in the form of skating our asses off for two hours.

My buddy curls up into a sitting position and lets out a

long breath that puffs out his cheeks. "Wanna grab a beer at The Hideout?"

"Can't. I have to finish that paper for tech writing."

"You still haven't done that?" The disbelieving grin he tosses my way doesn't have any judgment in it. "I thought you were doing that last night when I crashed early."

"Nah. I ended up playing video games with the guys across the hall. Then some girls from the volleyball team brought up a bottle of Malibu."

"That explains the high-pitched noises coming from your bedroom when I got up to shower this morning. I thought you were singing along to Celine Dion again."

"Hey, Celine's got great pipes. So did Abby, or was it Anna?"

He gives his head a playful shake and then gets to his feet. "Finish it and then meet up with us." Liam struggles to get his practice jersey over his head. We all look like we took a dip in the swimming pool after practice without removing our gear.

"I thought you said *a* beer?" He hardly ever drinks, especially during the week.

"It feels like a pitcher kind of night."

No freaking shit. "Doubt I'll make it but call me if you need a ride."

He tosses his jersey in the laundry bin. "I'm not staying out that late. I'll be home before you finish that paper, probably."

I snort a laugh. "Later."

Back at the dorms, I pull a half-eaten sandwich and a blue Powerade from the mini-fridge and sit at my desk. I scarf down the food while I pull up the document due tomorrow.

One sentence—that's how much I've written on the three-to-five-page paper assigned two weeks ago. Damn. I knew I was going to regret putting it off as long as I did.

I turn on some music and twirl in my desk chair, hoping an idea comes to me. I can bullshit for three pages no problem, but I need some inspiration.

A knock at our suite door snatches my attention, and I shoot up, glad for a distraction.

"Leonard," I say as I pull the door wide. "What's up?"

Stepping back, I give him room to duck his head to enter. At six foot six, Gavin Leonard's a good five inches taller than me and towers over the general population.

"Where's Price?" he asks.

"He and some of the guys went out after practice."

"And you stayed in?" He scans the suite I share with Liam, his gaze stopping on my open bedroom door. His voice drops to a whisper. "You got a girl in there?"

"Do you really think I'd be answering the door for your Gumby ass if I did?" I take a seat on the couch, and he drops into the chair. "What are you doing slumming it with us dorm-folk?"

He leans back with a smirk. Gavin lives at The White House with three other basketball players. It's a palace. They have their own gym, pool, and media room. Must be freaking nice.

"Warren lives downstairs," he says of one of his teammates.

"Uh-oh. What'd he do to deserve a visit from the team captain?"

A devious smile pulls at his lips. "Today's his birthday. The guys took him out to dinner, and we filled every inch of floor in his room with cups of water for when he comes back."

I bark a laugh at the image.

"For real," he says. "What are you doing tonight? There's a party at Sigma and a bunch of people at The Hideout."

I rake a hand through my hair. "I have a paper due tomorrow."

"So finish it and let's go out. I'm meeting the guys in twenty."

Indecision wars inside of me. "I shouldn't. Practices have been awful, the team isn't meshing, and we have a game on Friday."

"Staying in while the rest of your guys are out isn't going to magically make it come together."

He's probably not wrong about that. Still, I hesitate.

"What time is your first class tomorrow?" he asks.

"One I'm actually planning on attending?" I ask with a laugh. "Not until one."

"Practice or workouts?"

I shake my head. Coach gave us the morning off to recover from the brutal conditioning we did today.

He stands tall. "What are we even talking about then? Come on. At least come say happy birthday to Warren, and then you can come back and finish it and still get a full eight hours of beauty sleep in."

"Yeah, of course." I stand. Warren came out for my twenty-first celebration. It'd be shitty not to go and at least have one beer with him.

When we walk up to Sigma, the scene is insane. I can barely see the front door with all the people standing in the front yard. And the party is in the back.

"Whoa," I say as adrenaline hits. I love a good party.

"I told you." Gavin pushes at my shoulder and stretches his long legs to hurry up to the house.

I texted Liam on the way to see if he wanted to meet up with us, but he was already headed back to the dorm. *Be like Liam,* I tell myself. One beer, and I'm out.

A booming voice cuts through the silence, and the ground beneath me shakes. "Gotta get up, man. Class in twenty."

"Unnggh." My mouth is dry, and my head splinters in two when I open my eyes.

Liam's amused smile greets me. "You look like shit. I thought you were taking it easy last night."

I pull myself up and crack my neck to work out a kink. "Sigma was crazy. Biggest after hours I've seen all semester."

I reach for the water bottle on my nightstand. One beer turned into two or three, and then several rounds of birthday shots.

"The Hideout was packed last night too." He backs out of my room, stopping in the doorway. "Did you finish your paper?"

Ah fuck. I had my alarm set for eight this morning to get up and finish it, but I must have turned it off and passed right back out. Not surprising since I didn't crash until almost three.

My face must give him the answer because he laughs. "Bring it to lab. You can work on it there."

"Thank you."

I have just enough time to shower and grab my shit before we head off to the Emerson Building for our physics lab. I'm finishing off a bag of chips when we walk in. Dr. Green pauses his lecture and waits for us to take our seats.

For twenty minutes, he talks, giving us all the relevant information for today's lab. My grades are decent. I pull Bs and Cs, thanks in large part to sharing most of my classes with Liam. He keeps me in check with school, and I like to think I've helped him learn to cut loose a little. Freshman year, when we got to Valley, he'd never had a drop of alcohol, and he spent every night studying.

I'm not saying there's anything wrong with either of those things, but it's college—you have to live a little.

When Dr. Green finishes, Liam nods toward my bag on the floor. "We've got this. Just make it look like you're feverishly taking notes."

"We?"

At my question, Daisy steps up to our table. She pushes a lock of dark blonde hair behind one ear. "Hi."

"Stuck with us again, huh?" Liam asks, shooting her a charming grin.

She eats it right up, dropping her gaze to the floor with a smile. "Yeah. My partner must have dropped the class."

Liam grabs an extra stool and sets it next to her. "You're our partner now."

"Thank you." She moves like a scared rabbit, perching herself on the very edge of the seat. I'm not sure I'd heard her say a single word all semester that wasn't a direct response to a question until two days ago when Dr. Green put her in our group. She's smart, though. Our professor always calls on her when no one else knows the answer.

She's pretty cute. The shy, quiet thing she has going on is a whole vibe.

My buddy is into it, too. I can tell. They're perfect for one another: Barbie and Ken, brainy, introvert edition. Liam's a good guy, the best, actually. If anyone can make her feel at ease, it's him. That's probably why Dr. Green put her at our table.

"How should we break up the work?" she asks as she leans forward and reads the lab handout. Her nails are painted a bright, fiery red. That makes me smile. They're so much bolder than anything else about her.

"It's just you and me today," Liam says and tilts his head toward me. "Jordan needs to finish a paper. Is that cool?"

Her gaze slides over to me briefly, not meeting mine before she pins another shy smile at Liam. "Perfect."

As planned, I start on my paper while the two of them work on the lab. I sneak a glance at them huddled together, smiling and laughing like physics is a freaking blast. Her cheeks are pink with a flush, and she looks at Liam like he's the freaking moon and stars.

I'm closing in on three pages and reading over it again to check for errors when they finish the lab.

"Done?" Liam asks me as they clean up the lab supplies.

"Yeah. I just need a closing sentence to wrap it up."

"What's the paper about?" Daisy's voice almost blends in with the noise of the classroom. She's so quiet, but she's talking a little more today.

"Time management." Liam snorts as he responds for me. Okay, it's kind of funny. Still, I glare at him.

"You had to write a paper on time management? For what class?"

"Technical writing. It's tips and tricks, that kind of thing. We drew out of a hat for topics."

She nods slowly. "Maybe you should end it with a cautionary tale of what happens when you don't have good time management, and you have to finish assignments during other classes."

Liam chuckles softly. Damn, is this girl burning me?

"Maybe I was sick yesterday or at a funeral."

"Were you?"

I huff a laugh and grin at her. "No."

The three of us pack up to leave. Liam has to haul ass across campus to meet with his adviser, but I take my time and walk out with Daisy. Even the way she moves is gentle and unassuming. She side-eyes me when I fall into step beside her.

"Thanks for today. I'm sorry you had to pick up my slack."

She regards me carefully, like she isn't sure if I'm being genuine or not. I don't even know why I'm apologizing. They still finished early, even without my help.

I get the briefest of nods from her, and she takes another tentative step down the hall.

"Are you coming to the game tomorrow night?"

"Oh, umm..." She has this habit of tucking her hair behind her right ear, and she does it again now. "I'm not sure."

"A big hockey fan like you?" I tease.

She blushes again but doesn't say anything.

We come to the outside door, and I hold it open for her. The wind whips her long hair around her head, sending the strands and their fruity smell into my face.

She looks over her shoulder as she corrals her wild hair.

"I'm going that way." I jab my thumb in the opposite direction toward my tech writing class. "Are you heading to another class?"

"No, I'm done for the day."

"Are you in the dorms?"

She hesitates like she's confused why I'm asking so many questions. Me too, but I find her sort of fascinating. "No, I live off-campus."

"Huh."

She looks at me quizzically. I can hardly tell her I find that surprising even though I do.

"You shouldn't spend so much time socializing between classes."

"What's that?" Now it's my turn to be confused.

A ghost of a smile crosses her pink lips. "It's another tip for better time management."

Chapter FOUR

Jordan

"I THOUGHT YOU TWO HAD FORGOTTEN." GAVIN TOSSES a wad of material at me. "New shirts."

"Sorry. Coach held us late again." Liam sets his bowling shoes down on the floor and takes a seat. "Just the three of us tonight?"

Gavin nods. "Jenkins had a study session."

I hand Liam a shirt and hold up mine in front of me, then drop it to look at Gavin. "Lucky Strikes?"

He stands and picks up his blue bowling ball. "We couldn't be Team Blue Balls again this year."

"Why not?" I ask and slip the black Dickies shirt with our new team name printed on the front over my T-shirt. "It's funny."

"It's really not that funny," Liam says.

I flip him off as he moves to the computer.

"Same order?" he asks as he punches in our names.

"Sounds good to me."

I'm rusty from not playing for a few months. The three of us, plus Gavin's teammate, Andy Jenkins, joined a bowling league freshman year when Gavin and Andy lived across the hall instead of their sweet new digs at The White House. We were bored and heard this place never carded for alcohol. At the time, it seemed like as good a reason as any to join a bowling league. But two years later, we're still doing it even after we've all turned twenty-one except Gavin.

At the end of the first game, we pause to grab a pitcher of beer and shoot the shit.

I stretch out my legs in front of me and rub at my left quad. "Coach is gonna kill us if he keeps running us like he has the past two weeks."

"Practice is still that bad?" Gavin asks as he fills our glasses. Liam waves him off in favor of his water.

"It's pretty bad. Coach doesn't know whether to keep yelling or give us the world's longest pep talk," I say.

We lost another game last weekend. There is nothing worse than losing at home.

"What's the problem? Are the rookies struggling that much to mesh with the rest of the team?" Gavin's question is innocent enough, but I feel the prickle of discomfort wash over my buddy.

"I'm going to get some air." Liam starts toward the doors without pausing for our response.

Gavin waits until he's out of earshot. "Did I say something wrong?"

"Nah. It isn't you. He's feeling the pressure." Coach made Liam captain this year, and ever since, his game on the ice has gone downhill.

"Is it just hockey, or does he have other distractions?"

"Like?"

"I don't know. A tough class schedule?"

I shake my head. "He has straight A's."

"New girlfriend?"

"No." Another shake.

"Good," he says. "Nothing like a new chick to make a guy lose focus. Trust me on that. New girlfriends are the worst kind of distraction. Women weaken the legs."

"What?" I bust a laugh at his last words.

"It's from *Rocky*."

I keep staring at him.

He jumps up and hops from leg to leg, tossing punches like a boxer. "The movie. *Rocky*?"

"Oh, I understood the first time, but don't stop making an ass out of yourself on my account."

He stops and flips me off.

The next afternoon, Liam shows up late for practice. His face is red, and his shoulders are stiff.

"Sorry, Coach," he says as he skates onto the ice.

He's never been late for practice or a workout. Never.

I fall into line behind him for drills. "Is everything okay?"

"Yeah." He stares straight ahead, jaw set.

I stop him with a glove to his bicep before he can skate forward. "Are you sick?"

"I'm fine. I overslept. No big deal."

I let him go, but now I'm more worried than before. He wasn't in his room when I left. I know because I checked. I needed a clean pair of shorts. But why the hell would he lie?

At the end of practice, Coach stops him.

"Price. Do you want to tell me why you were late today?" Instead of waiting for his answer, he continues. "You're late, you're missing passes, you're slow on your feet. If you keep it up, you're going to find yourself next to me during games."

"It was my fault." My chest heaves as I struggle to catch my breath. "I shut off his alarm before I left. I thought he was up."

Coach's mouth falls into a hard line.

"It won't happen again," Liam promises.

"Good." Coach motions with his head toward the locker room. "Get out of here."

When we sit in our stalls, my buddy finally speaks. "Thanks."

"Where were you?"

"I told you. I overslept."

"I know you weren't in your room."

His brows pull up toward the blond, matted hair on his forehead. "Checking up on me?"

"I forgot to do laundry again," I admit. I pull the band of my hockey pants down to show him the shorts I borrowed.

He chuckles lightly. "I was in the library. I passed out with my head on the desk trying to look over econ notes."

"I should have known."

Despite the lousy practice, Liam seems to be in a better mood when we get back to the dorms. I'm playing video games, and he brings his laptop out to the living room to work on an assignment.

"I'm thinking of asking out our lab partner," he says without looking up from the screen.

"Who?"

"Daisy. The girl in our physics lab."

"Right." I ponder that, not liking how it sits with me. "Really?"

"She's nice."

I pause the game. Liam hasn't really dated in the three years I've known him. He hooks up so infrequently it still surprises me when I wake up to find him walking a girl out. But something tells me him asking out Daisy wouldn't be like that. It'd be real. They'd go on actual dates and shit.

"Won't that be weird if shit goes south, and we have to team up with her twice a week for class?"

"Look at you all glass half empty."

"I'm just saying, maybe now isn't the best time to start something."

The insinuation is clear, and he pulls his bottom lip behind his teeth and bobs his head. "Yeah. You might be right about that. I'm one screw up away from Coach benching me."

"Of course, I'm right. When have I ever steered you wrong?"

He cocks a brow.

"Okay, yeah. Don't answer that, but dating is distracting. You can trust me on that."

"And partying and hooking up four or five nights a week isn't?"

"You're not me. You have to ease into being as awesome as me. Maybe try getting a polite hand job at a party or something first."

Thursday, during our physics lab, Daisy joins our table again. She and Liam fall into easy conversation, and I take my usual role, reading through the steps and calling them out. It's how Liam and I always worked. I learn better by writing things down, and he's a hands-on guy.

A pit forms in my stomach as I watch my lab partners interact.

Liam would never intentionally sabotage the team. He's too good of a guy for that, but the way Daisy is looking at him with hearts in her eyes sends warning bells off in my head. She isn't the kind of girl you take out once, hook up, and then maybe call for a repeat a few times in the future when your schedule is clear.

Daisy is the kind of girl that would have someone like Liam wrapped around her little pinky finger. She's the perfect sweet, smart, naïve catnip for him.

We're doing a projectile motion lab that involves launching a ball onto carbon paper. It's an easy lab, and as Liam loads up the ball in the launcher, Daisy smiles and moves the carbon paper a few feet away, which brings her closer to me.

"It's probably easier if I sit in the middle," I say.

She hesitates, then looks between Liam and me.

"I can walk around to the other side of the table," she says.

I fight a smile. She wants to be near him. How cute.

"You know what." I drop my pencil. "Give me a turn on that thing."

On my feet, I step toward Liam and the launcher.

"Yeah?" he asks with an apprehensive smirk.

"Looks fun." It absolutely doesn't.

He tosses the silver ball at me and takes my seat.

Since I've read the handout, I'm already adjusting the angle to thirty degrees and preparing to fire when Liam gives me the instruction.

"Ready?" I ask Daisy.

Her blue eyes flit over me through the safety goggles, and she pushes them up higher on her nose.

The ball shoots out and bounces onto the paper, then directly at her. She tries to catch it, misses, and a series of metallic pings ring out as it bounces along the floor.

Her cheeks are pink as she circles, trying to capture it. Liam and I both move to action. He gets there first, snatching it up and holding it out for her. He winks. On anyone else, it would seem like a skeevy move, but he pulls it off, and Daisy swoons at his feet.

"Why don't you have a turn?" I motion toward the launcher.

She nods and moves into position behind it. I stand near the paper, ready to catch the ball after it lands.

Her blonde hair falls forward like a curtain blocking half of her face as she leans down to set the ball in place. She glances up at me, or in my general direction anyway, before she fires. I nod, giving her the go-ahead. As the ball comes my way, I'm temporarily distracted as her shirt gapes hinting at a little cleavage. The daisy charm around her neck dangles seductively. Her boobs are small, but the cleavage is still nice.

The ball bounces while I'm still staring, but I easily catch it in one hand. She stands tall and takes a tentative step toward me like she wants to switch spots again.

"Nah, you go again," I say and hold the ball up to indicate I'm going to toss it to her. She places both hands out in front of her apprehensively. I smother a laugh and throw it directly into her hands.

I'd be lying if I said I didn't look down her shirt the next three times she does it, but I convince myself it's better this way, so she doesn't fumble around trying to catch the ball as it shoots out at her. And I think she kind of likes sending flying objects in my direction.

When we're finished with the launcher and start calculating velocity, I find myself back on my side, and the two of them huddled together.

I keep waiting for my buddy to ask her out, but he doesn't even after we finish the lab and start packing up to leave. Huh. Maybe he wasn't that serious about it. Or maybe I'm just that good.

Or he caught sight of her small tits or terrible ball catching skills and decided against it. It doesn't sound like him, but whatever. I'm just thankful he didn't.

Crisis adverted.

Chapter FIVE

Daisy

OVER THE NEXT TWO WEEKS, I CONTINUE TO SIT WITH Liam and Jordan during physics, and it actually starts to feel normal. Or as normal as sitting next to your popular crush while trying not to physically combust ever feels.

Sometimes the way he smiles at me, I convince myself that he likes me too. But when class is over, he says goodbye and races out the door like he can't wait to get wherever he's going.

Today when I slide into the chair next to Liam, he gives me the same smile and greeting, but his face doesn't light up the same way, and he drops his gaze to the table while Professor Green talks through the lab.

While we work through the lab, he barely speaks—even to Jordan. I've never seen Liam like this. He's sullen, broody even. He ducks out to refill his water bottle halfway through, and Jordan scoots closer.

"The next step is to measure the amplitude." He taps his pencil on the paper.

I nod, then ask, "Is he okay?"

"Yeah," he says as he hitches the sleeve of his T-shirt up on his shoulder. The movement lifts the cuff showing off his bicep and the bottom of a tattoo. He has a few. A long, skinny cross on the back of his left arm, then a hockey player and a puck going into a net—one on each thigh, that I've seen on days when he has worn shorts. Today his jeans cover them, and I imagine he has even more ink hidden underneath his clothes.

"He doesn't seem okay."

"Just a tough practice today."

"Oh." My brows knit in confusion. I expected something, I don't know, bigger? "That's all?"

"Were you hoping for more? Maybe a dead pet or incurable disease?"

"No, of course not." My face heats.

He grins and brings his pencil up behind one ear.

"You were at practice too?"

His dark brows pull together slightly as he nods.

"And yet you haven't lost your sparkle."

His deep chuckle does something funny to my stomach. "Part of my charm, I guess. I don't let things get to me like Liam does."

I finish the measurement before I prod a little more. I want to understand Liam—what makes him tick and what gets to him. "A bad practice really gets him that upset?"

"Sometimes, yeah," he says.

My face must show my surprise because Jordan shakes his head. "I wouldn't expect you to understand."

I start to ask what he means, but Liam returns, and Jordan moves back to his spot. The time to himself seems to have done Liam well. He smiles a little brighter as he takes his seat and sets his bottle in front of him. "All right. Where did we leave off?"

Liam is more talkative for the rest of the class, and I forget all about Jordan's remark until we're leaving.

"Have a good weekend," Liam says.

"You too. Good luck at your games." I have the hockey team's schedule memorized, so I know they're traveling Friday and Saturday for away games.

His smile dims ever so slightly. It's such a small change. I think it's only because I've watched him so long that I'm able to notice. I steal a glance at Jordan. He's watching for his friend's reaction, too. I've hit a sore spot, which obviously isn't what I wanted.

He recovers quickly, and his mouth pulls into a forced smile. "Thanks, Daisy. See you next week."

Jordan tips his head to me and departs with him.

"Stupid, stupid," I mutter softly as I head in the opposite direction.

I meet up with the girls at the cafeteria for dinner. Violet is in full-on planning mode for the ball. She flips through images from her Pinterest board, showing us everything from table designs to a photo background. As I suspected, she's gone way overboard.

Jane is all about it, and Dahlia is busy cramming in homework. She has the craziest schedule of the four of us since she is on the golf team. They have practices in the afternoons and workouts in the evenings or mornings, sometimes both.

So, while my friends are preoccupied, I think about Liam. I can't believe I was so stupid to bring up hockey when Jordan had just told me that was why he was upset. I guess I didn't really believe that was all it could be. I know student-athletes take their sports seriously, but even on bad days, Dahlia seems more like herself than Liam did during lab.

"Everything is still good with the flowers?" Violet asks me, shaking me from my thoughts.

"Yes." I take a drink of water. I've said so few words during this dinner my throat is dry. "She can deliver everything that Saturday afternoon, or we can pick it up as soon as Friday on the weekend of the event."

"Saturday afternoon?" Violet's eyes widen. "That's too late."

I nod. Hence the need for a backup plan—aka picking it up ourselves.

"I don't think you understand how many flowers we're talking about here, Daisy," she says.

"So, we'll take more than one trip."

I look to Jane and Dahlia for backup.

"I don't think we have a vehicle big enough for the archway," Jane says. "Unless it comes apart somehow."

"It doesn't," Violet says. "We need a van or a truck or something."

I hadn't thought of that. Honestly, I've given the flowers very little thought at all beyond the specific instructions Violet gave me. But I can practically see the stress rising as her shoulders lift toward her ears.

"I will figure it out," I say. When she doesn't look convinced, I add, "I will. Leave it to me."

"Thank you." She exhales.

"Why are you putting so much pressure on this? We had a blast last year, and it wasn't nearly this..." I search for a word that doesn't make her extreme planning seem negative.

"Decadent?" Dahlia offers, looking up from her homework.

"Yes, that." I point to her.

"Because..." The energy around Violet shifts as she struggles to put her feelings into words. She gets this way when she's really passionate about something. "For one night, I want our friends to feel like they are part of something as amazing and unique as they are. How many times have we been turned away or left out because we're not cool enough or outgoing enough or don't have the right friends? It's dumb. We're awesome. I want this party to be so incredible that people are begging to be invited."

"That's sweet, Vi." Also, slightly delusional. "The flowers will be there Saturday morning."

She tilts her head to the side and narrows her gaze.

"I mean Friday night." I smother a laugh.

"Thank you." She smiles. "Dahlia, do you have the fliers?"

"Yeah. They're in my backpack." She stops working to pull out a stack of fliers.

"They turned out amazing," Vi squeals and hands Jane and me each one to examine.

I groan when I see the bold title. "Wallflower Ball? You're officially calling it the Wallflower Ball?"

"Wallflowers are awesome," Jane says.

The fliers are amazing. Dahlia designed them with girls in big gowns and fierce pantsuits—a mix of her and Violet's designs. And around them a big, floral archway like the one causing the current floral nightmare.

Violet divides the stack into four. "We should post these around campus, and I have the digital file we can post online."

"Where?" I ask.

"We split up. I'll take the dorms. Daisy, take the library and University Hall. Jane can get the theater and music buildings, and Dahlia can get the rec center and athletic facilities. Anything else, we'll hit together tomorrow afternoon."

"Can I take the dorms? Or at least Freddy?" I ask as I wrap my fingers around the fliers.

"Sure," Violet says the word slowly. "Why? What are you up to?"

"Nothing. I need to talk to someone from class that lives in the building, so I'll be there anyway."

My friends are quiet for too long, and my face gets hot.

"Doesn't *Liam* live in Freddy dorm?" Violet's smile widens, and she bats her lashes.

Dahlia and Jane are watching me expectantly for more information.

With a smile, I stand. "See you guys back at the house."

Sitting and talking about him will talk me out of my plan. And the plan isn't half bad.

Freddy dorm is where most of the jocks live. Even a lot of the upper-class students stay here instead of moving out. The dorm is one of the nicest on campus, and the setup is in suites with two or four bedrooms and shared living space.

I only know this because it was in the housing packet when I was accepted to Valley U. I didn't know then it was reserved for student-athletes, but I should have guessed as much.

In high school, well-meaning guidance counselors and teachers tell you that in college, it's less about labels like jock and nerd and more about finding your people. They were half right. It was easy to find my people here. By the second semester, I had a group of people I called friends. They are all physics or art majors or girls from the same dorm hall. Then Violet, of course, once she stopped hanging with her sorority roommate. The point is the division in groups still exists. I guess because there are more of us, we're supposed to stop caring.

I haven't, but as I walk through the front entrance of Freddy, I wish I could. If just for a few minutes, I would love to be blissfully unaware that I am different than the other people walking in.

A girl in a Valley U volleyball tank top holds the door open for me and smiles. "Coming in?"

"Thanks." My gaze sweeps over the large lounge area.

Girls and guys hang out in front of a TV. The sound is muted on a basketball game, and there's music coming from somewhere—upbeat, party music. Which is exactly what it feels like—a fun, little Thursday afternoon party. Our dorm lounge never felt like that.

"Are you looking for someone?" she asks as I pause, still looking for which direction to go.

"Is there a bulletin board for announcements?"

She points to the left side near mailboxes and the front desk.

"Thanks again."

With a nod and a smile, she bounces away from me, ponytail swaying with each step.

I hang the flier and then hesitate on my plan. I don't know what floor Liam is on or if I can even get there without being stopped. Freddy is a co-ed dorm, but I don't know which are boys' floors and which are girls'. This was a terrible idea.

Not to mention, how am I going to ask him to haul something for me, therefore admitting I know he drives a truck when I have no reason to have that knowledge. No reason except when he's around, I have some sort of sense. I can spot him across campus, across parking lots... I just see him. But, yeah, I don't think that explanation is going to convince him to help me. More like run far, far away.

I'm about to leave when Jordan walks through the front doors. I look behind him, hopefully for Liam. I'm not that lucky.

His black backpack hangs on one shoulder, and his Valley Hockey hat is turned backward. He has this ease about him, from the way he dresses to the way he walks like he doesn't give a single fuck about anything. I admire it as much as I dislike it. Would it kill him to care a little about something?

It should say something about my feelings for Liam that I'm able to put one foot in front of the other and catch Jordan before he reaches the stairs.

"Jordan," I call his name, then quicken my steps to a jog so he can hear me over the music. "Jordan, hey!"

He glances over his shoulder while still moving up the stairs, but when he sees me, he stops, and his brows lift. "Daisy?"

The confusion on his face isn't malicious, but I still pray for the floor to swallow me up. I'm the last person he expected to see here.

"Hey," he says when I don't respond. "What are you doing here?"

"I..." My explanation is stuck somewhere inside of me. Why did I think this was a good plan?

"If you're looking for Liam, he isn't back yet. He had a meeting with Coach."

"Thanks." I spin on my heel to flee, but I can't seem to force myself to go. I came here for a reason, and I need to see it through or die of embarrassment trying. Spinning back around, I face him again. "Do you know what time he'll be back?"

"No, but it shouldn't be too long. You can wait for him if you want or if it's something with physics, I can probably figure it out."

"It isn't about physics."

"I figured." He flashes the smallest of grins. He tips his head, motioning for me to follow, and bounces up each stair, somehow moving slowly but energetic at the same time.

I keep a two-step difference between us as he leads me up to the fifth floor. He holds open the door for me, forcing me to go ahead of him. I stop and let him retake the lead. Lots of doors are open, letting the noise from the rooms bleed out into the hallway—music, video games, laughter. Two guys are tossing a football the length of the hall.

"Heads up," Jordan says as we pass them. "Hey, Ry."

"Thatcher." The guy he called Ry smiles and holds the football in one giant palm. "How's it going?"

"Good, man."

Ry gives me a knowing smirk that takes me a second to decipher, but when I do, I once again wish I could disappear. Ry thinks I'm on my way to hook up with Jordan. *Kill me now.*

Jordan eventually stops about halfway down the long hallway and opens a door on the left side. He walks in, holds the door open with an elbow, and flips on the light.

I'm staring at a living area. A couch and a chair face a TV with various gaming systems. Hockey jerseys hang on the wall, there are skates, sticks, and other gear shoved next to the TV, and it smells a little like a gym locker, but it's not as messy as I might have imagined.

On either side of the living area are what I assume are the bedrooms, but I can't see inside of either.

"It's even bigger than I expected," I say.

Jordan's lips pull into a wide smile.

"The room," I grit out.

"I knew what you meant."

"Then why are you smirking like that?"

"Knew what you meant, but I still thought it was funny." He drops his backpack onto a chair and points to another empty seat. "You can sit if you want."

I do and then instantly regret it. Jordan rubs the back of his neck like he's not sure how to entertain me now that I'm here. The movement lifts the hem of his T-shirt to expose an inch of flat stomach above his jeans. He's about the same height as Liam, but Jordan is leaner, and his muscles are more defined.

He disappears into the bedroom on the left side. "Do you want something to drink? We have Powerade or beer."

He comes back with one of each.

"No thanks."

He sets the Powerade on the coffee table anyway and opens the beer. He moves his backpack out of the other chair and takes a seat.

"What's that?" he asks, nodding to the fliers in my hand.

I shove the forgotten fliers into my bag. "Nothing. What time did you say Liam would be back?"

"I'm not sure." He shrugs. "I could pass on a message if you want."

"I'd really rather just ask him myself."

"Okay." He leans back and extends one long leg. "Physics and art, huh? How does that happen?"

"My parents are physicists, and art makes me feel beautiful."

Jordan stays quiet as he studies me. My answer feels too heavy. It's definitely more than he bargained for. It's the truth, but not something I usually tell people.

I fidget with my hands in my lap. "What about you? Why did you choose civil engineering?"

"Do you really want to talk about our majors?"

"*You* brought it up."

He's quiet a beat and then says, "I like being outside, and engineers make decent money. It's a good fallback plan."

"Fall back from what?"

He takes a drink of his beer. "I was drafted by the Kings over the summer."

I don't immediately put it together until he adds, "They're a pro hockey team."

"Oh. Wow. Congrats."

"Thanks."

Silence falls between us again. He taps his finger on the side of his beer can. "Are you sure I can't pass on the message? I could write it down and everything."

Standing, I start to move past him. "I should get out of your hair. I'll just send him an email or something."

He grabs my hand to stop me. The pads of his fingers are warm and calloused, and an unexpected thrill shoots up my arm. He smells like soap and beer.

I pull away first.

Jordan brings his hands together, gliding his palms together slowly in front of him. "Don't go. Stay, have a drink. I'll text Liam and see if he's on his way yet."

Chapter SIX

Jordan

"He's leaving the rink now."

Daisy's blonde head bobs, eyes downcast. "Thank you."

Her fingers wrap around the red bottle. She hasn't taken a drink, but she looks maybe the slightest bit more at ease. What the hell am I doing, letting her get comfortable and practically rolling out the red carpet for her to ask out Liam?

The last thing he needs is another distraction. The past week he's gone from bad to worse. And if it were only impacting him, that'd be one thing, but the whole team is suffering.

Besides, the more time I spend with him and Daisy in class, the less I can see them together. I mean, the guy spent the entire two hours of class moping while sitting next to a girl who just wanted him to pay attention to her. He's too caught up in his own shit to see how much she likes him.

"What did you mean today?" Daisy asks with the slightest edge to her voice.

When I look at her, she's no longer staring at her feet but right at me. She has these big blue eyes and dark lashes that are hard to look away from when she has them trained on me.

"When you said that you wouldn't expect me to understand about Liam and hockey," she clarifies.

"Oh, uh, nothing. He had a rough day. Practice was awful, and Coach was on his case. I wouldn't take anything he did or said today personally."

"The only thing I took personally was you implying I couldn't possibly understand. Is that some sort of dig at my intelligence?"

A chuckle escapes, but the look she cuts me has me reining it back. "No, of course not."

"I'm a straight-A student."

"I'm not surprised."

"So?"

She's pretty cute all wound up. In class, she seems all timid, but I like the fire in her eyes now.

"Have you ever been on a sports team?"

"No." Her shoulders stiffen.

"Then you don't know what it's like to be a part of something, have people depend on you, and then fail them."

"Liam feels like he's failing the team. Why?"

"Do you follow the games at all? Never mind, it doesn't matter. Liam is in a funk. As our captain, he needs to lead us even when he's not playing well. He's still figuring it out."

"You're right. I don't get it. I mean, I understand, but that doesn't sound fair. Because he's not playing well, the team blames him for the losses? Isn't the whole point of a team that you're stronger together? If he were playing well, you wouldn't say he won you the game. Why should a loss be blamed on a single guy?"

I mull that over. It isn't exactly the way I'd put it, but she isn't wrong either. No one is blaming Liam for us losing. We just know we can be a hell of a lot better with him playing well.

Before I can respond, the door opens, and Liam walks in.

"Hey." His gaze goes straight for Daisy and his face breaks out into a wide smile. "What are you doing here?"

She stands and pink dots her cheekbones. "Hi."

An awkward beat passes before she blurts out, "I'm sorry to drop in like this. I have sort of a favor to ask."

"Sounds interesting." Liam continues to smile at her. "Let me just toss my stuff in my room."

I guess that's my cue. Liam comes back out and sits next to her on the couch. That's the last thing I see before I stand and start toward my room to give them some privacy.

Sitting at my desk, I open my laptop to do homework. Liam's voice carries through the thin wall, but I can't make out Daisy's quieter words. Adrenaline vibrates under my skin. What are they talking about out there?

"Yeah," Liam says so enthusiastically that a pit forms in my stomach.

She did it. I can't believe she did it. She actually asked him out. Damn, I knew I shouldn't have invited her up. *Fuck.*

Daisy's voice climbs as she thanks him. I stare at the screen of my laptop, then snap the lid closed. Their voices move closer, and the door to the hallway opens. Leaning back in my chair, I can see Liam standing with the door held open and the slightest sliver of her dark blonde hair in front of him. I push back a little more until I can see her through the crack in the door. She has a nice smile. Full lips hide straight, white teeth. When the corners of her mouth pull high enough, she gets a cute little smile wrinkle on the left side of her cheek.

Balancing on the back two legs of the chair, I tilt back another inch to watch as Liam steps closer. It'd be a bold and uncharacteristic move for him to kiss her, but my heart stops as I wait to see how far he'll go. His arms lift at the same time my legs go over my head, and I'm unceremoniously dropped on my head.

I curse the chair and groan as I pick myself up. She's gone by the time I glance toward the door again.

"Everything okay in here?" Liam steps into my room and eyes the chair overturned in front of my desk.

"Fine." I right the chair and rub my elbow. "Daisy left already?"

"Please." He sits on the end of my bed. "Like you weren't in here eavesdropping."

Sitting back at my desk chair, I smile. "She talks too damn quiet. I assume you said yes?"

A deep laugh leaves my buddy. "Yeah, it's no problem. It'll only take an hour or two."

His shrug is so blasé I struggle to find the words. "Only take an hour or two? I'm confused. That's a good thing?"

He tilts his head to the side. "What is it you think she asked me to do for her?"

"To go out on a date. What else?"

His shoulders and chest shake with laughter before I hear it.

I toss a pencil at him. "What the hell is so funny? She's obviously into you."

"You think?"

"It's painful to watch someone be so oblivious," I tell him. "Yes, that little mouse just tracked you down and waited for you to get home so she could… well, fuck, I don't even know what now. But whatever she asked, what she was really hoping for, was a date."

"That sounds better than what I signed us up for." One side of his mouth lifts. "She needs a couple of strong guys to move some flowers for an event in January."

"Oh." I can't hide my surprise. "That's it?"

Liam nods. "Yeah, man. That's it."

I take in a deep breath and lean back in my chair. "You're not going out with her then?"

He shakes his head and gets to his feet. He gives my door two taps on his way out, then takes a step back inside my room. "By the way, she said to tell you the answer is Pascal's Law."

"The answer to what?"

"I'm not sure. That's all she said. PlayStation?"

"Nah, I need to finish a couple of assignments before we leave tomorrow."

"Cool." He leaves my room for real this time, and I open my laptop and type Pascal's Law into the search engine. I know it, of course, but I don't understand what she's trying to tell me.

I pace the room, equal parts annoyed and intrigued. I really do have some homework to finish up before the bus pulls out tomorrow for Utah, but I can't focus on anything else but Daisy's cryptic message.

I pull up my email and type her name into the directory. Daisy Johnson.

From: jthatcher@valleyu.edu

To: djohnson3@valleyu.edu

Subject: Pascal

I give up. How is Pascal's Law the answer? And what was the question anyway?

I grab another beer and wait for her reply, hitting the refresh every thirty seconds.

From: djohnson3@valleyu.edu

To: jthatcher@valleyu.edu

Subject: Re: Pascal

The question is how to stop putting the pressure of success on one man's shoulders. Hence, Pascal.

Hence? Seriously.

From: jthatcher@valleyu.edu

To: djohnson3@valleyu.edu

Subject: Re: Re: Pascal

I don't think Pascal's Law works in this situation, but I'd love to hear your take.

I pull up the assignment for my strength of materials course and read it over, but as soon as an email notification pops up, I click over to read her response.

From: djohnson3@valleyu.edu

To: jthatcher@valleyu.edu

Subject: Re: Re: Re: Pascal

I was simply trying to say that maybe if you all took a little of the pressure, instead of piling it on one guy's shoulders, the team would be the better for it. Pressure applied to any part of the boundary of a confined fluid is transmitted equally in ALL directions. You all have to take some of the stress.

I know, I know. Don't @ me. A hockey team isn't a fluid, but it's the best I could do on the fly.

Go, team go!

I laugh, picturing her face typing out that cheery last line. I doubt she's ever gone to a single sporting event. But, at this point, I might even take an unathletic physics major's advice if it'll help Liam.

Chapter SEVEN

Daisy

VIOLET COMES INTO MY ROOM FRIDAY AFTERNOON AS I'm sketching. "We're going out in thirty minutes."

"Where?" I drop my pencil and smooth my hair back out of my face. I blink several times to focus my eyes after staring at the paper for so long.

Instead of answering, she comes around to look at my drawing. "What are you working on?"

I flip the paper. "You can't see yet. Not until it's done."

"You always say that." She rolls her eyes playfully.

"Then you should know better than to ask."

Smiling, she motions toward my left cheek. "You have black all over your face." Her gaze drops to the side of my right hand, and the black smudges. "Shower and meet us downstairs for a drink before the Uber gets here."

"You didn't say where we were going?" I call after her.

I see Dahlia as I'm heading to the bathroom. She yawns and stretches like she just woke up from a nap.

"Do you know where we're going?"

"No idea," she says. "How much are Violet and Jane going to yell at me if I just wear this?"

She's in a baggy white T-shirt and jeans. She looks great, but maybe a little wrinkled. Our friends treat nights out like a runway show. I guess it's because we don't do it that often that it always feels like a lot of pressure to look and dress a certain way.

"I could do your hair if you want," I offer.

"Distract them with killer hair and makeup." Dahlia grins. "I love it."

The four of us meet in the kitchen downstairs five minutes before the Uber is supposed to arrive.

Jane gives me an appreciative once over when I walk into the room. "Wow. Daisy. You look great."

She circles around me, taking in every detail. I feel so short next to her.

Jane is five foot eight without heels, but she's almost always wearing heels, so she looks even taller. She's technically a freshman, but she's the same age as the rest of us. She took a year off before starting school.

She's a music major and filthy rich. Not just rich like she had nice things growing up. Jane has the kind of money that makes her a little out of touch with reality. Her parents are... well, actually I don't know what they do, but something that makes them very wealthy. She once tried to offer me a thousand dollars to help her study for a calculus test.

She isn't snooty, and she doesn't really care about labels, though I think her shoe collection is mostly Louis Vuitton—even her sneakers.

Dahlia met her when she came to tour Valley U last spring. They kept in touch over the summer, and we jumped at the chance for all four of us to move in together off-campus this year.

"Will you please tell me where we're going now?" I ask Violet.

She grins. "The Hideout."

My stomach drops. "We can't drink at The Hideout. They've been cracking down hard on underage drinking, and I'm shit at lying."

"Don't worry. I've got us covered." She pours us each a shot of tequila. "And, despite all my strongly worded emails to the owner, I can almost guarantee that the TVs will be tuned in to watch your guy play Utah."

All three look at me.

"He isn't my guy." My face suddenly feels hot. "We're just lab partners."

I hold out my shot glass, and we clink them together, then toss them back. A shiver rolls through me at the awful liquor.

"For now," Jane says, her face still twisted up from the tequila. "But who knows, by the end of the night anything could happen."

"Exactly!" Vi exclaims. "Although he is a jock. Maybe we can find you someone else tonight."

"And you're both already drunk," I say as I take the shot glasses and put them in the sink.

The Hideout is a classic restaurant and sports bar. On the bar side, Valley students are jammed into tables and booths and every space in between, making it hard to walk through, let alone find a spot to sit down.

Jane stands taller than the rest of us and scans the bar area for somewhere to sit.

"There's a table in the back right," she says and makes a beeline for it.

A frazzled server approaches us as soon as we sit down, then gets shoved into the end of the table by a group passing by. It's vicious in here tonight.

"Can I get you something to drink?" She blows her hair out of her eyes.

"A bottle of your most expensive wine," Jane says with a dispassionate glance in the direction of our server.

"I need to see your IDs."

Jane sighs, and her posture loosens. "Just a glass of tonic for me. Lime on the side."

"Sprite," Violet says.

Dahlia orders the same, and then our server looks at me.

"Diet—"

Someone kicks me under the table.

"Ouch," I yelp.

"Sorry. My foot slipped," Violet's voice is sugary-sweet, but her eyes are wide like she's trying to communicate something.

"Diet Coke," I repeat. "Thanks."

"Got it." The server disappears, and I lean forward to rub my shin.

"Ow, Vi. That really hurt. I think I already have a bruise."

"I'm sorry, but I was trying to get you to order something that would mix a little better."

Jane lifts a bottle of alcohol from her purse on the seat between her and Violet and then hides it again.

"So the wine was just to throw her off?"

"No," Jane says, leaning forward on an elbow, so her diamond bracelet catches the light. "I really was hoping for wine, but I brought back up." Her words get quieter as the server reappears.

"Wow, that was fast," Violet says.

"You're my last table, and I am eager to get out of here," she says and sets our drinks on the table in the same order. "I'm closing out. Jordan will help you if you need anything else."

My head snaps up, and I instinctively look for him, only realizing she doesn't mean Jordan Thatcher but an entirely different Jordan that works here. He's been on my mind, though. The other Jordan. He and Liam, of course.

The game is on, but the angle to the TV is weird, and the players look like blurry dots on the small screen.

"Drink up, ladies," Jane says.

We make room in our glasses, and then she adds alcohol to each of our drinks.

I take a long sip and cough. "What is that?"

"Vodka."

"I tried to get you to pick something other than Diet Coke," Violet says. She takes a small sip from my glass and grimaces. "We need to order you something else after you drink that."

But by the time I get to the end of the glass, I've almost gotten used to the taste. And I'm definitely tipsy. It's been a while since the four of us have gone out together. Even living together, I don't see them as much as I thought I would when we moved in at the start of the year.

Dahlia is busy with golf, Violet is busting her butt this semester to put together a portfolio for an internship next summer, Jane volunteers with a local youth music program, and I'm just me.

Dahlia is the most like me, but without Violet and Jane, we'd be two sad friends staring at one another every weekend, wishing the other would force us out of our shells.

I think that's the thing people don't realize about being shy. Most shy people desperately want to be included, but to do something as simple as plan a night out makes us anxious. We tell ourselves a thousand stories of how awful it could go and decide the payoff isn't worth it.

It's different when Violet is with me. She understands me. She protects me. Which gives me the confidence to say and do things I might not otherwise. Being the shy girl doesn't mean I'm always quiet. Just when I feel out of my element or like I have a lot on the line. Like talking to Liam.

When it's time for new drinks, Dahlia and I weave through people to get to the bar. Jordan, not Thatcher, hasn't stopped by our table once. I can't really blame him since we're not ordering food or alcohol.

Two bartenders are working. It's busy, but even the people

coming up after us get waited on before us. Frustration builds. I stand a little taller and plead (mentally, of course) for one of them to notice us. Dahlia and I share a sympathetic smile.

"We might be here a while," she says.

Nodding, I glance up at the TV hanging behind the bar. It's the third period, and Valley is up by one. The camera zeros in on Jordan, coming off the ice and tapping his glove with a teammate. Sweat makes his dark hair curl around his helmet. His cheeks are red, and there's an intensity in his eyes that's so different than the easy, playful one I've seen so often. I think I spot Liam's blond head, but the camera moves on before I can get a good look.

"What is taking so long?" Violet asks, coming up behind me. She lifts an arm to get the bartender's attention, which she succeeds in almost immediately.

We leave a minute later with fresh drinks.

Valley wins the game, but I only know because the bar is loud with cheers and applause at the final buzzer.

"I bet your boyfriend is happy," Violet says. Her teasing gets infinitely worse when she's drunk.

"He is not my boyfriend."

"Not yet," Dahlia bumps my elbow.

"Tell me again what he said when you went to his dorm?" Jane asks.

"I still can't believe you just showed up there," Dahlia says.

"I probably would have chickened out, but I ran into Jordan on his way up."

"Oh, right," Jane says. "I forgot they were roommates. They're so different."

They fire questions at me after I retell the story.

"What was their dorm like?"

"When are you going to see him again?"

"Are you like friends with him now?"

"Does this mean we'll be invited to the hockey parties?"

"We're not friends," I say. "Aside from the favor, I've only talked to them during class. And Jordan and I exchanged a few emails."

Their eyes pique with interest, and I wave them off. "It was silly."

When it's clear they aren't going to stop staring at me until I tell them about the emails, I do. And then they spend the next thirty minutes talking about Jordan and the many rumors they've heard about girls he's hooked up with. The list is long, but I already knew that.

"You didn't tell me about Jordan," Violet says later when the two of us make a trip to the ladies' room.

"It was nothing."

"It doesn't sound like nothing." Her gaze narrows. "Do you have a thing for him now?"

"Jordan?" My screech gets the attention of two girls entering the restroom. I lower my voice as butterflies swarm in my stomach. "No, of course not. He's... no."

But he is intriguing and not exactly who I pegged him to be. He's playful and witty and even polite. He could have sent me away or made me feel like a real idiot for sitting around waiting for Liam, and instead, he sat there and talked with me until Liam got back. I always imagined him as Liam's opposite, but I'm not sure that's entirely true.

After another drink, the four of us head back to our house to watch movies and play dress up. It's Violet and Jane's favorite thing to do after a night out. Vi brings out her latest creations, and she and Dahlia play designer, dressing Jane and me from head to toe. It's kind of awesome.

"Wine or stick with vodka?" Violet asks, pulling both from the fridge.

"Wine," Jane says at the same time Dahlia says, "Vodka."

With a laugh, Violet puts them on the counter. "Help yourself."

Jane and Dahlia fawn over Violet's newest designs, and I take my vodka and Sprite to the living room and scroll through my phone. I pull up the email exchange from Jordan and re-read it.

I hit reply and then tap my thumb on the edge of my phone, unsure what to say. I lock my phone and set it on the couch beside me. Liam gave me his number to contact him about the flowers, but I can't make myself text him randomly even to say congrats.

My pulse thrums dangerously. I take a large gulp of my drink and grab my phone.

From: djohnson3@valleyu.edu

To: jthatcher@valleyu.edu

Subject: Congrats!

I heard Valley won tonight. Congratulations.

Chapter EIGHT

Jordan

We're staying in Utah tonight. The bus leaves early in the morning, and we have another game tomorrow in northern Arizona before we head back to Valley late Saturday night.

Liam snores lightly from his bed on the opposite side of the room. I pull on my headphones and turn on music, but sleep isn't in the cards yet. I'm keyed up from the game. We finally pulled out a win. It wasn't pretty, but we did it.

Scrolling through my phone, I respond to texts from my mom congratulating me on the game, then check email.

"No way," I mutter under my breath. I click on the new message from Daisy. Something like excitement bubbles under the surface as I read her few words. I check the timestamp. Only ten minutes ago.

Fuck it. I'm bored and a long way from sleeping.

From: jthatcher@valleyu.edu

To: djohnson3@valleyu.edu

Subject: Re: Congrats!

Thanks. I guess all we needed was a little bit of Johnson's Law. What are you up to tonight?

I send it and wait.

From: djohnson3@valleyu.edu

To: jthatcher@valleyu.edu

Subject: Johnson's Law?

I'm hanging out with some friends. I think you meant Pascal's Law. How'd that work out?

From: jthatcher@valleyu.edu

To: djohnson3@valleyu.edu

Subject: Yes, JOHNSON'S Law

Pascal's Law was a stretch, but I took your advice and chatted with the guys about us all stepping up and helping lead. It might have been a fluke, but it worked tonight.

What are you and your friends getting up to?

I try to picture her out at a party in her cute little dresses, hiding in the corner.

From: djohnson3@valleyu.edu

To: jthatcher@valleyu.edu

Subject: Re: Yes, JOHNSON'S Law

Drinking and playing dress up. Are you on a bus or something?

Drinking? Interesting. I wouldn't have thought that's how she spends a Friday night. And not because she's shy. Tons of quieter people come to parties and stand off to the side, but I've never seen Daisy at a party. And I've been to plenty of them thrown by all sorts of groups of people.

From: jthatcher@valleyu.edu

To: djohnson3@valleyu.edu

Subject: Dress up?

I'm going to need an explanation. What does that mean, dress up? Halloween is over. Or is this like cosplay? I'm intrigued. Tell me more.

We're at the hotel in Utah. Back on the bus in the morning.

From: djohnson3@valleyu.edu

To: jthatcher@valleyu.edu

Subject: Re: Dress up?

My roommate is a fashion design major. She makes a lot of dresses and skirts inspired by the Regency and Victorian eras. I suppose that could be considered cosplay, but we just do it for fun after a night out.

From: jthatcher@valleyu.edu

To: djohnson3@valleyu.edu

Subject: Re: Re: Dress up?

What in the hell are dresses inspired from the Regency and Victorian eras? Like big ass dresses with corsets and shit?

Her next email says nothing, but she attaches a picture of herself in a red dress with sleeves that hang off her shoulders. It dips low in the front, pushing up her small tits.

I never noticed how little she is, but the fabric wraps tight around her midsection and then flares out around her hips. The skirt has a large slit that comes up high on her thigh, and attached to her feet are these strappy gold shoes that tangle around her legs. She looks… well, she looks fucking hot.

She's not smiling, but her lips are coated a shiny pink, and her dark blonde hair falls around her shoulders. She's a tiara away from looking like a sexy, vintage princess. It annoys me, but I can't stop staring.

Heat rushes to my dick. Man, away games are the worst. Short of picking up a random at the hotel, there's no one to hook up with after games. I could use a release right now.

I can't say any of the things I'm thinking, but I'm hella fascinated to know more now. This is not the Daisy I've been sitting next to for the past few weeks. Sure, she always looks cute, but this… fuuuuck.

From: jthatcher@valleyu.edu

To: djohnson3@valleyu.edu

Subject: Re: Re: Re: Dress up?

Your roommate made that? There's more?

From: djohnson3@valleyu.edu

To: jthatcher@valleyu.edu

Subject: My friends are talented

Yep. My cousin, Violet. Do you like them?

She's attached more pictures. Her friends, I presume. I scroll back up to the one of just her. *Damn*. Look, a sexy little dress alone doesn't make a chick hot. Her friends are wearing similar things, and they all look great. Totally fuckable by just about any guy I know standards.

But that dress on Daisy. It's just so… unexpected.

From: jthatcher@valleyu.edu

To: djohnson3@valleyu.edu

Subject: Re: My friends are talented

Yeah, that's pretty cool. Now that you're all dressed up, what's the plan? Hitting after hours?

From: djohnson3@valleyu.edu

To: jthatcher@valleyu.edu

Subject: Re: Re: My friends are talented

No, we're in for the night. This could go on for hours. Violet just opened another bottle of wine.

P.S. Diet Coke and Vodka do NOT mix well.

From: jthatcher@valleyu.edu

To: djohnson3@valleyu.edu

Subject: Drunk Daisy?

Are you drunk, sweet Daisy? I can't tell.

From: djohnson3@valleyu.edu

To: jthatcher@valleyu.edu

Subject: Re: Drunk Daisy?

I am not sweet, but I am drunk. I think. My insides are warm and tingly. Do you get your own rooms at the hotel, or are you bunked up with a bunch of other guys?

From: jthatcher@valleyu.edu

To: djohnson3@valleyu.edu

Subject: Re: Re: Drunk Daisy?

Warm and tingly, huh? Yeah, I'd say you're drunk, sweet Daisy.

Nah, just one roommate on away games most of the time. He's sleeping.

I know she's probably asking specifically about Liam. Actually, it's probably why she emailed me at all. The thought puts a bitter taste in my mouth, and I glance over at my buddy sleeping.

Something like guilt pricks the back of my neck. I'm not doing anything wrong. So we're exchanging a few emails? It's a far cry from anything I should feel bad about. I'm not stepping on his girl. He's had plenty of time to make a move. Though that might be because of what I said when he mentioned asking her out.

I scroll up to take one more look at her in the red dress and then turn my phone on silent for the night.

We get back to Valley Saturday night with another win in the books.

"Are you coming out?" I ask Liam as we step out of the bus. A few of the guys are going to the bar, and others are heading to one of our senior's, Brad McCallum's, apartment.

Liam's smile is a little quicker tonight. He still struggled out on the ice, but we found ways to score without him. I hope it's taken a little pressure off him, and he can get back to playing awesome hockey. I know what it means to him. He wants to play professionally but hasn't been drafted yet.

"Yeah, I think I'll head to the bar for a beer or two. You?"

"I told McCallum I'd stop by."

"All right, man." He offers his hand, and I take it and pull him in for a one-arm hug. "See you later. Nice job this weekend, Cap."

McCallum's apartment is already packed when I arrive. Dallas, a sophomore goalie, tosses me a beer, and I take a seat next to him at the dining room table currently covered in cards and cans.

A hand snakes down my shoulder and onto my chest. Cybil leans forward, and her shiny, brown hair falls into my face. "Hey, handsome."

"Hey." I lean back and wrap an arm around her waist, and she moves to sit on my lap.

"You missed the most epic of parties last night. I hate hockey season." She sticks out her bottom lip.

Cybil and I have an easy friendship that often leads to sex. She's a civil engineering major, too, and parties more than anyone else I know. She's a cool chick—wild and always up for a good time.

"Then I guess we better make up for it tonight." I knock Dallas on the shoulder and motion for him to move down, so Cybil has a chair.

For the next two hours, I play catch up, drinking my weight in beer. I'm always a lightweight after a game.

"Be right back," I say after we finish a hand of poker. I get up from the table, saying hey to a few people on the way to the bathroom. I've barely got my pants unzipped when Cybil slips inside and shuts the door.

She giggles. "Oh, you really had to pee."

"Yeah, at least turn around. Spare a guy a little dignity."

She does but keeps giggling. "I heard a lot of people turned up at Sigma tonight."

"The only place I'm going after this is my bed. Maybe McCallum's bed." I am beat.

"Come with me," she whines. "A quick stop at Sigma, and then you can crash at my place."

I move to the sink to wash my hands.

"Do you like my dress? It's new." She pushes in front of me, so she's wedged between me and the vanity. It's red and has a zipper down the front. She pulls said zipper down slowly until it's past her bra.

It's a sexy dress, and Cybil has a banging body. Hooking up with her is always great, but a flash of a different red dress on a different girl stops me.

"Uhhh... another night. I think I'm done for."

"Stupid hockey season," she says, and shakes her head. "Text me if you change your mind."

She leaves me alone in the bathroom. I lock the door and then pull up the last email from Daisy. She's fucking hot, and I can't stop being aware of it.

She didn't email again to congratulate me on the victory tonight, and I don't know why I keep expecting one to show up. I start to email her but stop myself. We're not friends. She's my lab partner, and she's into Liam.

I wrap my fingers around my phone and bring it up to my forehead with a groan.

What the fuck am I doing?

Chapter NINE

Daisy

My laptop is open in front of me, and I navigate from the English assignment I should be working on to my email. Jordan Thatcher's name taunts me, but I don't dare click on it again.

We haven't talked since Friday night, but the humiliation is just as fresh two days later.

A dull ache presses behind my eyes, and I lean forward, head in hands.

"You looked at your email again, didn't you?" Violet asks from across the table.

"Ugh." I sit tall and take a long gulp of my energy drink. It isn't helping. Neither is the soft laughter from Violet that follows.

"There should be a law against using your phone when drinking."

"It was not that bad." She smirks. "You sent a couple of sexy photos."

A new flush creeps up my neck and my stomach rolls. Stupid technology. I groan and squeeze my eyes closed.

"*Tame*, sexy photos. It isn't like you were naked," she says.

I know she's trying to help, but every word jabs into my confidence, deflating it a little more.

"Can we just study in silence?"

"Sure. Yeah." She presses her lips together and sits back in the chair across from me. The grin on her face has been the same every time we've talked about… *shudder*. I can't even say it.

"I have to say one more thing." Violet clasps her hands together on the table. We're at the library studying, or I'm attempting to with little help from Violet. "You were having fun Friday night. More fun than I've seen you have in, maybe ever. Chalk it up to that. He's probably already forgotten about the photos. I mean, we're talking about Jordan Thatcher. He has no shortage of girls at his beck and call. Honestly, that's probably the least sexy photo he got from a girl all weekend."

That should make me feel better, but it doesn't.

"I just can't believe I have to face him in class."

I look at my cousin for another dose of encouragement. Instead, her gaze is stuck behind me, eyes wide. "You might have to face him a little sooner than that."

"What?"

I swivel around and spot him as he reaches the top of the stairs. He's alone, backpack over one shoulder, hat backward, Powerade in hand. He scans the second floor until he spots whoever he's looking for and juts his chin.

I follow his trek to a table with three other guys, including Liam.

"Did you know Liam was here?" she asks.

"No." My Liam senses are all out of whack. Stupid emails. Oh my god, did Liam see the pictures? I don't know why it didn't occur to me until now, but of course, Jordan would show him. I bet they had a good laugh. Oh man, I'm going to have to drop out of physics. Maybe out of Valley U completely.

"We should go." I close my laptop and shove it into my bag.

"No. Running away is admitting you're embarrassed."

"I *am*."

She doesn't budge. "Plus, there's a better chance of them seeing you if you get up and walk around."

That keeps me planted in my seat. I take one last covert glance at their table. Liam sits forward, smiling and nodding. Jordan leans back with a pencil behind one ear, staring at his phone. His phone. Double groan.

I have never concentrated harder on being invisible. I hunch over my laptop and focus on American literature. Every noise, every shadow behind me, sets me on edge, but I don't turn back around.

"Okay, they're leaving," Violet says sometime later.

I slink down farther in the chair.

"And they're walking, walking, almost to the stairs," Violet provides the play-by-play. "Oh, they're stopping to talk to someone."

"Guy or girl."

"Girl. Pretty. Really pretty."

Of course, she is.

"Okay. I think she's moving along. They're walking again."

My heart is racing, and I want to look so bad.

"Oh." Violet's voice squeaks, and she looks down at the table. "I think you've been spotted."

"What?!"

"Oh my god. Uhh... act natural."

"Violet." My blood turns to ice. "Please tell me they're not coming over here."

She keeps her lips closed as she mumbles, "Sorry. Can't."

"Daisy?" Liam's voice comes from behind me.

I turn slowly, shooting Violet a panicked look before I do.

"Hi!" I fake surprise as I look from Liam to Jordan, then back at Liam. "What are you guys doing here?"

"Studying," Liam responds for the both of them.

"Right." *Duh.*

"We have a killer Geotech test this week." His gaze moves past me to Violet.

I wave in her direction. "This is my cousin, Violet."

Liam takes two steps forward and extends a hand. "Liam. Nice to meet you."

"Likewise."

Her ability to play it cool is impressive. Then again, a year ago, she was partying with guys like Liam and Jordan.

"Liam and Jordan are my lab partners in physics."

Jordan smiles and tips his head in greeting. "You must be the design major."

"Yeah. That's right."

Oh, the mortification. My ears burn, and I'm certain my face is bright red.

"I saw some of your stuff. It's good." Jordan wears a smile that's neither mocking nor fake.

"Fashion design, huh?" Liam asks. "What kind of stuff do you design?"

Jordan holds my gaze until I can't take it anymore. He didn't tell Liam. I'm both relieved and surprised.

"All kinds of stuff," Violet says. "But dresses are my favorite."

Liam's phone lights up in his hand.

"That's my mom," he says, backing away. He looks at Jordan. "I'll catch you back at the dorm."

Jordan nods, and Liam waves at Violet and me. "Good to see you both."

"Bye," Violet and I say at the same time.

He hurries off, putting the phone to his ear as he reaches the stairs.

Jordan lingers, and when I turn my gaze back to him, he's watching me.

"Looks like he's in a better mood," I say.

"The wins were good for him."

"Yeah, it seems like it."

Violet leans forward and points to an empty chair.

Shaking my head, I can't get the words, *I'm sure he has places to be*, out of my mouth before he's pulling out the chair and dropping his big, intimidating frame into it.

"Which was your favorite?" she asks.

"Uh..." He looks between us.

"She means the dresses," I explain.

"Oh." He grins. "They were all pretty awesome."

Violet would never give up that easily. She keeps staring at him expectantly.

"The red one was my favorite." He glances at me as he says it.

My stomach does a thousand somersaults. Rationally I tell myself it's probably the only one he remembers, or he's just guessing, but there's something about the way he's looking at me that makes my heart race.

"That is some of my best work." Violet leans back, satisfied with his answer.

"How was the rest of your weekend?" he asks me.

"Fine. Yours?"

"Good. We got in last night and went out for a bit. Any more drinking and dressing up?" He smiles at me. Jordan Thatcher is freaking smiling at me.

I shake my head. I'm a mess, heart racing, palms sweaty, stomach still doing flips. And then there's Jordan. He always looks so comfortable, so relaxed. Then again, he wasn't the one that got drunk and sent sexy pictures.

To be fair, I wasn't trying to be sexy. Or maybe I was. The dresses are sexy, and I felt good wearing them. Some part of me wanted his approval. I can't quite wrap my brain around that.

Sober, I can see how it came off, but drunk, I just wanted to be noticed. I wanted Jordan to notice me.

He sits forward. Violet's gone back to her homework, or at least she's pretending not to be listening as Jordan says, "I'm glad I ran into you."

"You are?"

"I didn't know how to say this over email, still don't." He rubs his jaw and looks more unsure than I've ever seen him. I didn't know he was even capable of that look.

"O-kay."

"Just say it," Violet pipes in, still not looking up. "Because right now, she's going through every worst-case scenario in her head."

She's absolutely right about that.

A small chuckle leaves his mouth. "Liam's a good guy."

Of all the places I thought this conversation was going, this wasn't anywhere on the list. I wait for him to continue.

"He's a little slow to pick up the vibe when someone's into him."

"I don't understand what you're saying."

He gets to his feet and shoots a grin right at me. "I'm saying, if you like him, ask him out."

Ask him out? Just like that. Is he crazy?

"But I don't—" My voice breaks off. Denying seems stupid. And even if I could get up the courage, I'd never be able to face Liam again if he said no. Lab would be unbearable, and I joke, but I can't drop it. I need that class.

Jordan takes a step away, and his smile gets softer. "He won't say no. See you Tuesday."

I spend the next two days thinking about the weird interaction with Jordan, and playing scenarios in my head where I do what he suggested. Even in my daydreams, I can't say the words without blushing a hideous shade of red.

I hate that my crush on Liam was so easy for him to see. Okay, fine, he'd have to be an idiot not to notice. And Jordan isn't an idiot. I haven't totally figured him out, but an idiot he is not.

Tuesday afternoon during our lunch break, Violet corners me in the kitchen as I'm packing up for my final classes of the day.

"Have you decided what you're going to do?"

"I'm not asking him out." I've told her as much the other ten times she's asked.

"You heard Jordan; he won't say no!"

My heart is galloping in my chest. "Oh, well, Jordan said it, so it must be true."

"I don't think he would steer you wrong. Which is odd because I never thought Jordan Thatcher would be the type of guy to come over and tell you to ask out a guy." She shrugs. "There was something about the way he said it. He likes you."

"Liam?"

"No, Jordan."

"Oh yeah, that's why he told me to ask out someone else. Why are you pushing me to go out with Liam anyway? You hate jocks."

Violet fidgets. She doesn't really hate Liam or Jordan or anyone that I know of, except maybe our neighbor Gavin (they have history), but she'd never approve of me dating a popular jock. When it was theoretical, she played along but now...

"It's what you want, and at least Liam is a decent one."

I grab my backpack off the chair and start for the door. "I will see you later."

"He won't say no," she yells after me.

I'm usually the first person to physics lab, but today I walk so slowly that at three minutes until class starts, I realize at this rate I'm going to be late and have to book it the rest of the way across campus. Professor Green is beginning his lecture when I open the classroom door. All eyes are on me as I slip inside.

"Sorry," I tell him as I go to my table.

Liam pulls out the extra stool next to him.

"Thanks," I whisper.

For the twenty-five minutes that Professor Green covers today's lab, all I can do is focus on breathing. Frantic energy flows through my veins, and as the seconds tick by, I recognize it as adrenaline. The dangerous kind that makes you do things that shouldn't be physically possible, like lift a car or ask out your crush.

"You may get started," Professor Green says.

Liam angles his body toward me and smiles, then starts setting up the lab. I look at Jordan for reassurance. He meets my gaze with an intensity that makes my chest tighten. Oh god. He better be right.

Chapter TEN

Jordan

I CAN PRACTICALLY SEE DAISY'S THOUGHTS OVER HER HEAD like a thought bubble. She and Liam are working through the lab while I lead us through the instructions, per the usual.

She hasn't stopped blushing since she walked in late. Today she's wearing jeans and this oversized sweatshirt that hangs off one shoulder. It's even sexier to see her like this, knowing what she looks like all dressed up.

Tapping my pencil on the paper, I redirect my gaze to the table. She's never going to ask if I keep staring at her. And I need her to ask. Then the two of them can go out, just like they both want, and I can stop thinking about her.

The number of times I looked at her in that red dress is too many to count.

"Jordan?"

My head pops up at my name, and Liam's eyes narrow in confusion. "Everything okay?"

"Yep. Great."

"Can you read the next step then?"

I clear my throat and adjust the hat on my head. "Right."

For the rest of the class, I focus only on the handout in front of me. Well, that and Daisy's soft voice as she and Liam talk through their work. I'm no help at all. I have visions of drunk Daisy in that sexy, red dress and an irrational burn in my chest to stop her from asking out Liam and ask her out myself.

"I think that's it," Daisy says.

"We're a good team." Liam holds up his hand, and she presses her much smaller palm against it lightly.

I pack up quickly and wait for Liam. He's still chatting with Daisy, taking his sweet time. We don't have class together after this, so I don't need to wait for him, but I want to see if Daisy works up the courage to ask him out. He's obviously not going to. Which is why I told her she should ask him.

I wasn't lying. He won't say no. I don't know if he's hesitated because of what I said, or maybe he's just taking his damn time, but I decided to give them a little push.

I'm seriously regretting that now as she fiddles with the straps of her backpack. This is fucking painful.

"What time are you done with classes and everything today?" she asks him. It's her in. I can see the breadcrumbs she's laying out and smile to myself.

"This is my last class."

"Where are you headed next?"

"Probably just head back to the dorm. You?"

"I'm done for the day, too."

The three of us walk out of class, her and Liam leading the way.

She glances over at him, still clutching onto the straps of her backpack like a lifeline. "I was thinking about going to University Hall and getting coffee or something."

"Cool." He bobs his head. "I love the hot mocha."

Jesus, man, take a hint.

We continue another few steps before she summons the courage. I can see it, and I hold my breath.

Her shoulders lift and, even in profile, I can see how nervous she is. "Would you want—"

One big step puts me directly between them. "Hey, Daisy, can I talk to you for a minute?"

I take her by the elbow, and a rush of pure pleasure shoots up from my fingertips.

"Y-yeah." Her voice quivers, but I swear I see relief wash over her.

"I'll see you back at the dorm," I tell Liam, effectively dismissing him.

"Sounds good." He gives me a salute. "Later, Daisy."

"Bye," she calls after him.

I step back to give her room. The two of us stand in place. My heart is hammering like a drum in my chest.

"Is everything okay?" she asks. "You look nervous or something."

"Yeah, everything's fine. I just have a favor."

Her blue eyes bore into mine like she can see into my soul. I'm waiting for her to call me on my bullshit, but instead she asks, "A favor?"

"Mhmm." I shove my hands in my front pockets.

She buys it. Of course she does. In what world would I interrupt her and say I need a favor when I don't? Fuck my life.

"Are you going to ask me, or am I supposed to guess?"

Right. Uhh. Well, crap. I scroll through options quickly and blurt out the first thing that doesn't sound totally ludicrous. "I need you to tutor me."

She hesitates. Her pink lips part and then press into a thin line. "Favors are usually posed as questions."

"Right. Can you tutor me?"

"In physics?"

"And statistics." My throat is dry, and I clear it.

"I didn't realize you were struggling."

I don't say anything. Outright lying feels shitty, though so is asking someone to tutor you when you don't need it.

"I've never tutored anyone before. I'm not sure that I'd be any good at it."

I should give her the out. I've successfully stopped her from asking out Liam. At least for now. Was that the plan? Fuck, I don't know what I'm doing.

"How's tomorrow night?"

She thinks for a second. "Fine, I think. I'm done with classes at two. I could meet you at the library right after."

The fact that she's so accommodating just makes me feel worse for not really needing a tutor.

"Great." I start to walk off, then stop. "Oh, fuck. I have film review tomorrow night." I should have asked her to borrow a damn pen or something. "How about you give me your number, and I'll text you when I'm done?"

She looks like she might be seriously regretting agreeing to this, but she rattles off her number, and I put it in my phone under Sweet Daisy. "Perfect. I'll text you when I'm done, and I can come to you if it's easier."

She nods.

And I walk away before I say or do any more dumb shit.

Chapter ELEVEN

Daisy

"He's coming *here?*" Violet drops her phone to her lap and sits up on the couch. She glances around at the mess of her and Dahlia's sewing stuff around the room.

"Maybe we can move this upstairs," Dahlia offers weakly. Even if I wanted that, he'd be here before they got it all moved. Two fashion design majors can accumulate a lot of stuff.

"It's fine. Jordan and I will study upstairs."

"In your room?" Jane asks, peeking out of the kitchen. Her smile starts slow and builds until I'm certain I'm blushing.

"Is Liam coming too?" Violet asks.

"No. I don't think so."

Her brown eyes narrow. "It's weird that he didn't just ask Liam to help him. Don't you think?"

"Maybe. I don't know." Frazzled, I can't think through the

strangeness of the situation. Jordan Thatcher is going to be at my house. All weirdness pales compared to that.

A heavy knock on the front door pushes my pulse into overdrive. I smooth a hand down my dress and take a deep breath before I hurry to answer it.

Jordan stands on the other side in his standard backward hat, jeans, and T-shirt. A smile tugs at one side of his mouth. "Hey."

"Hi." My voice sounds entirely too breathy.

Instead of making a move to come inside, he points to the house next door. "You live next to The White House."

"Yep. That's right."

I open the door wider, and he steps through. "I didn't even know this place was here."

"We get that a lot." Violet waves from the couch.

"You remember Violet. And that's Dahlia and Jane," I say, introducing him to my roommates.

Dahlia's eyes are wide as she takes him in, but she doesn't speak. I forget how shy she is sometimes since it mostly surfaces around the opposite sex.

"Nice to meet you," Jane calls from the next room. She moves closer, unabashedly watching as Jordan walks in.

I have to say, Jordan in the middle of our living room is a strange sight among the fabrics and sewing machine occupying most of the space.

He nods to my friends and then looks back at me.

"Ready?" I ask.

My roommates are so intently staring at him and now me.

"Yeah." He adjusts his backpack and follows me to the second floor. The four bedrooms and the only full bathroom are up here. My room faces the house on the opposite side of us from The White House. This street, as well as the one behind us, are primarily rentals for the university.

As he walks into my room, I feel like I'm seeing it with new eyes—the simple metal frame, the light-yellow comforter, the raggedy stuffed bear that I've had since I was seven. The only other furniture besides my bed is a desk, chair, and my easel.

"You can have the chair," I say.

The wood floor creaks with his footsteps. He takes a seat and drops his backpack to the floor in front of him, then continues to look around the room.

"Drawing?" He points to the easel. "Or painting?"

"Mostly drawing."

"That's awesome. I can't draw for anything."

"It's just a lot of practice."

He nods slowly. "Bad at taking a compliment."

"What?" I ask with a light laugh.

"Just adding to the list of things I'm learning about you."

"Thank you," I relent with a smile. "Did you have something in mind that you wanted to work on? I pulled up some study notes from physics that might help."

"That sounds fine." He brings out a notebook and pencil.

My laptop is on my bed, but I suddenly feel weird about sitting on it in front of him. I perch on the very edge and open my computer.

He slides his pencil behind one ear, and I move so that I'm closer to him but still sitting on the edge of the bed. He smells like soap again, sans beer. Turning my laptop, I say, "Do you want to go through the lab questions or...?"

"Sure."

I start to read through the first one, explaining as best I can. His brown eyes are pinned on me so attentively my pulse jumps, and my voice quivers. I stop and sit back. "How about you read it and just tell me what questions you have?"

He sits forward and stares for a minute. The silence in my room is suffocating. Even my breathing sounds too loud. I try to do less of it, but then I feel like I'm going to pass out.

"I think I've got it."

"All of it?"

"Well..." He glances from me to the screen and back. If he expects me to read his mind and magically fill the gaps in his knowledge, he's going to be seriously disappointed.

"I don't know how to do this," I admit.

"Me either." He sits back in the chair. "Are you hungry?"

"No, not really."

"Thirsty?"

"I'm okay."

"A walk then?"

"If it will help."

"It couldn't hurt. There's a gas station up the street." He starts toward the door, leaving his backpack. He glances back when I don't follow. "Are you coming?"

Violet and Dahlia are nowhere to be found downstairs, but the evidence of their work is still strewn around.

"Whoa," Jordan says as he takes it all in. "It looks like this room exploded. How long were we up there?"

"This is how they are when they have a big project due. They take over the entire first floor. Fabrics and threads, measuring tapes, and scissors." I look at him. "Violet owns like ten different ones and still can never find a pair."

"Why do they call it a pair?" he asks. "A pair of scissors sounds like they come in two."

"It's a plural tantum."

His mouth quirks up on both sides.

Even in the cool night air, I feel my cheeks warm under a blush. "Like jeans or pants."

He's quiet a second and then says with a smirk, "Or panties."

We lock eyes in the darkness, and my heart flutters.

The gas station is on the next block. We walk up the street and stop at the intersection.

Jordan hits the crosswalk button. "Do they take over the first floor a lot?"

"Violet and Dahlia?"

He nods.

"Once a week or so. Sometimes they go to the design lab, but Violet says she's more inspired at home where she can play her music loudly and keep late hours."

"And Jane?"

"She is a music major, but she spends a lot of time in her room."

He hangs on my every word. "And what about you?"

"What about me?"

"What do you do when they're taking over your first floor and blasting tunes all night?"

"Oh, I don't mind."

The light changes, and we cross the street at a clip. The gas station/quickie mart smells like burnt coffee. I hang back and let Jordan grab what he wants, which includes a bag of chips, Twizzlers, two energy drinks, and a pack of gum.

"You don't want anything?" he asks as he places his items on the checkout counter.

"No thanks." I peruse the items up front and smile at the Fun Dip packets. "I didn't know they still made these."

"They're classic. No childhood is complete without Fun Dip and candy necklaces."

I run my hand along the pack and then pull it back. "I wasn't allowed to have either of those as a kid."

"You've never had Fun Dip?" Jordan asks, disbelief in his tone as one dark brow lifts.

I shake my head and move to the other side of him, closer to the door. He pays, and we head back outside.

Jordan opens the chips before we've crossed the parking lot. He tosses one in his mouth, chews, and asks, "What kind of deprived childhood did you lead, sweet Daisy?"

I swear he says things just to see me blush, which I, of course, do. "I wasn't deprived. I had candy and junk food sometimes."

"Sometimes?"

"At birthday parties and Halloween, Easter, that kind of thing."

He nods thoughtfully, and we walk across the street back toward the house.

"You didn't answer my question earlier," Jordan says. "Where do you hang out when they take over for these wild and crazy design sessions?"

The wind blows my hair around my face. I tuck it behind my ears and hug my arms to my stomach. "In my room or—"

"Hold up." He stops, sets the bag on the ground, and removes his hoodie. When he thrusts it in my direction, I stare at it, unsure what to do.

"Take it. You're obviously cold."

I wrap my fingers around the soft fabric, hand still outstretched. He nods, encouraging me.

"Thanks." My pulse kicks up a notch as I pull his sweatshirt on over my head. It's warm and smells faintly like fabric softener and something else I can't quite place.

"Welcome."

We continue in silence. Most of the houses along the street are quiet. The lights are on inside, but the yards and driveways are still. I walk this street almost every day, but I'm usually in a hurry one way or the other.

Jordan's long strides are slow, and his gaze roams around, taking it all in as he eats his chips. I get the feeling very little studying is happening tonight.

I take a step, looking over my shoulder at him as I do. "There's a tree house in the back yard."

His stare focuses on me, and my pulse races higher.

"Sometimes I go out—"

"Watch out!"

Brakes squeal against the pavement, and a flurry of red light flashes in front of me before I'm yanked backward, swallowing my words, and slamming into his chest.

A shocked gasp escapes as I glance from the car backing out of the driveway and into Jordan's dark eyes.

"Oh my gosh."

He curses under his breath.

My hands tremble. "Thank you. I didn't see it."

"No shit." His voice is quiet but forceful. He steadies me and steps away.

The guy in the car rolls down the passenger side window. He's a Valley student. I know because I see him walking toward campus sometimes. "I'm so sorry. They should really put streetlights up. Are you both okay?"

"We're fine," Jordan answers, his voice like ice. "Streetlights don't make you a better driver. Try watching where you're going."

The guy pales.

"It was my fault," I say, but the driver is inching backward while rolling up his window.

Jordan's steps toward my house get quicker. "He should have been looking where he was going."

"I should have too."

He stops in front of my house. Anger radiates off him, but I watch as he reins it in. "You could have been seriously hurt because that asshole wasn't paying attention."

I'm at a loss for how to respond. I don't know if he's pissed at me or the driver, or both.

"You're okay?" His voice softens.

"I'm good," I say.

When we get inside, Violet and Dahlia are in the living room, sitting on the floor with their sketchbooks and iPads laid out in front of them.

"Where'd you two go?" Violet asks.

"Gas station," I answer.

Jordan lifts the bag. "Anyone need snacks?"

They both shake their heads.

I follow Jordan back up to my room. He sits on the chair in

front of my desk, digging through the bag. He frees the Twizzlers, opens it, and pulls out two. He separates the strands of candy and offers one my way.

"No thanks."

"Live a little."

"I've had licorice, and I don't like it."

"Has bad taste in candy. Noted." He winks and bites off the end of both candies. He's back to the carefree guy of earlier, and I guess that means he's forgiven me for nearly getting squashed in front of him.

I point to my laptop. "Maybe it would help if we went over the last quiz?"

He nods.

Over the next half hour, I talk through each question on our last physics quiz. He asks me to explain a few points further, but I don't really feel like I'm being that helpful.

A text notification on his phone interrupts us on the final question.

He taps out a response before giving me his attention. "Sorry."

"It's okay. I think we're done with physics unless you have more questions?"

"Oh." He pockets his phone again. "Uhh. No. I'm good."

"Do you want to work on statistics?"

"I should probably get out of your hair for tonight."

I never really cared about being a good tutor, but the thought of him walking out of here no better off than when he came in doesn't sit well with me. I'm not good at a lot of things, but physics and math I can do.

"What about tomorrow night?" I offer.

He's quiet a beat as he studies my face. "Glutton for punishment?"

"I don't feel like I helped at all," I admit.

"You did," he says too quickly. "Thank you."

Downstairs, Dahlia and Violet are busy hunched over their work. I walk Jordan to the door.

"Oh, here." I pull his sweatshirt over my head and hand it back to him, missing the heat of it instantly.

"Same time and place tomorrow then?" he asks, raising his voice so I can hear him over the noise.

At my nod, he waves and starts off.

"How was it?" Violet pauses her sewing after I shut the front door.

"Fine." I hurry upstairs.

"We want details tomorrow," Dahlia yells after me.

On any other night, I might sit downstairs and tell them everything while they work, but I've been itching to draw for the last hour.

Something on my bed catches my eye as I pull my chair over to the easel. I walk closer, and a smile tugs at my lips. Fun Dip.

Chapter TWELVE

Daisy

THE NEXT NIGHT JORDAN APPEARS ON MY DOORSTEP just like the night before.

"Hey," he says as he steps inside the house.

Violet and Dahlia were up late, but they finished their projects, and our first floor no longer looks like a fabric shop got hit by a tornado.

I lead him into the kitchen area where we have a small table that we sometimes use for studying. My laptop and notes are already set up. I put more thought into this tutor session than I did all my classes today.

Jordan came prepared today, too, with snacks and his energy drink.

"Thank you for the Fun Dip," I say as I sit at the table.

"What'd you think?"

"I think I went to bed with a sugar high."

His deep chuckle fills the room. "Where is everyone tonight?"

"Violet is at the library, I think Jane is upstairs, and Dahlia has a golf tournament this weekend, so she's gone until Sunday."

"She's a golfer?" He bobs his head. "Nice."

We study for a while. I printed out some old quizzes, and we work through them together. Jordan picks up everything quickly. Even when I move to next week's chapter, he grasps the concepts and nods along. At some point, he turns on music, claiming he thinks better with background noise.

I thought he was full of crap, but I can see it. He mouths the words and taps his pencil, but he's in it, focused and working hard.

"You're different than I thought," I say as he mouths along with an old Nirvana song.

His head pops up, and he leans back in his chair. "How's that?"

"I'm not sure, exactly."

"Well, since my good looks are obvious, it must be my personality that you thought sucked."

"Your personality doesn't suck."

"Exactly." He grins. "For the record, you're different than I thought too."

"I am?" My insides are squishy thinking about Jordan giving me any thought at all.

Before he can tell me what he might have thought of me before, the front door opens, and Violet says, "I'm home."

She walks straight back toward the kitchen but stops when she sees Jordan. "You again."

He juts a chin toward her. "Hey, Violet."

"Does this mean I can't convince you to come out and celebrate?" She waves her hand, indicating me and Jordan studying.

"Celebrate what?" I ask.

"I got an A on the dress, and my professor said it was my best design yet."

"That is amazing. Congratulations." I look over at Jordan, who has his phone in front of him, staring at the screen. "We're still working. Maybe tomorrow night?"

Jordan pushes his chair back. "Actually, I totally forgot. I have bowling tonight."

"Bowling?" Violet asks.

"I'm in a league with a few buddies." A shy smile pulls up one side of his mouth. "I'm sorry to cut this short."

"It's okay. Did you get what you needed?"

"I think so. Thanks for your help." His smile makes my lips twitch to reciprocate the movement.

"Now we can go out," Violet says. She moves to the fridge and pulls out a bottle of white wine. "Anyone else want a drink?"

Jordan and I both shake our heads.

She pours herself a glass. "I haven't been bowling in forever."

"What about you?" Jordan motions his head toward me as he pushes back from the table.

"Are you asking me if I've ever bowled?"

He nods.

"Of course."

"In the last five years?"

"Yes." My voice climbs defensively. "We went last semester with a group."

"She's not bad," Violet says as she leans against the counter.

I give him a smug, satisfied look.

"All right, sweet Daisy. Prove it." He stands and hooks his backpack over one shoulder.

"Prove it how?"

"We're short a player tonight. Come fill in."

"Oh, no. I—" All my excuses die on my tongue because they admit I'm not really that good. I'm not, but I'd rather keep that to myself. "I can't tonight."

"Okay." He lifts his phone. "I guess I'll just text Liam and see if he can recruit someone else."

"Liam is on your bowling team?" Violet asks.

"Yeah. He's a founding member," Jordan says.

Violet glances at me with wide, expressive eyes. She mouths, "Go!"

The thought of embarrassing myself in rented shoes is almost enough to hold me back, but I blurt out, "We'll come."

"We'll?" Violet asks, my insinuation clear.

"They have alcohol there, right?"

Jordan nods. "Yeah. And food."

I see the second that Violet gives in. She's the freaking best.

"Okay, fine," she says. "But one of you is buying me a drink."

We ride with Jordan in his SUV. I sit in the front, second-guessing this decision. I do want more opportunities to talk to Liam, but I'm not the most coordinated person, and he's, well, he just is. He moves so gracefully and confidently. I'm not a walking disaster or anything, but I didn't play sports as a kid and have mostly avoided them as an adult.

We're the first to get there for his team. Jordan checks in, and we're told to go to lane two. Jordan has his own ball, which for some reason, makes me giggle. I switch out my shoes and then go in search of my own ball while Jordan buys Violet a drink from the bar.

The selection is intense. I avoid anything pink and overly girly. I find a green one that isn't too heavy and fits my small hands pretty well, and I am about to head back when Liam's voice startles me.

"Hey, Daisy."

I turn around to face him. An image of me dropping the ball on his foot flashes before me. Luckily for the both of us, I manage to hang on to the slippery ball.

"Hi," I respond, clutching it to my stomach.

"Find a good one?" His blond hair is covered with a white hat, and he's in a matching polo shirt.

"Excuse me?"

He points to the ball. "The right ball is everything."

He scans the rack until he finds the one he's looking for.

"There you are," he says softly to the blue marble ball as he inserts his fingers and holds it up like he's refamiliarizing himself with it. He glances at me with a sheepish grin. "I panic every time that I won't be able to find it. It's lucky."

We walk back over to the lane and put our balls down, then sit to wait for everyone else.

"How's your week going?" he asks. He removes his hat and sets it on the bench next to him. He might be the only guy I know who can wear a hat and not get hat hair.

"Good. Yours?"

"Not too bad." He smiles. "Ready for this?"

"Not really," I admit. "I'm not very sporty."

I flounce the hem of my skirt to further my point.

"Ah, well. Don't worry." He reaches into a bag underneath the bench and pulls out a shirt. He holds it up to show me the front with the name, Lucky Strikes.

"Cute."

He hands it to me. "Welcome to the team."

Jordan and Violet come back with drinks—Violet a hard seltzer and Jordan a pitcher in one hand and a stack of cups in the other.

"Look at you," Jordan says as I slide on the oversized bowling shirt.

Violet giggles as she takes me in.

"That bad?" I ask.

"No, you're totally pulling it off."

"Adorable." Jordan's lips twitch with a hint of a smile as he extends a cup toward me. "Beer?"

Liam's already filling one for himself, so I nod. "Thanks."

Jordan pours my cup almost to the top, and I take a sip as another guy joins us. One I recognize.

"You have got to be kidding me," Violet's voice cuts through the noise of the place.

"Hey, guys," Gavin says. "New recruits?"

"Daisy is filling in for Jenkins tonight."

"And you?" Gavin asks, looking at Violet.

"I was here for the drinks and socializing, but I guess now I'm just here for the booze."

"You two know each other?" Jordan asks.

"We're neighbors," Gavin says.

"Oh, right." Jordan shakes his head. He looks to Liam. "They live next to The White House."

"Really?" Liam asks me, smiling.

"Yeah," I say quietly.

Liam moves to the chair in front of the computer to input names and motions for me to follow. My heart rate skitters along as I sit, and his arm brushes mine.

"You're filling in for Jenkins. He usually goes second, but I can put you anywhere in the lineup you want."

"Wherever is fine."

"I'll put you between Gavin and Jordan," he says, focusing on the screen in front of him. He puts himself first and then Gavin, me, and Jordan. He sits back. "We're all set. Ready?"

"No." I laugh.

"I've got you."

Liam puts on his team shirt, grabs his lucky ball, and gets in position. He throws a strike on his very first turn.

The guys give him fist bumps, and he takes a seat next to me again.

"Nice job."

"Thanks."

When Gavin has the same result, my stomach sinks. I glance at Violet whose smile and big eyes meet mine, silently communicating the horror. These guys are good. When Violet said I was pretty good, she meant my ball mostly stays out of the gutter, not that I knock down a lot of pins.

"You're up," Liam says.

I glance at a girl on the lane beside us, watching as she takes her turn. Her ball flies down the lane and knocks all but one pin down. I swallow thickly. Oh god. What was I thinking agreeing to this?

I grab my ball and glance back. All eyes are on me. Awesome. Slowly, I walk to the center of the lane.

"Let's go, Daisy," Liam cheers behind me.

It's only because the sooner I take my turn, the sooner I can go sit back down, that I move my feet and hurl the ball. It isn't as fast or straight as the others, but it manages to get all the way down without going in the gutter, and I knock down four pins.

I let out a sigh and go back. Then I remember I have to go again.

"That was great." Liam smiles and claps, encouraging me.

Jordan's sitting off to the side with Gavin and Violet, his cup of beer up to his lips. Even so, I can tell he's smirking at me.

I suffer through the rest of my turn and manage to get seven total pins.

I pass Jordan on the way to my seat. His confidence in rented shoes is aspiring.

Like the others, he throws a strike. I move to sit next to Violet when Gavin gets up.

"Oh my god, they're good. Like really good."

"No kidding," she says. She watches Gavin. "I didn't realize *he* was going to be here."

"Me either. Sorry."

"Whatever. I'm going to get another drink."

"Hey." I stop her. "Congratulations. I'm really proud of you."

Her face softens. "Thank you."

"And I totally owe you a real night out. Promise." I hold up my pinkie, and she links hers with mine.

"Yeah, you do." She starts to get up. "Now go talk to Liam, so this night isn't a total waste."

There isn't a lot of time for talking. The guys move fast through their frames. I could count the number of times they don't get a strike or spare easier than I could the times they do.

As I prepare for my last turn (thank you sweet baby Jesus), Jordan appears beside me. "You throw so politely."

"Politely? What does that mean?"

"Like you're afraid to hurt the pins' feelings."

I open my mouth to protest, but he laughs and adds, "Get angry, sweet Daisy. Those pins insulted you. They said your shoes were ugly."

I cock my head to the side. "We're all wearing the same shoes."

"They said I look great in them." His gaze slowly sweeps over me and down to my feet. "But not so much on you."

I scoff and return the once-over, stopping on his identical shoes, only bigger. "How dare you."

He grins and jabs his thumb toward the end of the lane. "Tell it to them."

I know he's messing with me, but I really do feel a wave of irrational anger as I launch the ball. When all ten pins fall, I stand frozen, completely dumbfounded.

Everyone cheers behind me. When I turn around, Jordan is grinning so big.

"You told them," he says, and wraps me in a playful hug, then swings me around. My face is buried in his neck, and I inhale his increasingly familiar scent.

"Yeah, I did."

His chuckle vibrates against my chest.

When he sets me down, Liam is waiting to offer me a high-five.

I get to go again, but my luck is out, and I only hit three pins.

"Are we done?" Violet asks, a little too hopefully.

"One more game," Jordan tells her. He points toward the entrance. "Look who showed up."

The tall, lanky guy making his way over to us is Andy Jenkins. He's a basketball player like Gavin.

Jordan introduces us. I know of him, of course, the same way I knew Jordan and Liam, but we've never met.

"I've been replaced, huh?" Jenkins asks.

"I think they'll probably be happy to have you back," I say.

"It was fun," Liam says and bumps me with his elbow.

The six of us sit and have a drink. The guys catch up while Violet and I listen in.

When they get ready for the second game, I pull off the bowling team shirt and hand it back to Liam. "Thanks for letting me play."

"Did you play too?" Jenkins asks Violet.

"No. I was just here for the drinks."

"And to heckle," Gavin chirps.

Violet gives him a haughty glare. "I wouldn't want to show you up."

"Oh, please do." He takes the shirt I just gave Liam and holds it out to her. "You can have my spot."

"Nah, you play. I'll sit this one out and keep Daisy company," Liam offers.

I can tell Violet would love to object, but Liam just said he was going to keep me company, and that's exactly why she agreed to come tonight in the first place.

"I'm not wearing that, but I will play," she says.

"You have to wear the shirt," Gavin tells her.

She rolls her eyes but pulls it on and tugs the hem to better see the logo. "Who designed these?"

"I did," he says. "Why? Not up to your standards?"

"I was going to say I liked it."

"Oh. Thanks." Gavin smiles.

Liam rests a hand on my arm. "I'm starving. Want to get some food?"

I catch Jordan's eye as he, Jenkins, Gavin, and Violet get set for the next game. He looks between Liam and me. His brows pull together, and his jaw flexes before he turns away.

"Yeah. That sounds great."

Chapter THIRTEEN

Daisy

LIAM ORDERS PRETZEL BITES AND A COKE. I GRAB A WATER.

"Are you sure you don't want one?" He holds out his plate for the second time since we sat at the counter that overlooks the lanes.

Violet is up, and Gavin stands behind her. I can't hear his words well enough to know if he's being encouraging or taunting. Her annoyed glare suggests the latter, but I get the sense that even if he was telling her how great she was, she'd still find a way to be irritated with him.

"No thanks." I sip on my water as he chews happily.

I've never had a serious boyfriend. I've dated a couple of guys, but one was in high school and the other was last year and only lasted for a few months before he transferred to another school. Both of those relationships started as a friendship and slowly grew into more, so sitting and talking with Liam is as close as I've been on a date with someone I have a real crush on.

And I'm not nailing it.

He has no problem with the silence between us. He comments on the game in front of us, and he smiles at me a lot, but there's no conversation about school or life or really anything except bowling.

I can't help but compare it to hanging out with Jordan. Silence with him feels different, and even though I know Liam is objectively more my type, I kind of wish it was Jordan sitting here. Which, of course, makes me feel ridiculous. This is everything I've wanted.

"Where are you from?" I ask as he pops a pretzel bite into his mouth.

He chews and washes it down with soda before answering. "Washington. You?"

"Here. Well, not Valley, but Arizona. Near Flagstaff."

"That's cool. Do you go home a lot on the weekends and stuff?"

"No. Not really."

His stare isn't menacing, but the way he looks at me tells me he's surprised by my answer.

"Well, I have Violet, so I have family here. And our families visit us."

It isn't a lie, they do visit us, but it's a sunny spin on it. Mine have been twice—once to bring me freshman year, and the second to a homecoming game last year that Violet's dad, my uncle Mason, organized.

"Right. Yeah, that makes sense." He pushes the plate away and leans back in his chair. He calls out to Gavin when he gets a seven-ten split. "You can still do this." He claps and nods to him.

"I can see why they made you captain."

A slow smile lights up his face. "Thanks."

I ask him a little about hockey, and we eventually get to talking about physics and school. It's weird. We're having a nice conversation, but I don't feel like I know him any better. Or that he learned anything new about me except where I'm from.

When the game is over, we all say our goodbyes. Gavin gives us a ride back since he's next door. In the back seat, I watch the houses go by and replay the night in my head. What a weird turn of events.

"Here is fine," Violet says as he goes past The White House.

"I can take you all the way. It's no problem."

He pulls up in front of our house. Violet doesn't give him so much as a goodbye before exiting his SUV.

"Thank you," I say for the both of us.

He turns to smile at me as I get out. "Any time."

Violet is already inside, shoes off, raiding our fridge when I walk in the house.

"You could have at least said thank you."

She rolls her shoulders as she scoops leftover pasta into a bowl. "He gets under my skin."

"I really didn't know he was going to be there. Sorry."

"It's fine. I can be the bigger person."

"Is this still because he hooked up with your roommate?"

She shoots daggers my way.

"I get it. I do. You liked him. He pretended to like you and then slept with your awful roommate. Just making sure nothing else happened tonight."

"That and because he thinks he's all that." She sits on the counter while her pasta is heating in the microwave. "You and Liam looked cozy."

"Did we?"

"Yeah. Did you finally ask him out?"

I sit beside her. "No."

"Why not? I saw the way he was with you. He likes you."

"I'm not sure."

"Do not play the dumb girl on this one. He likes you. Everyone can see it."

"I'm not playing dumb. I know he likes me as a friend, but I think that's all it is to him. I can't explain it. His touches are playful and sweet, and we talked all night, but..."

"But?" she prompts when I don't finish my sentence quickly enough.

"I was kind of bored."

"Wow."

I feel silly admitting it out loud. I've been dreaming of hanging out with Liam for months.

"Maybe you just set him up to some impossible fantasy of who you thought he was."

"Maybe." I hop down. "I'm beat. Thanks for coming tonight, Vi. I don't know what I'd do without you."

"Love you," she says.

I kiss my hand and fling it toward her, then head upstairs.

In bed, I think about what she said. Did I make Liam out to be so amazing that even he couldn't compare? He's a great guy. No question about it. I'm almost asleep when my phone pings.

I didn't get a chance to talk to Jordan much after the first game. I meant to ask him about tutoring. Looks like he had the same thought.

Get home okay? Tutoring tomorrow?

Turning on my side, I tap out a response with a smile. **Made it home just fine. Let's try tutoring at your place. Maybe a change of scenery will help.**

Chapter FOURTEEN

Jordan

"Hey, come in." I hold open the door for Daisy, and she enters my dorm. Her backpack weighs her down. She slips the strap off one shoulder and the other dips.

Liam waves from the couch. He and our neighbor across the hall are playing video games, so it's the perfect excuse to lead Daisy into my room, where she can't spend the evening chatting with Liam.

Watching the two of them at bowling yesterday was killer. I thought for sure he was going to ask her out, but he must not have because neither of them said anything or acted any different in lab today.

Daisy's cute and sweet. Funny, too—usually when she doesn't mean to be. She's tougher than I thought too. I mean, watching her bowling last night, all that determination and grit when she was clearly out of her element—it was hot.

The point is, the more I get to know her, the more I'm convinced that Liam's all wrong for her. She needs someone that'll push her to try new things and break out of her shell. She has fire inside of her.

"I like your room," she says as she turns in a circle in front of my bed.

I'm lost for a second as I picture her on the bed with that dress cinched up around her waist. Damn.

I clear my throat.

"Thanks." I move to my desk to grab my laptop and books. "You can have the chair."

"That's okay." She sits on my bed, angling her legs, so her feet hang off the side like she's trying to keep her shoes off the comforter.

"You're okay to get your shoes on the bed, sweet Daisy."

A flare of annoyance sparks in her eyes. "I am really not that sweet."

I sit on the opposite side of the bed from her. The mattress dips with my weight, and her knees hit mine. If I'd punched her, I doubt she'd move any faster than she does now as she scrambles to move away from me.

Laughing, I shake my head. "Never met a chick quite like you."

"Like what?" She rearranges herself so that she's facing me on the bed but too far away for us to accidentally touch.

Smart, hot, quiet, fiery. All of the words describe her, but they aren't enough. Instead of trying to explain that, I ask a question that's been floating around since we met. "Do you date a lot?"

Her brows lift, and slowly she smiles, then giggles. "I've spent the past three nights tutoring you. What do you think?"

"Off guys at the moment?" I lean on an elbow and kick my legs out toward the end of the bed.

"Do you date a lot?" she asks. Her tone is full of accusations like she thinks I'm some sort of serial dater.

"Not really."

"Oh, come on. Even I know about your reputation for..." Sweet

Daisy looks a little flustered as she realizes she doesn't want to finish the end of that sentence.

"For?" I prompt.

"Dating." She waves a hand in the air and looks away. "Partying and sleeping with lots of girls."

"I didn't realize my reputation made me out to be such a badass."

She rolls her eyes. "So it isn't true?"

"I didn't say that." I grin.

"Doesn't it feel… I don't know, shallow or something?"

Her face is full of uncertainty and not the judgment I expected.

"No," I answer honestly. "Connection never feels shallow. Not to me."

She nibbles on the side of her lip as she studies me. Sometimes the way she looks at me is unnerving.

"Should we?" I motion toward our books.

"Yes. You're right. We should." She looks more at ease as she pours her attention on the material. I already knew she was smart, but it's reaffirmed every time she jumps into tutor mode.

She breaks down the information for me and takes her time making sure I've cemented each point before going to the next. The way her brain works is fascinating. She can take each piece apart, but she never loses sight of the big picture.

If I were struggling, I think she'd really be helping me.

As we're finishing physics and moving on to statistics, Liam knocks on the door and opens it a crack.

"Hey, sorry. I don't want to interrupt, but I'm ordering pizza. Do you guys want anything?"

"Grab an extra cheese for the morning," I say.

"Already done," he says. "Daisy?"

"No, thanks."

I glance between them for any unspoken communication. Is he still into her? I can't tell. He's so damn polite it's hard to tell the difference with him.

He backs out of the room with a wave.

I can't read anything about her feelings for him either. She's not flushed like she used to be during lab, but that just might be her getting comfortable around us.

Daisy looks down at her book and tilts it where I can see the page. "Is this what you covered in class today?"

"Yeah." I nod. "Let me guess. You don't like pizza? Or you weren't allowed to have it as a kid?"

"I like pizza."

"But?"

"No but." Her slim shoulders rise and lower. "I ate before I came over."

"What's your favorite pizza topping?"

"Pepperoni or green peppers."

My lip curls. "I don't understand veggies on pizza. It's pizza. It isn't supposed to be healthy."

"It makes more sense than a plain cheese pizza," she retorts.

"I like what I like."

"And what you like is cold cheese pizza in the morning?"

"Exactly."

"I've never had pizza in the morning." She purses her lips. "Or at least I don't think I have. And before you ask, it wasn't that I wasn't allowed or anything."

"Leftover pizza in the morning is the best. Especially after a night out."

"Are you going out tonight?"

"Nah. Game tomorrow."

"Oh right."

"Are you coming?"

"Probably not. Violet has a thing against sporting events."

"A thing against them? Why?"

"Freshman year, she was friends with some of the jocks. Specifically, the basketball team. She and Gavin had a thing briefly. They didn't date or anything, but I think she wanted to, then he hooked up with her roommate. After that, she stopped going anywhere she might run into him. That was over a year ago."

"And yet she moved into a house right next door to him."

"That was actually my doing." Daisy looks mischievous as hell as she grins. "Violet had the flu the day we were supposed to go see places with Jane and Dahlia. I fell in love with that house, and we put a deposit on it before she had a chance to see where it was located."

"I'm shocked, sweet Daisy."

"Told you I wasn't that sweet. Honestly, though, I thought she was over it."

"Didn't seem that way last night."

"No, it didn't."

We spend another half-hour reviewing my statistics homework. I've studied more this week than I have in my entire life, so when she asks if I'm getting the hang of it, I can answer without hesitation, "I've never been so clear."

"You're a quick study. I thought it would take weeks or maybe months."

Right. I probably should have dragged this out more. I'm digging spending time with her. Who knew studying was such a blast?

"Maybe I can convince you to keep tutoring me once or twice a week, so I stay on top of it?"

"Yeah. I don't mind." She stands next to the bed as she packs up her stuff. Her gaze goes to the nightstand, and she picks up the lone picture there.

"Is this you?" she asks with a broad smile.

"Yep. Me and a buddy from high school."

"You look exactly the same."

"I'm like three inches taller," I protest.

"It's your smile." She looks from the picture to me. "You always look like a cat that got the canary. Is he at Valley too?"

I scoot closer and take the picture. The edges are bent, and the photo is blurry where water spilled on one side, but I always keep it next to my bed. "Nah. College wasn't for him. He got a job working for the county. He passed away my first year at Valley."

"Oh." I don't look up, but I can hear the sympathy in her voice. "I'm so sorry."

"He was always flipping off the camera or turning away. This is the only photo I have of him where I can really see his face." The familiar pang of sadness hits me square in the chest as I stare down at the two of us, young, carefree, drunk off our asses.

Liam calls that the pizza is here, and I toss the photo back on the nightstand.

"Are you sure you don't want to stay for pizza?" I ask as I open my door.

"I should get back. I have some studying of my own still."

"Okay." I lead her out into the living area. Ry across the hall is gone, and Liam's setting the pizza boxes on the coffee table. The smell of cheese and grease hangs in the air, making my stomach growl.

Liam invites her to stay, too, but she gives him the same answer.

"Good luck at your game tomorrow," she tells us.

"Are you coming?" Liam asks.

"I don't think so."

"Bummer." He smiles. "See you next week in class."

I walk her to the door. "Thanks, sweet Daisy."

"I'm not sweet," she says, but she's smiling as she does.

When I close the door, Liam asks, "What's she helping you with?"

He passes me a box of cheese pizza.

"Statistics, mostly." I flip open the box and take a slice. "She's really fucking smart."

"So are you," he says. "But it's good to see you studying. You haven't even overslept for classes the past couple of weeks."

"Oh, man." I pause. "Am I a nerd now?"

I bust up laughing, and Liam rolls his eyes.

"Nerds are hot," I say and think of Daisy.

"She is. You? Not so much." He laughs it off, but a prick of guilt hits me for being into the girl he likes. I've never hooked up with a girl a buddy dated or wanted to date. Never. My friendships are everything to me.

"You two looked like you were hitting it off last night." I struggle to look at him, but I need to read his face and get some idea of just how into her he is.

His brows lift slightly. "Me and Daisy?"

I nod and take a bite of pizza.

"We were just chatting and getting to know each other a bit."

"So you aren't going to ask her out?" My pulse thrums quickly.

He gives me a weird look. "What is with you lately?"

I've never nagged him about when and who he was hooking up with, so he's rightly confused about my bringing it up. Still, I push a little. "Just wanted to know if I should be putting in a good word for you while we're studying."

"Please don't." He barks out a laugh. "I can just hear you telling her I have a big dick or something."

"Well, I mean you do, but I'd probably lead with your awesome personality. Or maybe how you pair your socks before putting them away."

"I think I can handle it on my own, but thanks." He laughs and stands with his pizza. "I'm heading out to the library to meet a buddy from history class. See ya later, nerd."

On game days, we do a light skate in the mornings. It's mostly a way to ensure guys don't go out and do anything dumb the night before. Or if they do, they sweat out the alcohol and still have all day to recover.

And when I say they, I mean all of us because I've totally been there before.

After leaving the arena, I run into Violet coming out of University Hall with a to-go coffee in hand.

"Hey." I hold open the door for her as she steps out and pulls her sunglasses down over her eyes.

"Thank you."

"Daisy with you?" I look inside, but it's packed with people in line for coffee before classes.

"No. She was up late studying for a big test today."

"She has a test today?" My stomach drops.

"Mhmmm." She takes a sip. "And she was busy helping someone else all week."

"I didn't know."

"I figured," she says. "Daisy is like that. It's easy for people to take advantage of her."

"Damn. It's not even eight o'clock. It's too early for a guilt trip." I rub at my chest. Fuck. I didn't even think to ask if our nightly tutor sessions were messing with her own schedule.

Her lips twist into a smirk. "Be nice to Daisy."

"Will do." I mock a salute, and she starts off. "But maybe I'm not the only one that needs to remember to be nice."

She pauses and faces me. One brow lifts over the frame of her sunglasses. "Meaning?"

"What's your issue with sporting events? Liam's invited her twice. I know Daisy. Or I'm starting to. She wants to go."

"I'm not stopping her from going."

"She won't go without you."

"Why do you care so much?"

"I don't." My skin burns with her accusation. Why am I meddling? It isn't for Liam's benefit that much I know. I flick my gaze away from her and step into University Hall.

Chapter FIFTEEN

Daisy

THE NOISE IN THE ARENA REACHES A DEAFENING LEVEL that vibrates inside of me. Valley just scored another goal, and it's impossible not to get caught up in the excitement. Or almost impossible.

"Ouch!" Violet yelps as the person on the other side of her jumps up and down, stomping on her foot in the process. "Watch it."

"Sorry," the guy apologizes, yelling over the roar of the crowd as it starts to die down. His face is painted—half yellow and half blue—and he waves his beefy arms around. "We scored!"

He turns back to the ice, and Violet's annoyed glare softens when she sees my expression.

"You're enjoying this?"

Shrugging, I smile. "It's kind of amazing."

I've been to sporting events before. Admittedly it's been a

few years, but I saw a football game or two in high school. I think I even went to a swim meet. However, the number of people crammed into this arena to cheer on the Valley hockey team is double or triple anything I've ever attended.

Hockey is fast and fierce. Watching the players race up and down the ice makes my heart gallop like I'm out there with them. I feel like I'm a part of something.

Violet would roll her eyes, and I get it; I will leave here tonight and never speak or see some of these people again. But as someone who is always watching from a distance, it's nice to be one of many sitting on the sidelines for a few hours.

The Valley bench is all smiles and high-fives as the buzzer sounds. It's the end of the second period, and Violet bounces beside me, ready to flee. She doesn't say that, though. She might not want to be here, but she's committed to seeing it through for me.

I was shocked when she suggested we go to the game tonight. Honestly, I thought she was joking at first and laughed in her face. When she confirmed that I had heard her correctly, and no, she wasn't kidding, I didn't ask any more questions.

Dahlia is still at her golf tournament, and Jane went over to her friend Eric's house to hang out and play some music.

"Do you want to get something to drink?" I ask. People around us are filing out of their seats to the concessions and bathrooms.

"Sure."

We fall into a slow-moving line with the rest of the crowd, moving up to the nearest mezzanine.

"Thank you for coming tonight."

She attempts a smile that looks more like a grimace. "It's nothing. If the roles were reversed, you'd have done it for me."

"I'm surprised that you even knew there was a game tonight."

Her brows lift, and her mouth presses into a thin line. The response only lasts for a second, but it's long enough for me to realize she isn't telling me something.

"*How* did you know?"

She lifts onto her toes to peer over the line in front of us. The smell of burnt popcorn is stronger the higher we climb up the stairs. "I think Liam or Jordan must have mentioned it at bowling. Or maybe I heard it around campus."

The line is at a complete standstill, and eventually, she has to look at me.

"Okay, fine. I ran into Jordan this morning at University Hall."

My stomach lurches. "And?"

"He told me that Liam's been inviting you to home games but that you wouldn't go unless I did."

Flames tickle my cheeks. It's a lot to process. Jordan and Violet were talking about me? Vi felt guilty for something as ridiculous as my insecurity to attend an event without a friendly face?

She tilts her head to the side and smiles at me as if she can read the thoughts spiraling in my head. "I should have offered before. And it isn't… *that* bad."

I can't think of what to say, so I hug her. "Thank you."

We grab sodas, and Violet gets popcorn, then we go back to our seats. The Valley players are near our end of the arena. Jordan skates behind the net to retrieve a puck, spotting us as he does. He juts his chin in acknowledgment and smiles.

I wave and then feel silly because he's around the net so fast, facing the other direction, that he doesn't even see it. But Liam does and waves back. Then I wave again. A few people look my way to see who is getting attention from the players. So I wave again like I'm just a waving kind of gal. *Oh my gosh. I'm going to duct tape my hands to my legs.*

Violet offers me some popcorn. I take it to keep my hands busy. Thankfully the third period starts, and I no longer have to worry about Jordan or Liam noticing me.

They're both on the ice, and they play so differently, like everything else about them. Even the way they skate. Liam has this slower, unassuming way he moves from one end to the other. He's fast, don't get me wrong, but he doesn't really look like it. In contrast, Jordan seems to be everywhere at once. He's quick and aggressive, darting one way and then the next. I'm exhausted just watching him.

I would have sworn I preferred Liam's style of play better before seeing it in person, but it's Jordan I can't stop watching.

His dark hair curls around his helmet and the wet strands stick to his skin. His dark eyes blaze with an intensity that makes my stomach flip. He never seems to let up or relax. Even when he's on the bench, he tracks the action on the ice with complete focus.

I'm so enthralled that it catches me by surprise when the game is over.

"It's over already?" I ask, pulse racing with excitement.

Violet laughs, then stands and stretches. "Already? We've been here for almost three hours."

I take one last glimpse at the Valley bench where the guys disappear down the tunnel. I don't see Jordan, but Liam stands where he can fist bump each guy as they go.

"Thank you again for coming," I say to Violet as we push outside.

I breathe in the cool air and try to hang on to the thrill of tonight.

"You're welcome." She stares down at her phone. "Jane is still at Eric's house. They're playing games and drinking. Could be fun."

"Yeah. It could be." Eric is Jane's friend. He's a business major but also plays in a local nineties cover band. He's nice, but nights at his place always end up with him and his friends super drunk and jamming out or talking about the stock market. And he lives kind of far from campus.

Since Dahlia is gone, my options are: go to Eric's, knowing I might be bored, but at least I'll be with Violet and Jane, or go home by myself.

Violet looks to me with a hopeful smile. She came here tonight for me. I can suffer through some drunken singing and guitar.

"Let's go to Eric's," I agree. "But can we stop at the house first? I want to change."

She gives me a once-over in my blue Valley Hockey T-shirt, her eyebrows lifting. "Definitely."

At home, I send Jordan a congrats text. Then do the same for Liam. My crush has waned a little after hanging out with him at the bowling alley. Liam and I make sense on paper, but in reality, I think we might be better as friends.

"Daisy," Violet calls from downstairs.

"Coming," I call back. I change into a dress and add another swipe of mascara on my lashes, then grab my phone and purse. Liam texts back, and that small part of me that still wants him to notice me, feels a blast of happiness as I read his words, **Thanks. So glad you made it to a game!**

"I'm ready." I shove my phone in my purse and start down the stairs. I lift my gaze from the steps to the person hovering at the end of the stairway. Jordan's appearance throws me off balance, and I stumble down the rest of the way.

"Whoa." He steps forward and steadies me.

I wish I were graceful enough to extract myself and recover quickly, but I basically faceplant into his chest, breathing in his freshly showered scent. One hand goes around him, and the other braces on his stomach—his very hard, defined stomach.

My fingers have a mind of their own, stretching to cover as much surface area as possible and then gliding along his abs.

His laughter eventually snaps the remaining, sane brain cells back to life, and I jump back. My face is on fire as I smooth a hand down my dress and then over my hair.

"I am so sorry."

"For copping a feel?" He shrugs. "I can hardly blame you."

His mouth lifts in a cocky smirk.

"For falling into you," I clarify. I'll die before admitting I was enjoying exploring his muscles. "What are you doing here?"

"You came to the game," he says as if that explains his presence.

I look around the living room and kitchen for Violet.

"She's out front yelling at Gavin because someone parked her in."

"Ah."

"I take it that's a usual occurrence?"

"Something like that."

"Meaning?"

"Let's just say, our yard and driveway see a lot of action on big party nights."

"People park in your yard?"

"No, but they do dump trash—beer cups, bottles, and one time we found two used condoms."

"Two?" His brows lift. "Impressive action for a front yard."

"They were in the back yard."

He looks past me. "Oh right. Your back yard butts up against the action."

I nod. "You still didn't say why you're here."

"To bring you to the party."

"The party?" Anticipation bubbles up inside of me.

He nods. "It isn't the full home game experience without celebrating after a win."

"We were just about to go to a friend's house."

"Invite your friends to The White House. That's where everyone will be tonight anyway."

"Violet will never go."

My roommate storms through the front door with a scowl. "I'm completely blocked in!"

"I heard. I'm sorry."

She looks between Jordan and me. "Are you going with him or me?"

"You don't want to come?" I ask hopefully.

"No chance, but you should go. I'm sure Liam will be there."

The displeasure on Jordan's face at the mention of Liam is only there a second, but I catch it, and my stomach dips at what it might mean. If he didn't come here for Liam, then he's here for himself. And wait, Jordan Thatcher wants to hang out with me?

"Definitely," Jordan says. "Liam will be there."

There's a knock on our door, and Violet must be expecting him because she grunts and rolls her eyes before opening it for Gavin.

"I'm sorry. I will send a freshman out to watch your driveway next time." He waves at me and Jordan.

"Creepy," she retorts. "And that doesn't help me right now."

He takes two steps backward. "I'll figure out whose car that is, or I'll call and have it towed."

She rolls her eyes. "Okay, let's not be dramatic."

I stifle a laugh. Jordan doesn't, but his laughter is friendly.

"I can give you a ride," he offers.

"It's fine. I already called an Uber."

Gavin wisely retreats to his house with another apology.

"Ready?" Jordan asks me.

"I don't know."

"Uber's here," Violet says. "Do you want to come with me?"

They're both looking at me expectantly.

Violet takes the decision out of my hands with a smile. "Go. If it's awful or you just decide you want to come to Eric's, text me, and I'll find you a ride."

"Okay." My heart races.

She looks to Jordan. "If you ditch her, I will cut off your nipples."

She rushes out to meet the waiting car, leaving me with Jordan, who's covering his nips with both hands. "She's violent."

He drops his hands and motions with his head toward the door. "Ready for this, sweet Daisy?"

Chapter SIXTEEN

Daisy

THE INSIDE OF THE WHITE HOUSE IS EVEN BIGGER AND more extravagant than I expected. Violet would die. Or maybe she'd already seen it during those few months when she was hanging with Gavin and his friends.

I hate to be glad that things didn't work out between them, but I'm thankful that we've become so close since then. We've always had a few core things in common: being the same age, loving art, wishing our parents were less strict, and that our fathers were less embarrassing; but because we grew up living two hours apart, we only saw each other on holidays or the rare occasion my parents stopped working long enough to join them on family vacations.

It wasn't until Violet and I both chose to attend Valley U—the same college our fathers had attended—that I've really gotten to know her. Our first semester, we only hung out to study or to grab an occasional cup of coffee, but after everything went down with Gavin and her roommate, she basically moved into my dorm with me. And now I can't imagine not living with her or seeing and talking with her every day.

Jordan rests a hand on my lower back as we squeeze through the crowded hallway to the kitchen. My body responds to the attention with far too much excitement. Especially considering his focus is everywhere. Some people call out their congrats. Others that are closer fist bump or hug him. One girl yells across the party for him to come sign her boobs.

"Is she serious?" I ask.

"Oh yeah," he says. "Want me to sign yours?"

I don't respond but send him a pointed look that makes him laugh.

He stops to grab our cups then tips his head toward the back yard. "Keg is outside."

My gaze travels over the large kitchen. I want to wander around and scope out this house, but there's a real chance I'd get lost. It's massive.

Jordan starts outside. I stick close to him, which isn't strictly necessary since it isn't as crowded out here as we make our way to fill our cups with beer.

Jordan fills mine, then his, and looks around the party. "I don't think Liam is here yet."

"It's okay." I take a large gulp of beer. "I don't really want to see him right now."

The honest admission catches me by surprise. There's no one else I'd rather come to a party with than Jordan. He's all chill, and I feel like it balances out my anxiety in this situation. And I think he might want to hang out with me too. I mean, why else would he have asked me to come tonight? That, or he's really shipping Liam and me.

Jordan nods thoughtfully. "Need a little liquid courage first?"

I open my mouth to tell him that isn't it, but I'm suddenly not so sure I've read things right. Maybe he didn't bring me here for

Liam or for himself, but because he felt sorry for me. That would be the absolute worst. I don't want his pity.

It makes the most sense, though, as I glance around the party. Girls openly stare at him. Two eventually approach, hugging Jordan and then falling into conversation with him about the game.

I take another sip of beer and try not to eavesdrop. More girls are looking this way—at Jordan and then to me. I was prepared to be invisible, but the looks these girls are shooting me tell me: 1. They see me, and 2. They don't understand why Jordan walked in with me.

I know that no one cares I'm here, or, let's be honest, would have even noticed if it weren't for Jordan. I'm nobody. And while being here is everything I've wanted since I moved in next door, coming with one of the most popular guys on campus was not the smartest decision. Talk about being thrown into the lion's den.

"This is Daisy," Jordan's voice cuts through my thoughts. He introduces me to the girls and steps closer to me.

"Are you in Chi Omega?" one asks.

"No."

The other squints at me. "You dated Jenkins last year?"

I shake my head.

They're trying so hard to place me. They can't fathom why Jordan would hang out with me.

He touches my elbow, sending a jolt up my arm. Then, with a smile at the two girls, he says, "We'll see you guys later."

Gently, he tugs me with him. I offer a brittle smile and wave at the girls now glaring at me.

"Where are we going?" I ask as he leads me onto the patio that spans the width of the house.

"Liquid courage."

"You don't have to do this." I pull free of his hold.

"Do what?"

"Hang out with me."

He chuckles. "Thanks, but I like my nipples."

On the patio, a large group sits around a long table. Beer cans cover almost every surface. A timer goes off, and someone yells, "Drink!"

All around the table, people lift shot glasses and toss them back. I watch as people finish and refill the glass with beer.

"Ever done century club?" He nods his head in greeting to people at the table and then pulls out a chair for me.

"Is that supposed to mean something to me?"

"You've never heard of century club?" He takes the chair next to me and grabs us each a shot glass.

"Trust me, I don't relish being dumb, so just assume if I'm asking, I genuinely don't know."

Laughing, he fills our glasses. "The rules are simple. You take a shot of beer every minute for one hundred minutes."

"Drink!"

Everyone around us takes their shot, and Jordan holds up his glass, then waits for me.

"Like power hour," I say.

"Yep, except longer."

"Yeah, that's a lot of beer in less than two hours."

"It's the fastest way I know to get drunk," he says. "Unless you can stomach Everclear?"

"This is fine." I take the shot, and Jordan immediately refills our glasses.

We're at the end of the table, and the people around us are coupled up and not paying us a lot of attention.

Jordan's wearing a hat, as usual. He lifts it and drops it onto one knee.

His black hair is messy, but it still suits him. I like how the ends are always a little unruly, just like him. "You have nice hair."

"Careful, that almost sounded like a compliment." He pauses. "Wait, are you drunk already?"

"You're shit at taking a compliment."

"Oh, like you're so good at it?" He shoots me a knowing glance.

It's time to drink again, and he leans back casually in his chair as he takes it.

"Fair point."

It takes very few shots of beer before my stomach feels too full. So I skip the next several. Jordan smirks, toasts the air, and keeps going. I wonder if he needs some liquid courage tonight, too.

"Who's Eric?"

It takes me a second to figure out who he's talking about. "He's a friend of Jane's. He has a house off campus."

"Is that where you usually party?"

"Occasionally. Mostly, we hang at our house." I take the next shot. Jordan continues to refill my glass each time.

"Do you only go places your friends go?"

"You ask that like it's a terrible thing. Isn't that why you're here? To hang with your friends." I wave my hand toward the party that's growing in size with every shot we take.

"The difference is if I wanted to go somewhere and my friends didn't, I'd go by myself."

"Girls don't do that."

He bobs his head. "Yeah, I guess that's not a quirk unique to you. Still, must be limiting."

"I've survived just fine."

"Says the girl that'd never had Fun Dip before." His dark eyes lock on mine. "What else haven't you done before?"

"I'm not a virgin," I protest too loudly and gain the attention of people around us. I consider jumping over the fence to the safety of my own house but am afraid I'd trip and fall or make a spectacle trying to climb over.

"Oh, sweet Daisy. You're blushing." He rests an arm around the back of my chair. The position puts just the smallest amount of contact between his forearm and my shoulder. "That wasn't what I was asking, but now you have me thinking about you naked."

My face is boiling, and my cheeks must show it because he chuckles then lets his thumb glide along my arm in a reassuring caress. "Relax. I'm sorry. I didn't mean to make you uncomfortable. Will it help if I tell you how I lost my virginity?"

"Nope, probably not."

He tips his gaze up and pulls his bottom lip between his teeth. "Know any jokes?"

The beer and the absurdity of this situation mixed with all the anxiousness and uncomfortable feelings I've been repressing comes out in a giggle. It starts small and builds. I can't stop, and soon I'm hiccuping along with it.

"Okay, I think we've accomplished our mission." Jordan stands and holds out a hand.

"I'm fine." I get to my feet without his help but then sway. "Or not."

"Catches up with you fast."

I slip my palm into his. It's warm and rough, and my pulse kicks up as I slide my fingers through his.

One side of his mouth lifts in a smirk, but he holds my hand as we walk away from the table.

"What's next?" I ask.

"It's a choose your own adventure. We have swimming." He waggles his brows as he stops us in front of the pool. People are stripped down to their boxers or panties and bras, swimming and splashing.

"No, thank you."

"Dancing?" He turns us to an open section of the yard where the DJ booth is set up, and people are dancing.

"Maybe later."

He continues through the options, which include more drinking games.

"Can we just sit and chill for a while?"

"Absolutely. That's my favorite party activity."

We refill our cups, where he sadly drops my hand to do so, and then Jordan leads me to an area of the party I know well. The spot where so many times I've watched him and Liam sit and hang with the guys on the team. I glance over at my house and up at the tree house. It's hidden really well. Not that most people would look over into the darkened yard next door when there's so much going on here.

"Thatcher!" the guys call out in a chorus. Liam is with them and stands when he sees me.

"No way. I didn't know you were coming," he says.

"It was a last-minute decision."

Jordan stays at my side. He introduces me to his teammates, and then we sit in a circle. I'm next to Liam, but Jordan takes a chair across from us.

It's a rare night that Liam is drinking, but he goes through beer at a much slower pace than his buddies. Now that my stomach has settled, I'm happily buzzed and content. Someone passes around a bottle of Fireball. Liam takes a drink then passes it to me. His fingers brush mine, and I wait for the sparks to shoot up my arm or a fluttering in my stomach—for any sign that there could be something more between us.

"You got it?" he asks when I don't pull the bottle away.

"Yeah. I think I do." I take a sip, stealing a glance at Jordan. I find him looking back at me, and those sparks and flutters I was waiting for finally arrive.

Oh shit. I went and fell for the wrong guy.

Chapter SEVENTEEN

Jordan

"NICE GAME TONIGHT." GAVIN STEPS OUT OF THE circle of guys he's with when I approach. His lips pull into an easy smile, and we slap hands.

"Thanks." I take a long drink of beer. "I heard you guys won too."

He nods. "We did. One more for the W column."

"We might both be playing in April next year."

"God, I hope so," he says. "Did you just get here? I saw Liam and McCallum come in, but you've been MIA."

"Nah, I've been here. Been… around."

He waits for me to elaborate, smiling like he thinks I was off hooking up or some shit. Don't I wish.

"I came with Daisy. We were doing century club for a while."

"Daisy? Violet's cousin?" His brows raise in question.

"Yeah."

"Really?" Gavin tips his head toward where she and Liam sit together, laughing. "I thought those two were a thing."

"Nope, but that might be on me. And you."

"What the hell did I do?"

"New girlfriends are the worst kind of distraction," I mimic his tone, repeating the words he said to me that night at the bowling alley. "I stopped him from asking her out."

I stare at her, cataloging how happy she looks. Daisy's drunk, I know, but still, she looks so fucking happy. They both do. I want to squash it. I want her to only look like that with me.

"If you're trying to keep them apart, maybe you shouldn't have brought her to a party and then left her alone."

"Doesn't matter. He likes her. She likes him. It's inevitable." I take another drink of beer, wishing it were something stronger.

Gavin laughs, and it snaps my attention back to him.

"What?"

"You should see yourself. You look like you're about to spit fire. *You* have a thing for Daisy?" He brings a fist to his mouth and keeps on laughing. "Oh man, the great Jordan Thatcher has fallen hard for a girl. She's cute but not your type. Like at all."

"She's…" I stop myself from pouring my heart out on the lawn of the party. "Whatever."

"The night is young, and the booze is flowing." He steps back. "Go get the girl, Thatcher."

He juts his chin, and I follow his gaze back to Liam and Daisy. He's filling her cup with another beer. Fuck, what she needs is a water. Her eyes flit up, and she smiles right at me. I swear it hits me like a bullet to the chest, and I can't breathe for a second. Earlier, when she took my hand, I was transported back to middle school like it was my first time all over again.

I don't immediately move toward them. Maybe I should just duck out and let things happen with them.

Liam is finally playing well, but I want him to be happy. The decent thing would be to walk away.

My phone buzzes in my pocket, and I pull it out, smiling at the text from the last person I expected. **I choose dancing now!**

I look up at Daisy to find her grinning at her phone.

Daisy is drunk. So am I, but that's status quo for a Friday night.

Instead of replying, I move toward her. Whatever good intentions I had are gone. I can't walk away from her. Not tonight anyway.

She sees me at ten feet away, says something to Liam, and then walks from him to me. I catch his eye and give him a head tip to let him know I have her. We've both been keeping an eye on her by some unspoken agreement.

When she reaches me, she takes my hand again and presses her tits into my bicep.

Yeah, she's definitely drunk.

At the outskirts of the dance area, I face her. Her gaze darts around to the others dancing, but she doesn't move.

"Change your mind?"

"No. It's just, I'm not a very good dancer."

I lift our joined hands and force her to do a spin. Graceful, she is not. But this isn't *Dancing with the Stars*.

"Nobody cares. Just move however you feel."

Slowly, she sways to the beat. This is not on my usual adventure map, but I've been pulled out here a time or ten. Plus, I don't give a shit if I can dance. I'm sort of in awe of Daisy. She cares deeply, yet she still puts herself out there. Mostly for Liam's sake, but I'm trying hard not to think about that. Or how I'm lusting after a girl my buddy likes.

With each song, she gets a little more into it. When the DJ plays a slower song, she looks at me awkwardly and fans her face. "I think I need another drink."

"You need water."

"I'm fine," she insists.

"All right, sweet Daisy. Pick your poison. Beer or liquor?"

Her face scrunches up. "No more beer."

In the kitchen, our options are limited. Empty cans and nearly empty bottles line the counter. I make her a Sprite with a splash of vodka. She notices but only rolls her eyes.

"Thank you."

I grab a water and lead her back outside.

"You're not drinking anymore?"

"I'm plenty drunk. Don't worry about me." This is true, but I also realize that she's on the verge of needing someone to hold her hair back.

Liam and a few guys are still in our spot playing cards. The others are most likely in the pool trying to hook up.

Daisy takes a chair next to Liam, and I fall into the one beside her.

"Do you want to play, Daisy?" Liam asks her.

She shakes her head. I'm momentarily pleased that she's choosing not to do something Liam asked her to, but then it hits me there's probably another reason she said no.

I lean closer. "Want me to teach you?"

"No," she says quietly so only I can hear. "Please don't make a big thing of it. I'm fine not playing. You can if you want."

She finishes her drink and then closes her eyes. "I'm kind of tired. I should probably go home soon."

"Want a boost over the fence?"

Her blue eyes pop open and narrow.

"Kidding. I told you, I like my nipples." I stand and say bye to the guys.

Liam gets up, and I hold out my hand to pull him into a side hug and talk into his ear. "I'm going to walk Daisy home and make sure she's okay. She's pretty drunk."

I half expect and half hope that he's going to tell me to stay and that he'll do it. That's just the type of thing Liam would do even if he wasn't interested in the girl

"Yeah." He chuckles lightly. "She's fading fast. Let me know if you need anything."

"Will do."

By the time I've said goodbye to the rest of the guys, Daisy is fighting to keep her eyes open.

I help her to her feet and wrap an arm around her waist.

"I'm fine," she protests even as she leans into me. "But you smell good."

"Another compliment. A guy might start to think you like him."

"I do like you," she says. "We're friends, right?"

I pause inside of the house and find her big, blue eyes staring up at me from only a few inches away. It'd be so easy to kiss her, show her how *not* friends we are.

"Sure we are." I tighten my grip on her. "Did you bring anything else with you tonight?"

She shakes her head.

"All right. Come on, let me walk you back."

"No." She straightens. "I haven't seen the house yet. If this is my only chance ever to be inside, then I have to see it all."

"All right then. Let me be your tour guide, sweet Daisy."

"I need a new nickname." She huffs as I lead her through the kitchen, stopping in the theater room briefly where I wave to Jenkins and more people sitting around watching the giant TV on the wall.

"But this one suits you so well."

"Sweet makes me sound like a twelve-year-old girl selling cookies and lemonade."

I bark a laugh as we head upstairs.

"Is that how you see me?" She stops on the top step and faces me.

"No." I tuck the dark blonde hair hanging in her face behind one ear. The air crackles between us, but a couple is coming up the stairs, and we move forward out of the way.

"This is the gym." I point to the locked door.

"They have their own court?" Daisy asks as she peers inside through the little window.

"Yep, and the rest of upstairs is bedrooms and bathrooms."

"This is so much nicer than our house," she says.

"It's nicer than most people's houses."

"True, but they don't have an epic tree house like we do." She walks the length of the hall and then comes back. "Thank you for indulging me. I can cross this off my bucket list now."

"You don't think you'll come back sometime?"

"With who?"

"With me."

She stops again. Her blue eyes narrow on me, and then she takes the railing in one hand and steps down the stairs. "You and I don't make any sense."

"Why's that?" I ask as we step out the front door.

The breeze blows against us. She shivers and ducks her head into my shoulder.

"I'm a wallflower. You're a popular jock."

"Liam is a popular jock."

"Yeah, but he's different."

There's no denying it, he's definitely not your average popular jock, but it still nags at me. She pulls away at her front door and digs through her purse for a key. It takes her a few tries, but she lets us inside and flips on a lamp near the doorway.

"Thank you for walking me home."

"Do you have any Tylenol?"

"Advil is better when you've been drinking."

I lift a brow.

"See? I know things."

"Okay, smarty pants. Take some and drink a full glass of water."

"You drank as much as me."

"Yeah, but you weigh like half as much."

"I don't weigh *half* as much as you."

"God, you're exasperating. If I drink a glass of water too, will you drink one?"

She nods. "I'll get the Advil. It's upstairs."

I walk toward the kitchen, find two glasses, and fill them with water. I need to make sure she's okay and get the hell out of here. It feels like a betrayal of Liam just thinking the things going through my head.

She hasn't returned when I get back to the stairs. I wait, then call up to her. No answer. *Dammit, Daisy.*

I take the stairs two at a time. I check the bathroom first. Empty. All the lights are off upstairs, but her bedroom door is ajar. Light from the closet spills out. I set the glasses on her desk and then move toward the closet. I'm expecting her to be passed out on the floor, but instead, she's grunting and flailing with her dress up around her chest.

"Oh shit," I say and turn around. "Sorry. I yelled up but got worried when I didn't get a response."

"Help me," she whines.

"Uhh. What?"

"I'm stuck."

Slowly, I face her, taking in the scene in front of me—Daisy with her dress caught around her boobs—with amusement at first, but then my gaze drops to her tiny white panties and all the smooth, pale skin on display in front of me.

My pants grow snug in the crotch, but I step forward with purpose. I try to lift the fabric, but it doesn't budge.

"How did you get this on?"

"There are buttons in the back."

The view in the back is even worse, or better, depending on your perspective. Ripping off her dress and kissing her was not in the plan for tonight.

I fumble with the three tiny buttons running down her spine.

Her skin is smooth and warm. The fabric gapes and the clasp of her bra stares at me, begging to be undone.

"Did you get it?"

"Yeah." I step back and clear my throat.

She pulls the dress over her head and then uses it to shield her front from me. "I, uh, just realized I'm now mostly naked, and you just saw me in my underwear. I am mortified."

"Striptease was not on the choose your own adventure map, but I am happy to add it."

"Just turn around or something."

I do and step out of the closet but can't resist taunting her more. "Already seen your cute white panties, Daisy."

She groans. "I wasn't expecting for anyone to see me naked tonight, or I would have worn sexier ones."

Well, that's… intriguing, and my mind processes it in a fashion show of Daisy in an array of colorful panty options. Her easel is set up next to her desk, and I walk toward it to inspect her drawing. Even in the near dark, I'm impressed. It's a man—or the beginning of one.

She reappears next to me in a T-shirt and cotton shorts, holding a bottle of Advil. "Did you get water?"

I motion to where I set the glasses on the desk when I came in. "This is good. Who is it?"

"No one. It's for class." She moves the easel where I can no longer see her work. "Thank you for the water and for… you know."

"Getting you naked?"

"You live for embarrassing me."

"Absolutely, I do."

Her face pales. "The room is spinning."

"You should lie down."

She takes the medicine and another sip of water.

"What time will Violet be home?" I ask.

"Not until the morning. She texted earlier and said they were staying at Eric's."

She gets in bed then glances at the closet light.

"I got it." I turn it off and then hesitate. Every fiber of my being is yelling not to leave her like this. "Scoot over."

"What?"

I kick off my shoes and peel off my T-shirt. She's staring at me wide-eyed as I stalk toward the bed.

"I'm not having sex with you," she blurts.

"No shit." I pull back the comforter. "But I'm not leaving you alone like this."

"I'm *fiiine*," she whines and then winces and curls into a ball. "My stomach doesn't feel great, but if I'm going to throw up, I'd rather be alone."

"Been there plenty of times."

She makes room for me, and I lay down beside her. The bed is small, Daisy-sized, and my feet meet the end of the mattress.

"You look ridiculous in my bed." She giggles.

"I never look ridiculous in bed."

Her gaze falls over my bare chest, and I'd bet if I could see better in the dark, I'd find her blushing.

She reaches out and touches a tattoo along my ribs. The date we won the Frozen Four my freshman year. "Show me your other tattoos."

I shift to show her my left shoulder and bicep.

"These are cool." She runs her finger along the outline of the mountains, then the sun, and compass. Then she reads the three words inked into the design, "Friendship, strength, and honor."

I say nothing as she continues to touch me.

"What about the ones on your legs?"

"You've seen them?" I ask.

"You wore shorts a couple of times in class."

I nod, filing away the tidbit that she noticed me, or at least my tattoos, before we officially met.

Daisy snuggles closer. "Show me. You've already seen me in my underwear. Seems fair."

Except, I'm sporting a semi.

"Come on." She pushes my shoulder playfully. "Strip."

Laughing, I get out of bed and unbutton my jeans. "I like it when you're bossy, sweet Daisy."

"I am not sweet!"

I drop my jeans to the floor and step out of them. She isn't bashful about looking, and since I'm already on display, I draw her attention to my thighs. "I got these two last year."

She gets on her knees and inches to the edge of the mattress, then sits back on her heels. "Any others?"

I nod, swallow, and turn so she can see my back. The cross I got for Mark is the most personal of my tattoos and sharing it with Daisy makes the moment feel heavier. Her cool fingertips meet my skin, and my spine tingles. I know she's reading the name and dates and figuring out that it's a memorial. I continue to face away from her until her hand falls away.

"I'm sorry." Her voice comes in a whisper. "I'm assuming this is your friend from the picture?"

I get back into bed and roll to face her. "Yeah. Mark was my best friend all the way back to middle school."

"What happened to him?"

I take a breath, and she adds, "If you don't want to talk about it…"

I usually don't, but something in Daisy's meek expression compels me to tell her.

"He was killed in a hit and run. We were at a party, and he decided to walk home. The driver never saw him."

"Oh my gosh." Her bottom lip trembles, and I reach out and smooth the pad of my thumb along it without thinking.

"Do you have any tattoos?"

She shakes her head slowly. "No. I like them, though."

She sits back, and I lift my right hand to show her the tiny tattoo on my pinkie finger. "Almost forgot about this one."

She takes my hand and brings it closer to her face. "A stick man?"

"I thought it was funny. Might have been drunk."

Silence falls between us as we continue to stare at each other. She releases my hand and lies down. Her eyes flutter closed and then pop open, and a smile tugs at her lips. When they close again, she mutters, "I can't believe Jordan Thatcher is in my bed."

"I can't believe I'm in bed with Daisy Johnson," I mimic her tone.

"Just an average Friday night in bed with a random girl," she says in a teasing tone.

She places both hands under her head and hits me with that innocent, blue gaze. "Why did you ask me to come out tonight?"

"Because I thought you'd like to go, but wouldn't unless someone came and dragged you there."

She hums her agreement.

"Plus, I was hoping I'd get to see you in that sexy red dress again."

She laughs and buries her head in the pillow. "Why do I do the most embarrassing things around you?"

"How is that embarrassing?"

"Are you kidding? I sent a guy I barely knew a picture of me in a dress with my boobs pushed up." As she says the last part, she reaches down and pushes up her tits as if I don't have the image of her in that dress burned into my brain. Add this moment to the ever-growing album of images of Daisy I'll never forget. Her hands are where I wish mine were.

"Trust me. You have no reason to be embarrassed. I should be the one embarrassed by how many times I've looked at it."

She's drunk and half passed out, so I don't really expect the comment to hit, but an uncomfortable beat of silence hangs between us. Then she giggles, this soft, happy sound I want to capture with my mouth.

Fuck it, I do. Erasing the space between us, I press my lips to hers, far gentler than I want. She inhales a cute yelp, and then her mouth softens and pushes back.

I force myself to pull back and prepare for the possibility she's going to tell me to get the hell out, but instead, she smiles, melts into the pillow with her eyes closed, and says, "Thank you for tonight. I had a really good time with you."

Chapter EIGHTEEN

Daisy

A DULL ACHE THROBS AT MY TEMPLES AND MY CHEEK IS plastered against something hard. Slowly, I open my eyes, and awareness slams into me. Jordan slept in my bed last night. And I'm on top of him. I try to untangle myself, but we're in some weird pretzel position that might have been comfortable, but now has my face flooding with heat because he hasn't moved from his side of the bed. Which means I attacked him.

"Morning," his deep voice rumbles beneath me.

"Morning." My response is squeaky, and I basically jolt myself back to my half of the bed.

"Couldn't help yourself, huh?"

I fling an arm over my eyes to block the sun and my mortification. Then I remember. He kissed me last night. My stomach flips at the memory. Does he remember?

"I can almost hear you freaking out over there." He gets up

from bed and pulls on his jeans. I sneak a glance and then look away when I find him grinning at me. "It's fine. Your bed is so small. I'd be more shocked if we didn't end up snuggled together."

"It isn't that." Or not just that. "Did you see me basically naked last night?" I squeeze my eyes closed while I wait for his answer.

"Yep. Sure did."

"Thought so." I groan, and of course he laughs at me like it was all no big deal.

The mattress dips with his weight, and he pries my arm away from my face. "I have to go to practice. Drink lots of water and take some more Advil."

"Thank you for staying and making sure I was okay."

He drops his head, and his nose grazes along the curve of my neck. In a lower voice, almost like he's talking to himself, he says, "Who knew white cotton panties were so fucking hot?"

He's on his feet before I can process it. "Oh, believe me. It was my pleasure." He hits me with a playful wink. "What are you doing later?"

"I'm not sure." I sit up. Did we make plans for today that I buried with last night's humiliation? That dull ache gets a little more insistent. "Oh, your statistics test is Tuesday. I completely forgot. I'm probably not going to be a lot of help today. How about we study tomorrow?"

A flash of something like insecurity crosses his face. "Yeah. That'll work."

He pulls on his T-shirt. His cocky smirk returns as he backs out of my room. "Later, sweet Daisy."

Going back to sleep is not in the cards. Every time I close my eyes, memories of last night replay, making me too antsy to lie still.

I'm downstairs eating cereal when Violet and Jane get home. Violet goes straight for the fridge and pulls out the orange juice. "Remind me never to stay at Eric's house again."

"That bad?" I ask.

Jane's laughter follows. "Eric got a new harmonica."

"My ears were bleeding," Vi says with a groan.

"How was The White House?" Jane asks, her voice lifting several octaves.

"It was... kind of amazing." I sneak a glance at Violet. "I wish you guys had been there."

Except then Jordan wouldn't have stayed over, and that was my very favorite part of the night.

"Did you get to hang out with Liam?" Violet asks.

"A little."

Jane claps her hands. "I want to hear all about it, but I need a shower and a nap."

Vi nods her agreement. "Same. And we need to go by the ballroom to take measurements and pictures for the artist."

"I'm out," Jane says. "I didn't sleep at all last night. I have to crash, but I promise I will be at your beck and call the rest of the weekend."

"I'm going to hold you to that," Vi says as Jane starts out of the kitchen to go crash. She looks at me. "You'll come?"

"Of course."

After a shower and breakfast, Violet and I go to campus. The ballroom on the first floor of Moreno Hall is way bigger than I pictured.

"How many people are we expecting?" I ask.

"So far only fifty have RSVP'd."

"Fifty?! That's way more than last year."

"I know. It's going to be amazing." She twirls around the big ballroom. She looks so happy.

My face must not meet her enthusiasm because she stops and asks, "Do you not like it?"

"No, it's going to be great."

"But?"

"Don't kill me, but I sort of liked it last year when it was more casual."

"Says the girl who spent last night at the biggest party on campus."

"That was just one night."

"So is this." She plants a hand on her hip. "You're fine with a big production if it's with Liam and his jock bros but not with your friends. Is that it?"

I don't point out that the guest list is now well beyond our friend group. "That isn't what I meant. This just doesn't feel like us."

"Exactly."

I give her the big smile she's waiting for. "It's going to be a blast. The best party of the year."

"You bet your ass."

We get back in her car to head home. She sings along with the song on the radio while I stare out the window.

"Do you ever miss it?"

She stops her singing to glance over at me. "Miss what?"

"Going to the big parties and hanging out with the jocks."

"No."

"Even excluding Gavin and the awful roommate?"

"Not for a second."

"It was that bad?" I had fun last night. Sure, I was happily drunk for most of the night, but the more time I spend with Jordan and Liam, the less I understand why she hates "them" so much.

"No, it was a blast until it wasn't."

"What does that mean?"

I've never pressed her on the topic, and I don't expect her to divulge any more information.

"I was so naïve. I took everyone at their word and was genuinely surprised when they went against it. I guess that's on me, but I knew myself well enough to know I couldn't play the game."

"What game?"

"You know, it's like a guy says he likes you and that you're different, spits all these sweet words at you, but really what he means is he wants to have sex with you. And I'm cool with that, but just say that instead."

"Gavin?" I ask.

"No." She shakes her head. "I mean, yes, I thought he liked me, and I still can't believe he hooked up with Bailey. He always acted like he couldn't stand her."

I only met Violet's roommate, Bailey, once, but she was pretty unbearable. She's one of those people who's always been pretty and popular, and treats it like it's the most important part of her personality.

"But in this instance, I'm generalizing. We'd go to these parties, and it was so much fun, but then the next day, I was playing it all back to decipher what was real and what was drunken fun."

My stomach dips. Was Jordan kissing me just drunken fun, or was it real?

"I know I've said it before, but I'm so sorry."

"It's fine. I'm fine. Obviously, I dodged a bullet." She stares straight ahead but mutters quietly, "Or an STD."

I snort a laugh. "Are you really okay? You seemed pretty stressed over the blocked car situation last night."

"Living next to him has not been as easy as I thought. Stupid me. I thought we'd continue never seeing each other as long as I stayed on my side of the fence. Instead, I'm running into him everywhere I go."

"Sorry about that."

"You're not sorry at all." She smiles.

"I really love that tree house, but I love you more. We could move." It's a weak offer, but if she really needed that, I'd do it.

"No way. He's not running me off." She pulls into the driveway and turns off the engine. "I know you like Liam and think he's different, but just be careful. Okay?"

I get it. She doesn't want to be hurt again, but I've been hurt by plenty of unpopular people before. Being a dick isn't an exclusive trait to just jocks. In fact, it's probably more like ninety percent of the population.

"I will. And one last time, I'm really sorry that happened to you."

"Thank you."

Jane is still in her room when we get inside.

"I think I'm going to nap, too," Violet says. "Dahlia should be back this afternoon. Jane and I thought we could have a night in, just the four of us. Or are you going to hang with your new boyfriend?"

"Stop it." I laugh nervously. "Liam is so not my boyfriend."

"Okay then, Darcy and dress up?"

"That sounds perfect."

Hours later, after Mister Darcy and Elizabeth have confessed their love, I still haven't figured out how to confess to my friends that my crush is no longer on the guy they think it is. Crushing on Liam was one thing, but Jordan? He's the epitome of everything Vi hates about that crowd.

But the real reason I can't bring myself to say the words is fear. I like Jordan. Really like him. Not like how I had a crush on Liam from afar. I've spent time with Jordan, I've kissed him… and I don't know if it means anything or if I'm just setting myself up for heartbreak.

What I do know is that it's just getting more awkward every time they mention Liam.

"Did he walk you home?" Dahlia asks as she helps me into one of Violet's old dresses. This one is my favorite. It's a pale yellow with a big, poofy skirt like a princess.

All the girls look to me for an answer.

"No. Jordan did." I laugh nervously. "He was afraid Violet would cut off his nipples if he didn't."

"Ha!" she says. "Good. I'm glad he didn't ditch you."

"No. He was great, actually. We hung out a little before Liam got to the party." I run my hand down the lace skirt.

"Hung out?" Jane asks. "Meaning he showed you his beer pong skills or let you observe him pick up other girls?"

"We played century club, but someone did try to get him to sign her boobs."

They all laugh. It might not sound like it was a good time, but it was. I think it was the best night of my life.

Jordan comes over Sunday evening. I'm in the tree house sketching when he calls up from the ground. "Daisy?"

"One sec." My heart races. I lost track of time, which isn't all that unusual when I'm really into it, but I've been anxious about seeing Jordan again all day, and I wanted time to prepare before he showed up.

"I'm coming up." His voice is closer this time, and I freeze because there's no other exit route and nothing to do now but wait for him to get to the top. His dark head covered by a black backward hat pops into view. He looks around and then continues up, so he's hunched over in the entryway. "You really do have a tree house."

"Yep." I wring my hands in front of me.

He shrugs out of his backpack and takes a seat with his long legs stretched out in front of him. "This is kind of badass, Daisy."

"It's my favorite spot. I come out here to sketch or think." *Or to watch parties across the fence.*

Jordan's gaze roams around the walls of the tree house. Some of my sketches are hung up with tacks, and he smiles as he gives each one attention. "All of these are yours?"

"Yeah." Several are from parties where I watched him and his friends hang out. They're just figures—backs of heads, broad shoulders, girls with small waists and big hair. He takes it all in.

"They're good. Really good."

"Thanks. How was the rest of your weekend?"

"Fine." We're crammed together in a tight spot where there's basically no way to avoid being close. He taps his shoe against my thigh lightly. "What'd you do yesterday?"

"Not much. We stayed in. You?"

"Pretty chill. We went over to my buddy Brad McCallum's apartment."

My gaze zooms in on his lips. So many questions. Why did he kiss me? And more importantly, is he going to do it again? And do I want him to?

That last one isn't a real question. Kissing him again is everything I want. I need to confirm that those sparks I was feeling Friday night weren't because I was at a party I'd dreamed of attending.

He unzips his backpack and pulls out a thick textbook.

"You do own one of those, huh?"

One side of his mouth quirks up as he also gets a notebook and pencil, then shifts to get comfortable.

"We can go inside if you want."

"Are you kidding? This is awesome."

"Okay." I'm pleased he likes it. "What areas do you still need help with for tomorrow?"

He adjusts his hat and gives me a sheepish grin. "All of it. I haven't looked at it since the last time we studied."

"O-kay." I hold my hand out for his textbook.

He places it in my palm, and I flip through it to refamiliarize myself with the material.

"We could work some problems," I suggest.

"Hit me." He flips his notebook to a clean page.

I give him a problem, and he jots it down.

With his eyes on the paper, he asks, "Have you even taken probability and statistics yet?"

"Noooo." I smile. "But I spent some time this past week looking up anything I didn't know."

He looks up and grins. "You did that for me?"

"It's no big deal."

"Are you kidding? That might be the nicest thing anyone's ever done for me." He points the end of his pencil at me. "Sweet Daisy. Told you. It fits."

Together we work through problems until the sun has set, taking the heat of the day with it. I rub my hands together and then bring them to my face.

Jordan packs up his stuff and then scoots forward, his knees bent. He takes my hands and covers them with his own. His thumb glides along the pulse point on my wrist. "I should get going."

"Why did you kiss me?" The question spills out with no regard for my ego. If he says he was drunk and doesn't remember it, I might have to jump from this tree house.

"I wanted to," he says simply.

"Why?"

He chuckles lightly.

"I'm not fishing for compliments. It just doesn't make any sense."

"That's your problem." His long fingers wrap around my wrists, and he tugs me closer. His minty breath hits my lips, and he stares at my mouth as he says, "Stop trying to make sense of everything."

There's an unspoken challenge in his words, or at least that's how I take it. I inch forward. He lets me come to him, but he reassures me with more soft caresses where he holds my wrists.

My mouth hovers near his, my breaths shallow and my heart hammering in my chest. I bring my lips to his in a ghost of a kiss. And there they are, the tiny sparks all over my body. I tremble everywhere, and Jordan groans quietly, bringing one of his hands to the back of my neck.

I forget to be timid. I forget that we don't make any sense because it feels so damn good.

His tongue strokes mine in the same rhythm of his thumb

along my neck. I raise a hand to his cheek and lightly run my nails along the light scruff and then higher where I thread my fingers through the thick locks of dark hair. He lets me explore.

He's a good kisser. Playful but intense. Gentle nips and then hard presses of his lips over mine as he steals the air from my lungs.

He pulls me between his legs and wraps his arms around my waist. His fingers dance at the hem of my T-shirt, caressing bare skin and sending goosebumps racing up my side. I want to be closer still, and press into him until his back is against the wall of the tree house and my boobs crush into his chest. My nipples ache at the contact, and heat rushes between my legs.

"Daisy!" Violet's voice is slow to register above the blood pounding in my ears. When she calls my name a second time, I jump back.

I scramble off Jordan and fix my clothes and hair before answering her. "We're studying in the tree house."

She comes to the bottom of the ladder and looks up. My cheeks are on fire, but I hope she thinks it's just the cold air.

"Take a break and come inside. I have a surprise."

Chapter NINETEEN

Jordan

CLIMBING DOWN FROM A TREE HOUSE WITH A BONER IS a new experience. Thankfully it deflates at record speed as Violet gives us a weird look.

"Why were you studying up there?" she asks. "It's freezing out."

"I like it up there," Daisy protests. "What's the surprise?"

"I finished your dress."

Daisy stares blankly at her cousin as we follow her inside the house.

"For the Wallflower Ball," Violet adds.

"The what?" I ask, brows raising.

"It's a formal Violet masterminds and has not-so-lovingly named." Daisy does a cute little eye roll to accentuate her comment.

"It's going to be epic," Violet tells me. "Jocks aren't allowed."

"Hey," Dahlia calls from the living room, where she's holding up a yellow dress. "I'm a jock."

"Sorry, *most* jocks aren't allowed," Violet corrects.

"This the thing Liam roped me into helping set up for?" I ask Daisy.

"Yeah." She nods, then turns back to her cousin. "And what do you mean you finished my dress. I thought it was already done."

"It was, but I think this one might be more you." Violet waves to Dahlia. The closer she comes with that dress, the bigger it seems to get. So much lace. I think it might swallow little Daisy right up.

"Wait. Is this..." Her words trail off as she takes the dress from Dahlia and clutches it to her chest. "Violet, you didn't!"

My gaze pings between them. I'm not sure what's going on, but it's obvious Daisy is pleased by the dress. I'm not sure I've ever seen her so unabashedly happy. Her eyes are fucking twinkling, and her smile is so big. Daisy smiling big like that is really something. And I want to see more of it.

She hugs Violet around the neck. "But you worked so hard on the other one."

"I know, but every time you put this one on, you look so happy. I hemmed it, and Dahlia helped me add the jewels around the waist. Do you like it?"

"*Love*," she says. "I love it."

I drag my backpack up to my shoulder and squeeze Daisy's bicep. "I'm gonna go. Thanks for your help."

Nodding to Violet and Dahlia, I start for the front door. I suck in the cold air and let it fill my lungs. Dammit. I kissed her again.

Actually, she kissed me. Sweet Daisy made a move on me. I never thought I'd utter those words. I thought I'd be good as long as I held myself back, which I was doing a pretty fucking epic job of until she started talking about us kissing.

I've barely made it to the end of the driveway when Daisy calls my name and jogs after me.

"I'm sorry," she says.

"It's okay. I'm good. I studied more for this test than any other in my life."

"Not about that. That we were interrupted," she says with a shy smile.

"Oh. Well, I've got another ten minutes if you want to make out in your front yard." *Shut the fuck up, man.*

She laughs. Damn, that sound shouldn't get to me the way it does.

"I should get back inside, but, uh, we could meet up tomorrow if you want." She blushes. "To study, I mean."

"I have a group project thing tomorrow night."

"Okay. No problem." Her smile dims.

"What about tomorrow afternoon? I have a break after practice."

And there it is again. Her lips curve up. "Sure. I'm done at two."

"Let's do it at my place." Liam is the perfect cock block for this scenario. I can spend time with her, but I definitely won't kiss her again.

"Okay."

"See you then," I say, and as I walk away, I realize that being the reason for that smile is the best part of my whole day. I take another step. "Send me some pictures in that dress?"

Her grin widens. "We'll see."

When Daisy shows up to study, Liam is in the shower. It's perfect because it means we can set up in the living room and not my room where there's a bed. Getting her near a bed would be game over.

Except, even sitting on our couch, shoes kicked off, legs crossed and a laptop resting on her knees, I have images of doing very dirty things to this sweet human.

"How can I help?" she asks. "What don't you feel like you have down for your test tomorrow?"

I take a seat next to her with my iPad and a notebook. "I feel pretty good. I thought I could work through all the problems in the chapter again."

"Yeah. Okay."

She goes to close her laptop, but I stop her. "Don't you have homework or something you should be working on, too?"

I drop my gaze to her mouth. She's wearing this pink lipstick that shines. I want to run my finger along her bottom lip to see what it feels like. And glide my tongue along it to see what it tastes like.

"I can work on it later."

"Nah. I can do this on my own."

"Then why am I here?"

Because I can't get enough of you.

I knock my leg against hers. "Moral support. And in case I get stuck."

She doesn't look convinced.

"I've got this," I say as Liam walks in. He's got a freaking towel around his waist and no shirt. Yep, I should have picked the bedroom.

"Daisy!" Liam greets her with his usual smile.

Daisy's eyes widen a fraction at his half-naked state. "Hi."

He goes straight to his room but leaves the door open. Is she thinking about him naked? I grimace. Fuck, now I'm imagining him naked.

He comes out in shorts and a T-shirt and sits in the empty chair. "What are you guys working on?"

"Stats," I say.

We both look at Daisy, who says, "I was just about to start reading for American Lit class."

"Cool." Liam drags his backpack from beside the chair to between his feet. "I need to do a little studying myself."

I turn on some music, and we all get to it. See? I can do this.

Studying with Daisy and Liam, and I am absolutely not going to kiss her. Or even think about kissing her.

Daisy leans over. Her hair falls onto my arm, and her pink lips open as she speaks, "Can we listen to something else? Something not so… angry."

Well, there went not thinking about kissing her. Not that I ever really stopped.

"Got a problem with my music?"

"Not if I'm jamming out in the car, but for reading Thoreau, it's a bit much."

I pick up my phone, unlock it, and hand it to her. "You pick."

She hesitates but eventually does take it.

"What type of music do you listen to?" I ask as she scrolls through my playlists.

"Whatever is on." She hits me with a shy smile. "I usually just go for the daily top hits."

She selects a new playlist, and an Ed Sheeran song plays.

"Favorite singer or band?"

She thinks for a second. "Don't laugh."

"I would never."

She doesn't look like she believes me, but she finally says, "Shawn Mendes. He's so hot."

Liam busts up laughing, and she blushes.

"Mendes is great," he says. "I'm laughing because Jordan got stopped once in the airport on the way to a game and asked if he was Shawn Mendes."

The girl was maybe fourteen and near hysterics. The guys are never going to let me live it down.

Daisy stares at me, and those pink lips fall open. "You do kind of look like him. I never noticed."

"He can't sing for shit," Liam says.

"Oh, like you can?" I fire back.

Daisy laughs as she hands my phone back. I tap out a text to her, **So you think I'm hot?** 😉

She checks her phone, smiling when she realizes it's from me. **I don't think I said that**, she replies.

That's what I heard, I reply.

She looks up and smiles at me. Neither of us looks away for several seconds. I lean forward a fraction and freeze. She's holding her breath like she's waiting for me to close the distance between us and isn't sure if she wants me to or not.

I don't, but damn, I really, really want to.

Tuesday afternoon lab we're in our usual setup with Liam sitting between us. They work through the lab with me guiding them, and it's all just like it's been every other time, but different too.

I catch Daisy's stare over her worksheet. She smiles tentatively and presses her lips together like she's fighting a smile.

This fucking girl. Why are all her little mannerisms so fucking adorable?

At the end of class, Daisy grabs her backpack and comes over to stand next to me.

I bump my elbow against hers. "Hey."

"Hey," she replies quietly. "How was your test this morning?"

"Aced it. Thanks to you."

"I didn't really do anything."

"Sure you did." She did, too. I would have passed on my own, but I did so well the professor is probably wondering who I cheated off of. "Celebrate with me tonight."

Liam hovers nearby.

"With us," I correct.

"It's a Tuesday night." Light laughter follows her reply.

"Drinking on school nights is allowed," I whisper playfully. "And, I promise to look out for you just like last time."

Her gaze darts to my mouth. "Okay."

I look at Liam. "Are you in?"

He smiles. "Sure, why not."

I pick up Daisy, and we get to McCallum's apartment just after ten. Liam hung back at the dorm and said he'd meet up with us, so I have some time with Daisy all to myself.

She doesn't ask about him, so I put my buddy out of mind, at least for now.

Only a few guys are here already, but the ones that are, are drunk and at the dining room table playing cards. I grab Daisy and me a beer and lead her to one end.

She leans in, her blonde hair tickling my face as she whispers, "What are we playing?"

I pull her chair against mine. "The game is Fuck the Dealer."

"I know this one!" She laughs. "But it's been a while."

"We'll do a practice round." I motion for McCallum to give me the deck, and I deal her three cards as practice. "What's your wager, sweet Daisy?"

She blushes at the nickname. "Three seconds."

If she were anyone else, I'd call her on such a low wager, but three seconds of chugging her beer, and she'll be halfway to tipsy land.

I rest my fingers along the edge of the first card. "Suit?"

"Diamonds."

I flip over a spade, and she frowns.

"Value?" I tap the second card.

"Umm..." She bites the corner of her bottom lip, drawing attention to her pouty mouth. I should have just invited her over to my dorm to celebrate so I could kiss her all night instead of playing games.

"Three."

A cute groan slips from her lips at the sight of the eight of spades.

"Last chance." I drop one hand to her knee.

Her breathing picks up. She licks her lips and stares at the last card on the table. "Higher."

I flip a deuce and smile. "Sorry."

Her eyes narrow in a playful glare. She lifts her beer and starts drinking.

I count. Slowly. I reach three as she looks like she can't swallow another drop.

With a grimace, she sets the can down. I pass the cards back to McCallum, and the rest of the table joins back in.

"How many nights a week do you go out?"

I shrug. "Depends, I guess."

"On homework and stuff?"

"On what's happening that week," I say.

She laughs at my answer.

My friends and teammates are important to me. Losing Mark put things in perspective.

"I could get better grades, but after graduation, am I really going to care if I got an A instead of a C?"

"Umm…" She holds back more laughter as she considers my question. "I'm not sure. I've never thought about it like that, I guess."

"Were you always super into school?" I ask.

She gets a slight blush to her cheeks. "Yes."

"No shame in being smart."

"I know, but it isn't like I set out to be super smart. I was just bored enough that it was something to do."

I want to ask her more, but my phone buzzes in my pocket.

"It's Liam," I say as I read his short text, **Something came up. Tell Daisy I'm sorry I couldn't make it.**

"He isn't coming."

I watch her for the disappointment that I'm sure is coming.

Instead, she smiles. "That's okay. I really just wanted to hang out with you."

Not even being mistaken for Shawn Mendes could compare to the way that makes me feel.

I slip my phone back into my pocket. "Same."

As the party gets bigger, Daisy and I make our way outside to the deck. Music from inside drifts out, and a few other couples are making out or cuddling under blankets, hands suspiciously missing from view. Daisy takes it all in, and her cheeks flush.

"Cold?" I rub my hands along her arms.

"I'm okay." She nuzzles against my chest anyway.

I tuck a strand of windblown hair behind her ear and bring my lips down to hers. Her mouth molds to mine, and she kisses me back, though tentatively. When I pull back to read her expression, she glances around, and it hits me. PDA is not her thing. And while I could tell her that no one out here is paying any attention to us, having her to myself sounds pretty damn good too.

"You wanna get out of here?" I ask.

She nods.

Dallas is sober tonight, and I get him to give us a ride. We take off toward Daisy's, both of us in the back seat. Her chest rises and falls in anticipation. I keep my hands to myself, but I am dying to touch her.

I know I need to talk to Liam, but if he was really interested in her, wouldn't he be here tonight? All Daisy has to do is look at me, and I want to say fuck it all.

Her house is dark from the outside. She pauses on the front stoop.

"Meet me in the tree house."

I raise a brow.

"If my roommates are awake, they will ask a million questions that I don't want to answer tonight."

"Hiding me from your friends, sweet Daisy?"

"Go." She pushes me lightly, and I head around the back of the house. I use my phone for light as I climb up into the tree house. I wasn't lying. I really dig it up here. It's so Daisy. Scraps of paper with unfinished sketches line the walls.

"Little help," she calls up while I'm still enjoying her art.

Daisy stands on the bottom rung with a big blanket in her arms. She lifts it over her head to me, followed by a pillow and a flashlight.

"Look at you. You're a regular camper."

She reaches the top, and together we put down the blanket so we can lie on top of it. "I've never been camping. Unless you count sleeping up here because I did fall asleep up here once."

"I love camping."

"Surprise, surprise," she sits in the middle and places the flashlight off to the side so it gives us a little light to see each other.

Sitting next to her, I ask, "What does that mean?" I mock her tone. "Surprise, surprise."

"It seems like you've done everything. What are your parents like?"

"They're cool. My dad is a high school baseball coach."

"Baseball?"

"Yeah, imagine his disappointment."

Daisy smiles and hugs her legs to her chest, then props her chin on top of her knees. "And your mom?"

"She's a dietitian."

"And were you always this…"

"Charming?" I lay on my side next to her. "Handsome?"

"Yeah. Those, too." She stretches her legs out, and I wrap an arm around her waist to pull her down, so we're facing each other on the blanket.

"I was into sports and video games, anything outdoors."

"I bet you had lots of friends and *girl*friends."

"Lots of friends. Only one serious girlfriend. In high school."

"You had a serious girlfriend?" Her tone is filled with surprise.

"Serious-ish. She went to college in New York. We lasted all of a week into freshman year." I breathe her in. "What about you? Was young Daisy as sweet as this one?"

Her shirt's lifted an inch above the waist of her jeans, and I run a hand along the soft curve of her waist.

"I guess I was the same, yeah. My parents worked a lot. They're both professors and researchers, so academics are sort of everything to them."

"What'd you do for fun?"

"Took extra classes, read." She shrugs. "They didn't really have time to run me to a lot of activities or friends' houses. And no one wanted to come to my house since it wasn't exactly party central."

"Sounds lonely."

"Sometimes, but I found ways to keep myself entertained. I taught myself to draw with books and online tutorials. I'd never taken a real drawing class until I got to Valley."

"You're really talented."

"I'm okay."

"And, as previously mentioned, great at taking a compliment." Pulling her closer, I let my hand glide around her back and down to her butt. Her breaths come quicker.

"Thank you."

"Better." I smile. "And boyfriends?"

"Two. One in high school and one last year."

"Why didn't they work out?"

"My first boyfriend only lasted a few months. We were friends, and I think we were both curious about dating and sex, and we just decided to go for it, but there wasn't much there in the way of chemistry."

"And the second?"

"He was great. We had a lot in common, but he transferred at the end of the year."

Her lips are warm and just as soft as the rest of her. I tug on her bottom lip until I feel her mouth curve into a smile.

"You have nice lips, sweet Daisy."

"Thank you." The words are quicker this time, and I reward her with another kiss and palm her ass in one hand.

"And a cute little ass."

She laughs, body shaking, bringing her closer. "Thank you, I think."

"Oh, it was definitely a compliment." I roll on top of her.

She stares up at me, hair falling around her shoulders. I twist my finger around one strand.

"You have a great nose." She lifts up to place the softest kiss on the bridge of my nose. It's a move that, from anyone else, would feel silly.

"Thanks."

"Welcome."

I wait for more. I think I could soak up compliments from Daisy all day long and never get tired of it. I want her to see the good in me, even if it's something as minor as a nose that's never been broken.

The desire to kiss her again eventually makes me too impatient to see if there are other things that she likes about me. Or at least things she'll admit. She likes kissing me, and the feeling is mutual.

My dick presses between her legs, and even between two layers of denim, she feels good. The longer we kiss, the more she starts to explore with her hands—up my side and down my back. The feel of her icy fingertips on my skin sets my insides on fire.

Eventually, when I'm so hard I can barely see straight, her hips rock up, needing more friction.

There is nothing I want more than to be inside of her. I want to fuck sweet Daisy so hard we bring the tree house crashing to the ground.

Rolling onto my side, I cup her through her jeans and press two fingers against her center. A shiver racks through her, and I swallow her whimpers.

I walk my fingers up to the button of her jeans. I swear my

hands shake like it's my first time shoving my hands down a girl's pants. Daisy may not be a virgin, but she isn't hooking up on the regular. She's trusting me in a way she's trusted few others.

Something silky greets me as I slide my hand down. I tear my mouth away and grin.

"Is something wrong?" she asks in a breathy pant.

I scoot down so I can kiss her at the top of her panty line. "No, sweet Daisy. Nothing wrong at all."

I work her jeans over her hips and down her legs. She kicks off her shoes so I can free them from her completely. She raises up on her elbows. Desire and nerves play on her face.

"I'm nervous."

"Do you want to stop?"

"God, no." Her quick admission makes her laugh. She sits up and reaches for the band of my jeans.

While she unzips me, I pull my T-shirt over my head and then hers.

It's no easy feat getting me out of my jeans in this small space, but with a little maneuvering and a whole lot of dedication to the task, I lay back down next to Daisy with only her silky panties and bra and my boxers between us.

I hold her face as I kiss away her nerves, then let my hand travel down her neck, over the valley of her breasts and her stomach, before resting on her upper thigh. I tease along the edge of her panties, finally sliding one finger underneath, then another.

She holds perfectly still until I brush the pad of my fingers along her slit. Her hips jump.

"If I come in like three seconds, should I be embarrassed and never show my face again?"

Chuckling, I push two fingers inside of her and drag my thumb along her clit.

She mutters something indecipherable under her breath.

"No, Daisy," I whisper against the corner of her mouth. "You shouldn't be embarrassed. But if you come on my fingers in three seconds, my ego might not fit in this tree house."

Her laughter is disguised under her whimpers as I glide in and out of her slick heat. My heart feels like it's going to explode in my chest.

It takes longer than three seconds, but her orgasm splinters through her in the most beautiful display. Her body arches and she kisses me like she needs the air from my lungs to survive.

As the last tremors die, she melts into the blanket.

"That was..." Her voice trails off. She smiles, eyes closed. "Thank you."

Yeah, that was definitely a compliment.

Chapter TWENTY

Daisy

I wasn't lying when I told Jordan that I wasn't a virgin. Only once with my high school boyfriend, but with Jonathon, a physics major I dated last year, we had sex lots. Okay, not lots, but pretty often. He ended up transferring back home at the end of the year. It wasn't exactly fireworks, but he was nice, and we had a lot in common.

So, while I haven't had loads of sex with a ton of people, I've punched in my V card. With Jonathon, though, we didn't do much else besides sex. Kissing led to undressing, and from there, it was pretty much straight to sex with maybe a boob squeeze or two for foreplay.

I didn't even know enough to realize how I was missing out. And oh, how I was missing out. I can say now without a doubt that what Jordan did with just his fingers was a thousand times better than what Jonathon did while actually screwing me.

And now I realize I don't know how to return the favor.

Jordan pushes his boxers past his hips, letting his dick spring up. He strokes himself once slowly as he scans my body from head to toe.

"Show me what to do?" I place my hand under his.

He's hard and smooth, and at my touch, his dick leaks with precum. He repositions his hand, so he's covering mine. I readjust so I'm holding him in the same spot he was, and slowly he pumps our hands up and down his length.

His gaze drops from me to his dick, and he sucks in a breath through his teeth. The muscles in his stomach contract, and I want to run my finger along the outline of his six-pack. Well, not now. You couldn't pay me enough to move my hand right now.

I'm dizzy with the excitement of touching him like this and the look of pure ecstasy that washes over his face.

He picks up the speed, moving our hands faster. I lean over and place a kiss on the head. He's salty on my lips, and my tongue darts out to taste more of him.

"Oh, fuck," he mutters. He guides me by the neck with his free hand, pulling me closer and crushing his mouth to mine as he lets out a guttural groan. He stills our joined hands but continues kissing me as his dick jumps in my palm.

With a final nip of my bottom lip, he pulls away and lets his head fall back. His fingers unravel from around mine, and he pulls off his sock to clean himself up.

It makes me giggle, and he shoots me a sheepish grin.

"Do you want to stay over?" I'm already imagining how to get him inside and up to my room without my roommates seeing.

"I should go."

"Really?" My face burns with what I guess is embarrassment at being so eager. He hooks up with lots of girls, this isn't a major thing to him.

He brings his hand back up to my neck and says, "This was

amazing. Tonight, you—all of it. I have an early workout in the morning, and all my shit is at the dorm."

"Okay."

A lump forms in my throat, and my eyes sting like I might cry. Stupid, I know. Of course he can't just stay over. Tonight was just… everything. And I don't want it to end.

We get dressed in silence, and then Jordan goes down the ladder first. I toss him the blanket, pillow, and flashlight, then start climbing.

Halfway, he grips me by the waist and lifts me in the air, spinning me around and loosening the knot forming in my chest. He sets me on the ground in front of him.

"My ankles are cold." He pulls his socks from the pocket of his jacket.

"Sorry about that." I laugh at his bare ankles.

"I'm not." He raises a hand to my face, stroking his thumb over my bottom lip before bringing his mouth down on mine.

I could keep kissing him all night, but he pulls away and backs toward the side yard that leads to the front of the house. "Later, sweet Daisy."

The hockey team has an away game during the week, leaving me by myself in physics lab. Professor Green moves me, yet again, to a new group for the day. It isn't the same without him. Jordan, that is. I don't know how it happened, but it stopped being Liam I was excited to see in class and who occupied my daydreams.

He texts every day, usually multiple times, but I still worry that whatever is happening between us means a lot more to me than it does to him.

Wednesday night, Violet gathers us all in the living room.

She's in full ball prep mode. Winter break is in two weeks, and the ball is the week we return.

"Table decorations are set," Violet says. She looks to Jane. "You're bringing everything back with you?"

"I'll have it shipped, but it will be here. I promise."

Violet nods. "Flowers are still good, Daisy?"

"Yes."

She keeps staring at me.

"I will go by tomorrow and quadruple check."

My cousin grins. "Thank you."

Once Violet is satisfied that everything is going to plan, the conversation falls to dates.

"Eric's coming with me," Jane says. "Unless I find a boyfriend before then. Do you think I could pay that cute boy who—"

"No," we all shout at once.

She just shrugs.

"I don't want the stress of asking someone to be my date." Dahlia shakes her head. "But I'm hoping to dance with lots of cute boys at the party."

"I'm going solo too," Violet says, then looks to me. "Are you going to ask Liam?"

"Oh." I swallow. All eyes are on me. "No. He probably has a game or practice or something."

"But he's bringing the flowers, right?"

"Yeah."

"So, he obviously doesn't have an away game that weekend. He can come after if they have a game."

"You should ask him," Dahlia encourages, and Jane nods.

"I'll think about it."

I don't like keeping things from my friends, but I'm not sure where Jordan and I stand. Plus, I know what Violet will say. He's a player, he'll hurt me, yadda yadda. And I don't want to think about how she might be right.

Jordan texts Thursday evening, and I go out to the tree house to wait for him.

I'm bundled up in a blanket, sketching, when I hear him on the ladder. I toss my notebook and turn the flashlight in his direction.

He holds up a hand to shield his eyes from the light when he gets to the top. "Whoa."

"Sorry." I set it to the side, and he walks hunched over to me.

He sits so that we're side by side. "Hey."

"Hey," I reply, feeling a little awkward. "Congrats."

The team won both of their games this week.

"Thanks." He leans back and adjusts his hat, so it faces forward. "What've you been up to this week?"

"Not a lot. Classes and helping Violet plan for the ball."

"Oh right, the Wallflower Ball. When is it?"

"The fourteenth."

"Might need you to send me a pic or two in that sexy, yellow dress."

It's on the tip of my tongue to ask him to be my date, but in what world does Jordan agree to go to a Wallflower Ball? He's anything but a wallflower. And if he says no, I fear it'll be the end of us right now. So I just say, "I can probably arrange that."

He bends forward and kisses me, scratching and tickling me with his scruff. It's grown since he's been gone, and it's a good look on him.

"I like." I run my hand over his cheek.

"Yeah?" He grins. "I figured you would prefer clean cut."

"It suits you."

He picks up my sketchbook near his feet and tips it toward the light.

"Don't look. It isn't finished." I try to grab it, but he holds it out of my reach. "Is this me?"

I climb into his lap and tug at his arm until he lowers it and lets me snatch it back. "You weren't supposed to see that."

His deep laughter isn't taunting, but I'm horrified anyway. When I've closed it and placed it under the blanket, I finally face him again. "We're working on facial features in class, and I needed the extra practice."

Those are both true, but I easily could have picked someone else to draw and now wish I had.

"I'm flattered," he says. "Did you do that from memory?"

"Yes. You have a very memorable face."

He traces a finger down the side of my face. "Well, from what I was able to see before you attacked me, it seemed pretty good."

"I can't get your mouth right."

"Oh yeah?" He brings his lips to mine. "Maybe you need to better inspect it."

I do, kissing him like I've wanted to all week. He slides his hands under my shirt.

It's movement next door that interrupts us as his thumbs glide over my nipples. The guys at The White House are outside, and their laughter draws Jordan's attention.

"Oh, wow. You have a perfect view into their back yard."

"Yeah," I say like I haven't spent many nights up here watching the parties next door.

"Can they see us?"

"I don't think so."

He glances around at the floor around us. "I wish I had something to toss at Gavin's head."

"Let's not give him any reason to come over and set off Violet."

"Those two really don't get along, huh?"

I shake my head. "Can't really blame her. He pretended to like her and hooked up with her roommate."

"Gavin?" He jabs a thumb toward where his buddy stands. "That doesn't sound like him."

I shrug.

He kisses me again, and I forget the reason he came over was to study until the light in Violet's room flips on.

"I need to finish my sketch," I say.

"Mhmm." He kisses down my neck and onto my collarbone.

"Finals are next week."

With a playful groan, he pulls back and gets his book from his backpack.

"You're cute when you pout," I tell him.

"Don't compliment me now, sweet Daisy, or I'll be tempted to toss our books over the fence and kiss you until you forget about school."

I almost do it. It's only because I know he needs to study that I don't.

The rest of the week and into the weekend, Jordan and I text but aren't able to hang out. He invites me to a party on Saturday, but Violet has planned an early birthday party for Dahlia, who turns twenty over the break.

We're at one of her teammate's apartment. The living room is filled with people. Some I know, more I don't. Dahlia refuses the Happy Birthday sash but has on a light-up shot glass necklace that flashes as Jane pours more champagne into it. She bought two bottles of Dom, one that was double the price because the outside was covered in rhinestones.

My phone buzzes in my pocket. Jordan's name flashes on the screen three times. He texts every thought in a different message, whereas I usually fit what would be several messages into one long one that he probably doesn't read all the way through.

I move off to the side of the room to read his messages. **Pick the suit,** the first one says with a picture of three cards facing down. I scroll to the next one. **Wanna fuck the dealer?** And last, **P.S. I'm the dealer.**

My heart flutters in my chest. **Hearts.**

A minute later, another picture arrives. The queen of clubs. **Uh-oh. Only two chances left.**

He follows that up quickly with, **Value?**

Eight, I guess.

Wrong again, sweet Daisy. The picture shows a ten of hearts.

Last shot, he texts. And, **Higher or lower?**

Lower.

Final answer?

I picture him at the party, sitting at a table, probably carrying on a conversation with his friends while texting me.

Statistically, the odds are in my favor.

He sends the picture of the jack of diamonds first, then a selfie of him flipping off the camera. I stare at it for a long time. His giant smirk aimed at me, eyes twinkling, backward hat, and scruff still going strong.

Looks like it's Fuck Daisy instead. ;)

I take a picture of me holding up my drink. I chug for three seconds and then send another text, **I think I'd rather us both be f'ed.**

Chapter TWENTY-ONE

Jordan

I fell asleep texting Daisy. I invited her over, but it's probably better she didn't make it because I'm not sure I could have made good on the sexy things I was texting her all night. Though I happily would have tried.

And I absolutely cannot have sex with her until I talk to Liam and tell him what's going on with Daisy and me. It's been weighing on me all week.

Liam's in the living room, picking up when I come out of my room.

"Hey." I glance around the small space. It's become a bit of a disaster area with all the practices, games, studying, and partying. "You got a minute?"

"Have you seen my phone charger?" He lifts a blanket from the couch.

"No, but I have an extra you can use." I run into my room to get it and bring it back.

"Thanks." He sits on the couch and plugs it into the nearest outlet. "I must have left it at the hotel."

"I'm usually the one leaving shit behind," I say as I grab a Powerade and have a seat with him. I have no idea how to broach the subject of Daisy, and my palms are sweaty. If Liam says he still likes her, I can't see her anymore (which will fucking suck). But it doesn't take back what I've already done. He might hate me for that.

He lets out a long breath and sinks into the cushion. "Man, I have never looked forward to winter break more than this year."

We only get a week because of games and practice, but most of the guys are excited about some time off to visit family and let their bodies rest.

"Yeah," I say, but I don't really mean it.

Going home and this time of year specifically remind me of Mark. It was an awful December night over break my freshman year that he died. Try as I might, I can't seem to feel the same excitement over visiting family and friends for the holidays anymore.

Friends from high school will be partying, and my family has big get-togethers. It's basically going to be a week of nonstop partying.

I'll attend all of it, putting on a happy face and trying to enjoy it like I know Mark would have. He was the life of the party, always smiling and having a good time. I swore after he died that I'd aim to live my life the same way, and in general, I've made good on that; but I know that week I'm home, I'll be faking it and counting down the days to return to Valley.

Liam's phone comes alive, and he sets it down next to him. "I'm going to shower and then head to the library to study for finals."

He stands and then pauses. "Wait, did you say you needed something?"

"Nah. I'll catch you later."

I'll tell him another time. Let him at least get through finals before I add to the stress.

It's in the last week of the semester that I realize how busy my schedule is. I've never tried to fit in spending time with a girl. Though I doubt she needs it, Daisy studies hard for her classes, and that's especially true for her final exams.

I meet up with her in the library one afternoon after practice. She's got her dark blonde hair pulled back into a ponytail, and she twists the end around a finger as she reads. She's wearing her daisy charm necklace today and it always makes me smile.

When she glances up to find me staring, she grins. "You're supposed to be studying."

"Oh, I am."

"I need to go find another resource book." She stands, and I automatically push to my feet.

Laughing, she slows her steps to let me catch up. I follow her to the back corner of the library where books line tall shelves. She stops and lets her fingers trail over the spines of the books. I wrap my arms around her waist from behind and place a kiss on her neck.

While tilting her head to give me better access, she pulls out a book and opens it. "I have to finish studying."

I bite her playfully. "What are you working on?"

"An essay on Thoreau for my final in American Lit."

I take the book and flip it open. Then I read from the biography. "American philosopher, poet, and environmental scientist. Best known for his book, *Walden* and his essay, *Civil Disobedience*." I close it with a snap. "Sounds riveting. I can think of a better way to fill the time."

I sweep my lips over hers and back her up against the shelves.

Her hands slide under my T-shirt and along my stomach muscles. The girl likes my abs.

"Born in Massachusetts in 1817. He attended Harvard College," she recites.

"Oh yeah?" I ask, kissing up the column of her neck. "Tell me more about Thoreau, beautiful."

She does, stating random facts as I glide my lips along her soft skin. I don't hear a lot of it. I'm too wrapped up in her. She consumes me. Kissing her, touching her, just being near her alters everything around me where it's only her.

"His later works include *Autumnal Tints, The Succession of Trees,* and..." Her voice wavers, and she lets out a little sigh as I suck lightly on her neck.

"And?"

"I can't remember."

I open the book. Who would have thought I'd be spending my afternoon reading Thoreau?

"Here it is," I say.

She looks up at me with hooded blue eyes. "What is it?"

"You tell me."

"I don't care anymore," she says, and tries to kiss me.

I take a step back. "Tsk, tsk, sweet Daisy."

She cares. Maybe not right this second, but no way I'm letting her off so easy.

She growls and tries to reach for the book.

"No cheating." I move closer, dip my head so my lips are within millimeters of her neck, and blow lightly, teasing her.

She leans into my touch, eliciting a laugh from me.

"Give me a hint."

"One of them starts with a W."

"*Wild Apples,*" she says quickly, looking so damn proud of herself.

I love it when she smiles at me like she's doing now. I feel a thousand feet tall.

"A-plus." I drop a soft kiss to her lips.

"You're a really good tutor." She wraps her arms around my neck. "And really, really good with your mouth."

On the last day of our lab, I stare at her, wondering how the hell she got so far under my skin.

"We did it!" she exclaims after we turn in our tests.

Liam holds up his hand for a high five. She slaps his palm and then looks at me. With a smirk, I lift my hand, let her slap it, then curl my fingers around hers, holding on a fraction longer.

I go to Daisy's Friday afternoon before she leaves for home. Violet opens the door with a scowl. "Finals are over."

"Uh, yeah," I say.

"Why are you here?"

"Vi," Daisy admonishes and pulls the door wider to let me in. "Ignore her. Come on. I have your notes upstairs."

"Notes. Right." I smirk and push past her cousin to follow Daisy upstairs.

"Sorry about that," she says as she closes the door.

I sprawl out on her bed with my feet hanging off the side. "What time are you leaving?"

"An hour. I'm following Violet. We're meeting her parents for dinner, and then I'm driving the rest of the way to Flagstaff."

"Sounds nice."

She shrugs. "What about you?"

"Not sure. Maybe tonight. Maybe tomorrow."

"You don't seem very excited," she notes. "Liam was practically bouncing yesterday to have a week off hockey."

"I like hockey."

"You can like something and still want a break from it."

I grab her by the waist and pull her down on top of me. I've barely had time to work my hand under her shirt when there's a knock at the door.

"Daisy?" Violet calls from the other side.

She scrambles off me, face bright red. "Just a sec."

I sit up, and she walks over to the door, then smooths a hand down her hair and over her mouth before she opens the door. "What's up?"

"How long until you're ready?"

"Uhh. I thought we weren't leaving for another hour."

"It took me less time to pack than I thought. Your stuff is already in the car, yeah?"

Daisy nods. They share some sort of silent communication, and then Daisy says, "Give me five minutes."

She shuts the door and then turns to face me.

"Five minutes, huh?"

She straddles me and glides her hands along my chest and around to my back. "Sorry."

"It's okay. I'll swing by and see if Gavin wants to grab food or something."

"You're really avoiding going home." Her brows lift in question.

"It's not my favorite time of year."

"You don't like the holidays?" Her expression goes serious. "Oh no, are you a grinch?"

I laugh. "No, it's just… my buddy, Mark…" I search for the right words. It isn't something I really talk about with anyone but my friends from high school. No one else really gets it in the same way. They're supportive, but unless you've lost someone like that, it's hard to understand.

Her mouth makes an O. "Oh my gosh. He died on the twenty-third."

I nod. "We were at a party to celebrate everyone being home for break."

She wraps herself around me and squeezes tight. "I'm so sorry."

"Thanks." I clear my throat and lift her off me. I stand, and then she does too, watching me with sympathetic eyes.

"I should go so you can get on the road. Have a nice break." I start toward the door.

"Wait." Daisy goes to her desk and grabs a black folder. She holds it to her chest as she walks to me. "Your notes."

I flip it open to see what she means. I thought that was just something she made up so Violet wouldn't know we were messing around, but inside is the sketch she was working on in the tree house.

"I finally got your mouth right," she says with a proud smile.

Behind it are a few more, one of me in my hockey gear, another of me sitting at a table a lot like the one from the physics lab. She drew my profile like she was sketching it the way she saw it in class. And finally, one of my back with the tattoo for Mark.

My chest tightens.

"Do you like them?" Her smile falters, and she sounds unsure. Probably because I still haven't spoken as I stare down at the pages. It's like she captured all the things that make me, *me*, in a few drawings.

"You can just toss them or whatever. I just wanted you to see them, so you didn't think I was creepily sketching pictures of you and tucking them away like some sort of obsess—"

I cut her off by bringing my lips down on hers. She squeaks her surprise and then flings her arms around my neck.

"I like them," I say.

Chapter TWENTY-TWO

Daisy

I DON'T HAVE A TREE HOUSE AT HOME, BUT MY EQUIVALENT happy spot is the formal living room on the first floor. Bookcases line one wall, overflowing with textbooks and a few fiction titles. It's a dark room off the west side of the house with old furniture in like-new condition. The only person that ever used this room was me. And it seems that hasn't changed.

With my sketchbook and phone, I sit cross-legged in the oversized leather chair. When I was younger, I'd hide away in here. My parents would be upstairs in their offices or in the TV room, laptops in front of them as they caught bits and pieces of their favorite shows.

They seem to be working less since I've been home but existing in our own corners of the house is par for the course. I like having my own space, but too much of it is lonely.

I've been home for six days, and if tomorrow wasn't Christmas

Eve, I'd be nervous that I'd die of boredom. Our traditional activities include Violet's family, as well as Grandma and Grandpa Johnson, coming here. We'll do our annual ham dinner, followed by exchanging presents. Aunt Serina arranges everything, but we do it in Flagstaff because she thinks it feels more festive here with the colder weather.

There isn't snow on the ground yet, but there's a chance of it tonight. I pull back the curtain to stare out into the dreary winter weather. Cold air seeps through the glass.

I haven't talked to Jordan, but I've been thinking about him. Today especially. It's the two-year anniversary of his friend's death, and I know whatever he's doing, it's with Mark on his mind.

Mom steps into the room and smiles at me. "Do you want some headphones?"

I glance down at my phone. Out of habit, I've started listening to music anytime I'm sketching or studying.

"No, I'm good."

Her brows pull together in confusion.

"I'll turn it down," I say.

"Thanks. Your dad is grading final exams."

I forgot the one house rule—silence. If I had been the kind of kid that wanted to get in trouble, I could have easily accomplished it so long as I did it quietly. Sometimes this house feels more like a library than a home.

When I'm alone again, I pick up my phone and turn off the music. Trying not to overthink it, I text Jordan. **Hi. Hope you're having a good break. Thinking of you today. X**

I warm up dinner, rummage the liquor cabinet, and take my food and drink back to my comfy chair.

Jordan FaceTimes me as I'm settling in. My pulse races as I answer.

"Hey," I say as his face fills the screen.

Eyes hooded, beanie pulled down over his ears, he smiles lazily back at me. "Hi, sweet Daisy."

"I wondered why you were calling instead of texting, but I think I see now."

His eyes practically close when he smiles. I've seen Jordan drunk enough to know that he's had way, way more than usual.

"Where are you?"

"Someone's house. I don't remember whose now. We started drinking early, bounced around a few places."

"Are you doing okay?"

"Yeah," he says, but it doesn't sound very convincing. "What are you up to?"

"Quiet night in." I lift my glass of vodka and Sprite to show him.

"Cheers," he says and brings his beer up to the screen. Music starts up in the background, and the lights go off in favor of a flashing red, blue, and green disco ball.

Someone yells something, and a chorus of voices call, "For Mark."

"We've been doing a shot every hour," he explains.

"Since when?"

"Fuck, I don't know. Noon."

"Maybe you should switch to water."

"You're right. I should hydrate. I'm gonna have a wicked hangover." He struggles to get up, but he navigates through the house until he reaches the kitchen. He fills a glass and chugs it. Then, he goes right back to drinking his beer, but well, I tried.

Instead of going back to the party, he goes outside. It's harder to see him, but it's quieter.

His breath is visible as he speaks. "I head back to Valley on Thursday."

"Christmas Day?"

"Yeah. I'll wait until the afternoon, but we do most of our celebrating on Christmas Eve anyway."

"I'm jealous. I'm already bored."

"Come back this weekend. We have home games, and I'm sure there'll be a party or two happening somewhere."

I laugh it off, but my brain runs with the possibility of it. I never considered going back early, but it does sound pretty great.

The noise from inside is louder, and Jordan lifts his beer and chugs.

"It's cold out." His shoulders lift around his ears.

"Even colder here. There's a chance of snow tonight."

"Fuck that," he says.

I can tell he's antsy to get back inside.

"Are you going to be okay? Do I need to come take care of you like you did for me?"

His deep chuckle seems to have a direct connection to the butterflies in my stomach.

"I can probably manage to find a bed or couch to pass out on, but if you want to come strip down in your white cotton panties, you'll hear no objection from me."

"Night, Jordan."

"Night, sweet Daisy."

Violet finds me in my room when she arrives the next night.

"Hey." She peeks in from the doorway.

I rush to hug her. "I missed you."

"Same. It's weird not seeing you every day."

I love that college has brought Violet and me closer. And she's right. I've gotten up to go talk to her so many times since I've been home only to remember where I am.

"I was thinking of going back to Valley this weekend."

Violet laughs. "Has it been that bad?"

"No. They're just busy and… you know what they're like. And I miss *our* house."

"Same." She links her arm through mine and rests her head on my shoulder. "Hey, your parents adore you. I know they don't show it the same way mine do, but they are always bragging about you. My dad is all, 'Daisy's parents said she's taking eighteen credit hours this semester. How come you're only taking twelve?'"

Laughter escapes my lips. Being quiet, being smart, and being an overachiever are the things that make my parents happy. Like it or not, they shaped who I am. And I like myself.

"Thanks for telling me."

"Of course. And, hey, at least your parents haven't spent the entire break asking why you're no longer interested in seeing your old friends from high school."

"Vi, not all jocks are shitty."

"I know."

I tilt my head to the side.

"I know," she repeats. "But I'm not the same person I was in high school."

We settle on my bed, facing one another.

"What are you going to do in Valley?" she asks.

"I don't know. Reorganize my closet, clean out our fridge, go to a hockey game."

"I knew it," she says, eyes widening. "You're going back for Liam."

"No."

She grins like she doesn't believe me. "Have you been talking to him this break?"

I hesitate, and she gasps. "Oh my gosh, you have!"

My phone lights up with a text, and my cheeks heat because I know it's Jordan. Just my freaking luck.

We both glance at it. It's too far away for her to read the name or text. She lunges for my phone. It's locked, but I still swipe it and hold it up to my chest. "I haven't been talking to Liam."

"Then who is it, because you are blushing so hard. I know it isn't Dahlia or Jane."

She tries again to free it from my grasp.

"Vi, stop," I say when she's nearly worked it out of my fingers. "It's not Liam. It's Jordan."

She pulls back and goes quiet.

I nod to confirm it because I can tell she's trying to decide if I'm joking or not.

"Jordan Thatcher?" The way she says his name speaks volumes.

"Yes. Jordan Thatcher. We've been spending so much time together while I tutored him, and things just sort of… happened."

"Daisy."

Okay, I like the way she says my name right now even less than the way she said Jordan's.

"I really like him. I know he has a reputation, but—"

"He's slept with half of the Valley population. That isn't a reputation. It's a fact."

"I don't care about his past."

"Past?" Her voice softens. "Honey, I say this with love, but you don't really think that he's only seeing you, right?"

I squirm under her scrutiny. "We haven't set any boundaries."

"So he could be with some other girl right now?"

"Would he text me if he were?" I unlock my phone to read his text and then show the image to Violet.

She stares blankly between the screen and me.

"Fuck the Dealer. It's this card game where—"

"I know the game. So?"

"So he's out and texting me. Therefore, not with another girl."

"I love your optimism," she says with a sigh.

Okay, fine. I admit there's a teensy tiny part of me that wonders if he's hooking up with other people. We mostly hang out alone in my tree house and around his schedule. It wouldn't exactly be hard for him to juggle. But the bigger part of me just doesn't care. Or maybe wants to stay in denial.

"I know that your past makes it hard to believe that he could be this popular jock who parties and sleeps around, and is also a decent guy, but I think he is, Vi."

"You're going back early to hang out with him?"

I nod. "He asked me to come back this weekend."

"What happened with Liam? I thought you were into him."

"I was, or I thought I was. I think I liked the idea of him more than anything."

"Jordan is so different from Liam," she says.

"Yeah." I laugh. "But also not. He's unexpectedly sweet and..." I trail off. "I never expected to fall for him."

"Fall?" Her brows rise. "Do not fall in love with him. Talk to him, get it out of your system or whatever, but absolutely do not fall in love with him."

I smile and roll my eyes, then shove at her leg lightly. "Don't worry. I will be fine."

Or I hope I will because I think I already have fallen in love with him.

Chapter TWENTY-THREE

Jordan

LIAM DISAPPEARED AFTER PRACTICE AND HASN'T COME back to the dorms yet. He was late again and just a total mess. I don't get it. These streaks of hot and cold are throwing the team for a loop. We get in a nice groove with him, and then BAM, he's late or having a bad day, and we all have to readjust.

I came back to the dorm thinking he'd be here beating himself up about it, but it's been hours, and he's not here and not answering my texts. Jenkins came over with his teammate Warren and Warren's girlfriend, Regina. We're playing video games when there's a knock at the door.

"Are you expecting someone?" Jenkins asks.

"No."

"Go away," he yells in the direction of the door.

"Nice," I say, and then call louder than he did. "Door's open."

No one enters. I wait for another knock. Nothing. I put down the controller. I wouldn't normally bother checking. In fact, it's only the thought that it's Liam on the other side, too drunk to work the door handle, that gets me to my feet and across the room.

A lot of athletes are still here over break, but the hallway lights are dim, and it's quieter on the floor than during the semester. I notice all of this because the girl in front of me is a shock.

Daisy's face is red from the cold. She's bundled up in a coat and hat that puts all the focus on her face and those big blue eyes that seem even brighter in this dark hallway.

"You're not Liam." That's what I say. It's all I seem capable of getting out of my mouth as I stare at her.

"Surprise!" Her smile is small and forced—hesitant. "Hi."

I'm still a little thrown that she's really here, and I don't move or say anything for too long. Regina's laughter breaks the silence. That moves me to action because instantly I can see the wheels turning in Daisy's head and her jumping to the wrong conclusion.

She takes a step back. "I'm sorry for showing up like this. You're obviously busy. I was trying to be spontaneous. I'll text you like a normal person."

She ducks her head and actually takes off down the hallway.

A laugh breaks free from my chest, and I take off after her, grabbing her around the waist.

"You're fast."

"Humiliation is a great motivator," she mumbles, and tries to keep moving forward. "Let me go. I'll text you later."

"But then I can't see your face when I tell you that I missed you."

She stops struggling and turns her head to look me in the eye. "You did?"

"Yeah. I did." It's true, too. I don't think I even realized how much until I saw her. Everything just feels better when she's around. Liam disappearing after practice has me worried, but here she shows up, and it soothes something inside of me.

I take her hand and tug her back toward my room.

"Are you sure?" she asks before I push open the door. I'm not sure what she thinks she's walking into, but I'm not the kind of asshole she obviously thinks I am.

"Positive."

Inside, she glances around and visibly relaxes at the scene in front of her. Warren's girl is halfway on his lap as they stare at the screen.

Jenkins looks up first. "Hey, Daisy, right?"

She nods and waves. "Hi."

"That's Warren and Regina." I point as I introduce them.

"Hi," Regina says. Warren tips his head.

"Do you want something to drink?" I go to the mini fridge.

"Water is fine."

I grab her one and take a seat on the chair, beckoning her to sit on my lap. She's all bundled up and the cold from outside is radiating off her.

I'm still a little stunned, so I just wrap my arms around her.

"Why'd you think I was Liam? He's not here?"

I shake my head. "No. He disappeared after practice."

"Uh-oh. That doesn't sound good." I can barely hear her over Jenkins' smack talk to Warren.

I lean closer. "Practice was pretty awful."

Her response gets lost in another wave of noise, but her mouth turns down in a sympathetic frown. I stand with her, and we go into my room. After kicking the door closed behind us, I flop down on the bed and hold my arms out. She sits on the edge of the mattress, looking all unsure and adorable.

"I can't believe you're here," I say, dropping my hands around her.

"I wouldn't be if I'd thought it through. I should have realized you'd be hanging with friends."

"You're a friend." I hook a finger through a belt loop on her jeans. The denim gaps around her hip bone. I don't pull, but she leans into me anyway.

"Is that what I am?"

She smiles as I bring my mouth to hers. Has it only been a little more than a week? Damn. I missed her lips.

"Hello, friend," I tease and sweep my tongue against hers.

Most of the time, when girls start trying to have the *what do we mean to each other* conversation, it freaks me out. I'm not anti-girlfriend, exactly. I did it once, and it didn't work out, but that isn't why I haven't seriously dated since. The truth is, I like hanging with my friends and doing what I want without worrying about another person.

With Daisy, though, I don't get the feeling that she's trying to trap me into a label, so much as she's taunting me. She's supposed to end up with someone smarter, nicer, just generally better. Someone like Liam. Fuck, they'd probably already be an item if I hadn't interfered. The thought places an uncomfortable weight on my chest.

She places a hand softly on my side. Unassuming and tentative, she's slow to touch me, like the week apart has made her more unsure. I tug her down on me and encourage her with deep, hungry kisses that only show her a fraction of how much I missed her—missed this.

My phone vibrates in my pocket, and I groan because I know I have to check it in case it's Liam. I dig it out without breaking the kiss.

"Is it him?" Daisy asks, pulling back.

"No. Still nothing." As a last-ditch effort, I texted some guys from class that I thought might be around, but no one's seen him.

Daisy leans over my outstretched legs and props herself up on an elbow. "I'm sure he's around somewhere. Where would he go? Bar? McCallum's apartment?"

Damn, she looks good laid across my bed.

I settle a hand on her hip and up the curve of her stomach.

"He's not at either of those places. Or The White House. I've texted everyone that's in town. No one's seen him."

"You're really worried about him?" It isn't a question so much as her pointing out a fact she just discerned. Her brows pinch together.

"It isn't like him to go off the grid."

"Yeah. That doesn't sound like him." She gets that contemplative look like she does when she's studying. She stands and moves to the door. When she opens it, she looks back at me. "Are you coming or what?"

"Where are we going?" And how do I get her back on my bed?

"To find Liam."

Campus is a graveyard. I pull the hood up on my sweatshirt, and Daisy zips up her coat and shoves her hands in her pockets.

"Any other ideas where he might have gone?" she asks.

"Not really."

"Where are his favorite places?"

"I don't know. The arena."

"Did you check there?"

I hang my head, and Daisy laughs. "We'll go there first."

Damn. It never even occurred to me that he might have stayed at the rink, but it makes sense. It's a good ten-minute walk to the arena, and we move slowly.

"Did you have a nice time at home?" I ask.

"Yeah," she answers immediately and then adds, "I was kind of bored."

I can almost picture Daisy sitting all alone in a room with her sketchbook.

"My parents aren't evil or anything." Soft laughter falls from her lips. "I realize I might have made them out to be awful, and they aren't."

I hold her hand, swinging it lightly between us. "I don't think that."

"I don't want to be like them," she says. "Someday, when I have a house, I want it to be loud and chaotic. That's my favorite part of living with Vi, Dahlia, and Jane. It's never completely silent."

My mouth hitches up with a smile. "You like loud, huh?"

She nods.

We've reached the arena. I tip my head back into the still night and shout as loud as I can, "Daiiiissy!"

She's laughing when I pull her against me. Her nose is cold against my face as I kiss her.

"You're cold." I slide my hands under her coat and shirt. She inhales sharply as my freezing fingers walk up her sides.

"So are you. We should go inside."

I pin her against the building, kissing her until we're breathless, and the only next step is getting naked. I'm so hard it's painful.

"I want you."

"I want you too." The words fall from her trembling lips. "We should hurry and find Liam."

Not a lot I wouldn't agree to right now if it clears the path for sex at the end of the night. I swipe my access card and hold open the door for her. The arena is silent. I check the locker room first, shaking my head at Daisy when I come out.

"He's not on the ice either," she says. "Is there somewhere else here?"

"No."

We walk down the tunnel to take another look anyway. I glance around at the empty seats. Daisy leans into me. The pressure of her small body against mine is a comfort.

"We'll find him." She links her arm through mine.

We check the weight room and then head back out into the

cold. I hold on to Daisy's hand, swinging our arms lightly, as we make our way back to the heart of campus.

"What made you decide to come back to Valley so early? Besides boredom, of course."

"Hmm. I'm not sure." She smiles like we're in on the same secret, then her eyes widen. "Oh my gosh. Do you not remember asking me to come back?"

"Uhhh..."

She groans and mutters something about being embarrassed as she tries to hurry off again. This time I have her by the hand, so she doesn't get far.

"What did I say, and when did I say it?"

She faces me, avoiding eye contact. "The night before Christmas Eve."

"I talked to you on the twenty-third?" I was wasted that entire day simultaneously trying to remember Mark and forget the horrors of the day. I definitely don't remember talking to Daisy.

"Yes. You were at someone's house. You didn't know whose."

"And I asked you to come back early?"

"Yeah, in hindsight, it's obvious you were drunk and not thinking clearly."

"I have some of my best ideas when I'm wasted." I circle my arms around her waist. "And I'm damn glad you're here."

"You have to say that now," she mumbles, but I get a smile out of her.

"What else did I say?"

"Not much. You were pretty drunk and sad."

I nod—no use in denying it. I miss Mark. He was my best friend. We shared so many good times together, and it's fucking sad that he's gone.

"I asked if you needed me to come take care of you."

"I hope I said hell yeah."

"Not exactly, but you did say something about wanting to see me in my white panties again." She shakes her head. "I can't tell if you really liked them or you're mocking me."

"I'm not mocking you." I drop my hands down until I'm cupping her ass. "Are you wearing them now?"

"I don't know. Guess you'll have to wait and find out."

"Damn. We need to hurry this up."

She laughs as I pull her down the sidewalk. The library is closed, but we go in the study rooms in the engineering building, then the laundry room and lounge in Freddy. I'm fresh out of places to look for Liam and growing more distracted by the girl next to me every step.

"I'm sorry," she says. "But I'm sure he's okay."

"Yeah." I'm not sure but saying as much won't help.

"Have we looked everywhere?" There's a hopeful lift in her tone.

"Yeah. Fucking finally." I stop. "Get it. Fucking, finally."

Her eyes light up. "Finally!"

We jog toward the stairwell. I stall on the last set of stairs. So close to being inside of her.

"Why are we stopping?" The whine in her voice assures me she's as excited as I am.

She stands on the step above me, making her a few inches taller.

Guilt claws at me. Liam likes her, and that should stop me, but everything with Daisy feels fleeting. Like as soon as we give in, whatever this crazy thing is going on between us will be over. She'll wise up and move on. We're a moment in time. And I'm starting to wonder if that'll be enough.

"Just wanted to look at you."

She holds my gaze in the quiet stairwell. When I can't take it another second, I blaze past her, pulling her with me onto the fifth floor.

Halfway down the hall, I lift her into my arms so I can kiss her sooner rather than later. She wraps her arms and legs around me and attacks my mouth with the same enthusiasm ripping through my body. I fumble for the door handle and lose my grip. She slides down my body, rubbing against the length of my dick.

Oh, damn, that feels good. I register that the living room is quiet, so I assume everyone took off and walk Daisy backward toward my room.

I peel her out of the coat, and it hits the floor. Her fingers fumble for the button of my jeans as I sneak both hands under her shirt to unhook her bra.

We make another stop against the doorjamb. I press into her until she moans.

Someone clears their throat, and lazily I move my mouth from Daisy's to see Liam sitting on the couch with both brows raised.

He's here. Good. Except he looks like shit. And *oh fuck.*

"Liam!" Daisy exclaims. Her arms shoot down to her sides, and she stands tall.

We tear apart. Liam's still glancing between us with a curious expression.

"Where the hell have you been, man?" I ask, rubbing a hand over my mouth. "We looked everywhere for you."

"Just with a friend," he says.

I catch Daisy's eye, and she nods as if she understands what I need. Actually, I'm starting to think she knows better than me most of the time.

"I should go home and unpack." She picks up her coat and holds it against her chest.

"I'll text you later," I say. "Thanks."

"Welcome." She smiles slightly. "Bye, Liam."

When she's gone, I take a seat in the chair.

"When did that happen?" he asks.

I ignore his question to ask one of mine. "Where have you been? I was worried."

"I should have told you already. I've been seeing someone, and I was with him tonight."

I nod, letting that sink in. "Wait. Him?"

"Yeah. I've been seeing a guy." He squares his shoulders like he's ready to take on the world to defend himself.

"Relax. I don't care who you fuck, but I'd be lying if I said I wasn't surprised to learn my best friend is gay when you've been hooking up with girls for the past few years." I thought we were close enough that he'd share something like that.

"I'm bisexual. And it's just been easier to date girls here because everyone assumes I'm straight. Hockey team parties aren't exactly hopping with dudes looking for dudes." He cracks the smallest smile.

"I guess not." Still, it hurts a little that he didn't trust me. I guess I'm in no position to talk. "So, you've been seeing someone?"

His head dips. "For a few months now."

My mind reels. A few months?

He nods and lets his shoulders slump forward. "He isn't out, so we've kept it quiet. I wanted to tell you, but it wasn't just my secret to tell."

"I get that."

"My head is all over the place. I've never felt this way about anyone, and it's like I can't stop letting it screw with everything else. I'm constantly letting the team down, but I'm just consumed." He rubs a hand over his chest. "He told me before break that he thought we should end things. I went over tonight to talk to him."

"And?"

"And I convinced him otherwise." He smirks, but it falls quickly. "For now."

"What about..." I trail off. It seems so stupid now. "I thought you liked Daisy."

"I do. I did. She's great."

"You know what I mean."

"If the timing was different, maybe."

"But you were going to ask her out."

"When?"

"Last semester."

"Oh right. Yeah, I almost did. Col—" He catches himself. "The guy I've been seeing thought we should see other people, slow things down. I tried." He shrugs. "Don't get me wrong, she's a cool chick."

"Cool?" That seems like such a weird way to describe Daisy. She's a lot of things, but cool isn't anywhere in the top ten of adjectives I'd use. The way he's blowing off any feelings for her pisses me off, and I'm pissed that I'm pissed off. Daisy isn't mine to be going all He-Man to protect her honor or some shit. And why do I care if he doesn't like her? That should make me happy.

"Yeah, she's cool, but it's hard to seriously think about dating someone when you can't stop thinking about someone else. Besides, it seems like *you* have a thing for Daisy."

My first instinct is denial, but he just caught me with my tongue down her throat and five seconds away from having her naked and bent over the couch he's sitting on. Of course, I have a thing for her.

"I know I should have talked to you first."

"Why?"

"Because I thought you were into her, and I know she was into you." Some part of me wants to believe that I'm better for her—I'm the chaos she needs. But it doesn't change the fact that I went behind his back. I know deep in my gut they would have gone out if I hadn't interfered.

He leans forward, elbows resting on his thighs. "You're the best friend I've ever had."

I try to laugh him off, but he won't let me.

"I'm not kidding," he says. "You don't give yourself enough credit. You just walked all over campus looking for me. Sorry, by the way, I should have texted."

"That was mostly Daisy. I was trying to get her naked, and she wanted to find you."

"I'm ninety-nine percent sure she did that for you, not me."

"Maybe." Daisy is always doing stuff for other people. She took on tutoring me like it was no big deal. She worked around my schedule. She freaking taught herself statistics so she could help me.

"Are we good?" I ask.

"You're worried I'm pissed because you messed around with a girl you *thought* I was into?"

"Yeah, I guess so. You did say you were going to ask her out. I talked you out of it, remember?"

He laughs. "You didn't have to try very hard, if *you* remember. We're good, all right? Finally, a chick I approve of you dating."

"I'm not sure it's that serious. We haven't really talked about it." A rough chuckle scrapes up my throat. "I mean, she's barely dated anyone, and I've..."

"Dated everyone," he finishes for me, smiling.

"Something like that."

"She's different. I can tell."

"She is, but I'm still me."

He shakes his head. "Uh-uh. I don't buy it. If you messed around with her thinking I liked her, that only means one thing."

"That I'm a shit friend?"

"Nope."

"What's it mean?"

He grins. "You *really* like her."

Chapter TWENTY-FOUR

Daisy

SITTING AT THE GAME BY MYSELF ISN'T AS LONELY AS I imagined. I'm in my Valley Hockey T-shirt in the student section. With so many people still on break, the arena is emptier than last time. I spot Gavin and some of the basketball guys in the front row. Good thing Violet isn't here.

I text her to see how she's doing, and she responds right away, **Fine. Bored. How's Valley and Jordan?**

I snap a picture of him on the ice and send it along with another text asking when she's coming back.

She doesn't reply before the game starts, and I tuck my phone away and get lost in the action. I really do enjoy watching. Especially Jordan. He's so fast and ruthless with every shift.

I talked to him earlier today to see how things went with Liam. He was vague, saying Liam had some stuff going on but that he was okay. I watch him now to see if I can tell any difference in him, but Liam rarely looks anything less than cool and collected. Even now, sweaty and tired, he's put together in a way that I don't find as intriguing as I once did.

I like that Jordan's emotions play out on his face and in his body language, even in his words. He's usually happy and playful, but when he's mad or sad, you know it. He isn't afraid of being exactly who he is at any given moment.

Valley wins, but there isn't the same excitement as the last game I attended. I told Jordan I was coming, but we didn't make plans after the game. They have another game tomorrow, so I doubt they'll be partying tonight, but I'm still hopeful I might get to see him.

I move slowly from my seat and toward the doors. I linger outside, cradling my phone. I could text him, but I came to the game. Just like I came back to hang out with him, and I showed up at his dorm last night. It's his move.

The crowd thins, and my fingers grow cold. I'm seconds from giving up when my phone vibrates with a text from him, **Busy tonight?**

Depends, I reply as my smile grows wide.

His response is one only I'd understand, **Tree house, white panties, twenty minutes.**

I rush home with butterflies in my stomach and a throb deep in my core.

It's more like thirty minutes before I hear Jordan's footsteps crossing the yard. He climbs up the ladder without calling up first. He has a plastic bag looped over one wrist as he steps up into my space.

"Hey," I say, unable to keep my breaths from coming out like pants.

"Sorry. It took me longer than I thought. Had to make a stop."

He drops down beside me. The smell of his soap clings to him.

"Congrats on the game."

"Thanks." He smiles and places the bag on his lap.

"To keep warm." He holds up the bottle of Fireball before setting it down between us.

"In case we get hungry." He tosses out three bags of chips, then grabs one of them back and opens it. He tosses several in his mouth and chews with a satisfied groan.

"We or you?"

"I got something for you too," he says, and his lips hitch into a satisfied smile as he holds up a candy necklace.

"You remembered."

"Of course." He pulls out Fun Dip, too, and finally a bottle of water.

I go for the Fireball first, wanting the warmth and maybe some of its courage. "We're supposed to just drink this straight?"

"I was in a rush to get here, babe. Mixed drinks were too many added steps."

The endearment doesn't go unnoticed, even if he said it without thinking. I laugh as I lift the bottle to my lips and let the dark liquor trickle into my mouth. It slides down in a trail of warmth. I pass the bottle to Jordan, and he takes a much longer drink before sitting back and finishing off his chips.

"Liam seemed okay during the game. Does that mean everything worked itself out?"

"Sort of." He tips his head side to side. "I think he's going to be okay. Thanks again for going to look for him with me."

"Of course. Being there for friends is important. If it were one of my friends, I wouldn't have been able to concentrate on anything else until I knew they were okay."

"I was worried, but I think I could have concentrated on something else." His heated gaze holds mine. My heart gallops in my chest, and I reach for the Fireball again.

With a light chuckle, Jordan sits back, and we pass the bottle back and forth a couple of times. I pick up the candy necklace and remove it from the clear plastic packaging. I lift it to my mouth and bite one of the hard candies. Jordan watches with amusement.

"You're doing it all wrong."

"Is there a right way to eat a candy necklace?"

"It's in the name," he says and takes it from me. He lifts it over my head and down around my neck. He moves closer. His head dips, and his lips brush my skin as he pulls the candy between his teeth.

I hold my breath as he eats one and then another, kissing my neck in between.

"I think I prefer your way."

He grins and positions us, so I'm lying flat on my back. One big palm slides under my shirt. He pulls back and looks me in the eye.

"Try it," he says. He uses his mouth to bring the necklace to my lips. The sweet candy crunches under my teeth. I let the necklace fall back around my throat, and Jordan covers my lips and cups my breast. His thumb circles my nipple, and I arch into his touch.

I sit up to remove my shirt and his. Jordan drops kisses to my shoulder and collarbone as he unhooks my bra. It goes in the pile of our discarded clothes.

His tongue leaves a wet trail along the valley of my breasts and down to my belly button. He places soft kisses down my stomach as he undoes my jeans and pushes them down. Lower and lower he goes until he reaches the band of my panties. White cotton. Not even close to the sexiest pair I own.

He takes off my jeans, then his own. A chill creeps over my skin, and goosebumps dot my arms.

He grabs one of the extra blankets I brought outside with this exact situation in mind. He covers me and then ducks underneath, reappearing in front of me. His erection hits along my aching core. He takes my mouth in a fast and hard kiss before dropping back to my neck. With every crunch of the candy necklace, he rubs along my panties until I'm sure there's a giant wet spot waiting for him.

I run my hands along his back and down to his hips. I have every intention of removing the thin barriers between us, but Jordan has other ideas. He kisses down my body again until his lips ghost along my panties. His finger runs at a frustratingly slow pace from hip bone to hip bone, barely sliding underneath the material.

My hips arch up. I need more. Finally, he gives it to me. His hand dips under my panties. When his fingers reach my clit, a jolt shoots through me. In a slow, steady rhythm, he works me until I'm writhing under him.

Only then does he slide my panties down my legs. He lifts them in a ball to his face and inhales. My pussy throbs.

"I'm so close it hurts."

"I've got you, sweet Daisy." His shoulders push between my legs, and he kisses my clit.

"Oh god." My head tips back.

He spreads my legs farther apart and pushes his tongue inside of me, then flicks it up. He sucks and licks in the same sort of hard, demanding kisses I've grown used to.

No one has ever made me feel so good and so… worshipped. It's in this moment that I refuse to believe it's ever been like this for him either. What we have is *more*.

When I come, crying out into the silent night, he only continues holding me tight as my body shudders. I see stars. Not the kind in the sky, though those are probably visible if I could pry my eyes open.

He sets another kiss below my belly button as he moves up to lie next to me.

I turn my head to look at him. He's smiling, definitely pleased with himself. I'm pretty pleased with him too.

He lifts my white panties up and lets them dangle from a fingertip. "Keeping these. Hope you have more."

"You are not keeping them." I grab for them, and he holds them out of my reach and kisses me. He doesn't play fair, but I'm not really complaining.

He rolls on top of me. His boxers are still on, and I push at them, eager to see and feel all of him.

He leans to the side as he takes them off. And finally, we're both naked. My fingers wrap around him, and his eyes fall closed. His jaw flexes. It's the only indication he's struggling to keep still. But he lets me have this. He doesn't move as I stroke him tentatively.

His skin is warm when I bring my lips to it. The muscles contract and his chest lifts and falls with his breathing.

He moves my hair away from my face and cups the back of my neck as he kisses my forehead, and it's the most tender feeling in a moment I expected anything but tenderness from him.

In a flash of confidence, I'll attribute to the Fireball later, I push him back and straddle him. Now that I'm here, I feel clumsy. That is until I find him staring at me as I've only ever seen someone in the movies do. He's Mister Darcy across the dance floor, pinning me with a look that can only be described as yearning.

"Condoms are in my wallet," he says as he rests both hands along my hips.

My heart beats wildly as I dig out his wallet from the back pocket of his jeans. Three condoms poke out of the top, and I hold up the strip.

He takes them from me, rips one off, and tosses it and his wallet back on top of our clothes pile. His mouth covers mine as he tears the foil and shifts to cover himself.

"Are you ready, Daisy?"

No sweet Daisy this time. No teasing. He's checking to make sure I really want to do this.

Nodding, I lift up so he can position himself underneath me. I sink onto him slowly, inch by inch. Tears prick behind my eyelids as he stretches and fills me.

His hands at my hips guide me—the pads of his thumbs dragging along my skin in a reassuring caress.

When he's buried inside me, I rest my weight on top of him and let my eyes flutter closed.

He sits up and kisses me. "Doing okay?"

"Divine." My muscles contract around him, and he lets out a guttural groan.

"Good." He smacks my ass lightly before he lies back. "Have your dirty way with me, sweet Daisy."

His hands take their place back at my hips, and ever so lightly, he sets the rhythm. Up and down over his thick length. Bliss hangs above me so close I can taste it, but I don't want this to be over.

Jordan must have the same thought because he wraps an arm around my waist and turns us, so he's on top. The playful softness of his face is gone and is replaced with a hard set of his jaw and cheekbones that look like they could cut glass.

He reaches between us to touch me. My legs spread open, and he sinks one finger in and then two. He removes them, and the head of his dick takes their place. I inhale, filling my lungs with air and holding it until he's deep inside.

"Sweet, sweet Daisy," he murmurs against my lips.

"I'm not that sweet."

"You are," he insists. "And it's the hottest fucking thing."

Then he crushes his mouth down on mine. Our tongues tangle with our groans. Each thrust is harder, more urgent. He kisses down my neck and latches on to my candy necklace, eating them one by one as he drives into me.

My want is a frantic, tangible thing. I cling to him, urging him impossibly faster and harder until every nerve ending explodes.

As I clench and pulse around him, he finds his own bliss. His hips slow, and his lips move along my skin. "Sweet Daisy. So fucking sweet."

My chin rests on Jordan's chest, and his fingers absently graze up and down my spine.

"Tell me again why we haven't been doing that every time you've been up here?"

He smiles lazily at me. He's tired. I guess he did play a hockey game tonight.

I sit up. "We might need to start our study sessions a little earlier if they're going to end like this. Speaking of, are you going to need my help again this semester?"

"That's a hard offer to turn down."

Happiness stretches through my limbs that he wants to spend more time together. "Thank god you needed a tutor."

He stills underneath me.

"I just mean this probably wouldn't have happened otherwise."

"I know what you meant." He clears his throat and rolls to his side. "I need to tell you something."

My heart squeezes in my chest. Tonight has been perfect. I know that sex doesn't necessarily mean anything else will change between us. I prepared myself for this.

"Tell me what?"

"Before we started studying together—" He stops, and his jaw works back and forth. "Remember how I told you to ask out Liam?"

"Yeah."

"You were into him, and I didn't want you to go out with him."

It's an unexpected thrill to think that Jordan was interested in me before I even realized it.

"You didn't?" I smile.

"No, I saw you in that sexy red dress and lost my mind, but I—" He sighs. "Fuck, I don't know how to say this."

It hits me slowly but doesn't strike me with as much

disappointment as I thought it would. He liked me, but it didn't stop him from hooking up with other people during that time. I assumed it but never would have asked. I can hardly blame him when I spent those first weeks still crushing on his roommate.

"I don't care about any of that," I say in a rush before he can confess names or numbers. God, I don't even want to think about how many.

"You don't?" His brows pinch together.

"No. How could I? I know you, and I know you don't really do the girlfriend thing. I'm not expecting this to change that." It's all true, but I hope he'll tell me I'm wrong.

He doesn't. His mouth opens and closes. Finally, he nods.

"Just promise me one thing."

"What's that?" His eyes continue to narrow as he studies me carefully.

"No hooking up with other people as long as this is going on. We can be casual, but I need it to at least be exclusive from here on out. I will not be very sweet if I think about you hooking up with other people."

He chuckles softly. "Me either."

"So exclusive?" I don't wait for his answer. "If you're not okay with that, then we'll just call tonight one amazing night together. But also, we should do it again if this is a unicorn night."

"I'm good with that." His playful smirk and tone return. He yanks me back on top of him. "And we're absolutely going to do it again."

Chapter TWENTY-FIVE

Daisy

STARING IN THE MIRROR THE FOLLOWING DAY, I SMILE at my puffy lips and the colorful dots around my neck from the candy necklace I still haven't taken off. The flimsy elastic strand is mostly empty. I find a pink circle and bring it to my mouth—the sugary-sweet taste dances on my tongue.

I spend a long time in the shower, enjoying the hot spray against my sore muscles. The hockey team has another game this afternoon, and after, Jordan invited me to come to a party at his teammate's apartment. I skip my Valley U T-shirt in favor of a dress and boots. I even curl my hair. I'm excited to go out with Jordan. Hanging out with him makes me feel like I belong in a way I never have before.

And I know, I know, it shouldn't matter, but being seen by

someone like Jordan feels amazing. He could have any girl he wanted, and he wants me.

This time after the game, I head around to the parking lot behind the arena to wait for him. I stand next to his SUV, crossing my arms over my chest to keep warm and to have something to do with my hands.

When the first guys start coming out the door, Jordan's among them. I step away from his vehicle and wait for him to see me. He says bye to his friends and comes toward me in long, quick strides.

The ends of his dark hair are wet and stick up around his head. One hand is wrapped around the strap of his duffel bag, and he hits the unlock button on his key fob with his other. He tosses the bag onto the back seat.

"You look nice," he says, circling both arms around my back.

"Thanks. Congrats again. I'm starting to think all you needed to start winning was for me to come to the games."

He laughs and hugs me tight against him. "A little sweet Daisy magic sure doesn't hurt."

He kisses me, but more guys are coming out and getting in their cars, and one of them calls out to him, "Yo, Thatch. Are you coming to McCallum's?"

"Yep," he answers without looking at him. He smiles at me. "Ready to party, baby?"

I expected McCallum's apartment to be as quiet as the rest of campus on break, but it seems like every single person still in town is crammed into the small space.

Jordan grabs us both a beer, and we're standing in the dining room where people are playing cards at the table. We're not playing, but it's a fun reminder of the last time we were here.

We stand close. The heat of his body warms my left side. He's talking to one of his teammates. They're talking hockey, and my gaze roams around the party.

In the living room, people are playing video games. A couple is making out next to the front door. Small groups stand in circles in every space that isn't occupied with furniture—music pumps from one of the bedrooms.

I can't seem to catch my breath. Nerves and excitement have lodged a lump in my throat. I feel different tonight being here with Jordan—really being here with him.

Two girls approach us—a pretty brunette and a blonde with the longest legs I've ever seen. The brunette makes a beeline for Jordan, not even seeing me beside him.

"Where have you been?" She launches herself at him, throwing her arms around his neck and plastering her curvy body covered by a sparkly gold dress flush against him.

He chuckles and lets the hand holding his beer, curve in to give her a small hug back. "Hey, Cybil."

She pulls back and swats him on the chest, then rests her fingers there. "Seriously, Thatch. Where have you been?"

My cheeks are on fire when Jordan glances at me. "I've been around."

He leans into me. "Cybil, meet Daisy."

She finally looks at me, and I can tell the second it hits her that I'm here with him.

"Oh," she says. "Hi."

"Hi." The word comes out so quietly I'm not sure she even hears it.

She turns her attention back to Jordan. "I'm going to do a lap but come find me later. I miss you."

As quick as they came, Cybil and her friend turn and go.

Jordan's teammate left in the middle of the Cybil tornado, leaving me and Jordan alone.

"Sorry about that," he says. "She's a friend. Civil major, too."

He's slept with her. I know this, but I've already made a big deal of leaving the past in the past, so I just smile and say, "She seems nice."

He chuckles and takes a long drink of his beer, then cocks his head to the side as if he's trying to decide what now. "You want to play cards?"

"Okay."

He nods and leads me to the table where he pulls out a chair for me and then takes the one next to me. It's a different card game tonight, with more rules that Jordan teaches me. I'm not as interested in playing as I was the last time. I want to kiss him again, maybe make out in the corner like the couple still going at it by the front door. I can't decide if it's some exceptionally good kissing that lasts that long or exceptionally bad, because every time Jordan kisses me for more than three seconds, I want to tear off my clothes.

At the end of the second game, I lean closer to him. "Where's the bathroom?"

"First door on the left." He tips his head toward the hallway.

"Save my seat?"

He lets his hand drift down to my leg and along my bare skin, leaving goosebumps in his wake. "Definitely."

"Be right back."

The hallway is crammed with more couples stealing kisses and small circles of girls whispering quietly. Cybil and her friend are among them, but neither looks up as I weave through them to the bathroom.

I text Violet while I'm locked inside. **I'm at a hockey party. Me!**

I send it with a selfie of me posing in front of the bathroom mirror making a funny face.

She responds immediately. **You look amazing. Have fun! See you soon.**

Clutching my phone to my chest, I breathe in her words. I miss her. I wish she was here with me. Not that I ever could have convinced her to come. I finish in the bathroom and open the door.

My smile falls when bits of conversation float my way.

"I have no idea who she is" and "You don't think they're actually together, do you?"

"Definitely not." It's Cybil's voice that cuts through the others. "She's so—"

Her friend elbows her before Cybil can finish her sentence. They both look at me. I muster a smile and hurry down the hallway.

Jordan's sitting in the same spot. He has one leg propped in my chair, saving my seat, and it gives me the most ridiculous rush. Who cares what they think? Maybe we don't make sense to them. I thought the same thing at first, but they don't feel what I do when he's around. Besides, some of the most interesting things defy logic, sometimes even physics. I figure Jordan and I are among them.

He smiles when he sees me and shifts his leg back to the floor. I take the seat because it's mine, and I kiss him for anyone that cares to see, but mostly I just kiss him for me.

I pull back breathless and find him smirking at me.

"Is that for saving your seat? Because I hate to admit it now, but it was also serving as a pretty bomb footrest."

"Just wanted to kiss you," I say.

He drops his mouth to mine. "If I kissed you every time I wanted to, I'd walk around permanently attached to your lips."

It hadn't occurred to me that he was holding back for my benefit.

"That doesn't sound so bad." I run my fingers along his cheek. He's shaved recently, but the skin is rough where the hair threatens to reappear. "I'd have to learn to skate, though."

"I could teach you." His legs shut around mine, and he pulls me closer. Now that I've made the first move I seem to have broken some invisible barrier in his restraint.

"Thatch, are you and your girl in this game?" one of the guys at the table asks him.

He looks at me for an answer.

"Maybe we sit this one out?"

He stands and hauls me up and onto his shoulder.

"Jordan!" I squeal. "I'm wearing a dress."

He places a hand over my ass and holds the material down as he walks. Giddy laughter bubbles in my chest as I hang over his shoulder.

When he sets me back on the ground, we're outside on the deck.

"I forgot our drinks," he says, and I swear he looks like he's going to pick me up again.

"What if we skip the drinks and go back to your place?"

"I thought parties like this were part of the charm of hanging with me."

"How do I put this nicely," I tease, placing my hands in front of me like a steeple. "You're more charming naked."

He barks a laugh into the night air.

"Fair enough, but first I wanna make out with my girl where everyone can be really, stupidly jealous of me."

My back presses into the railing, and he steps between my legs. My heart is pounding in my chest as his mouth drops to mine.

Our kiss is interrupted by someone calling Jordan's name.

He growls playfully as he pulls away.

"What?" he barks.

Brad McCallum laughs as he approaches us. "You two want to play flip cup?"

"Nah," Jordan says as I say, "Yes."

"You know I won't be naked, right?" he whispers in my ear.

I laugh. "It's finally a game I'm not bad at."

Which is true. Flip cup might be the great universal equalizer. Jordan and I line up with Brad and Dallas against four others I've met but can't remember their names. A rush of adrenaline hits me when it's my turn. I chug like I've never chugged before and flip over the cup on the first try. Jordan's grinning so hard at me, it slows his start, and the other team wins.

We play two more times before it breaks up, and everyone wanders off from the table. It's getting late, but neither of us mentions leaving again. I see Cybil as we're taking seats outside. She's making out with a cute guy that I assume is on the hockey team. When I check to see Jordan's reaction, he barely seems to notice. I guess it's then that I realize he might have hooked up with her, but it wasn't like us. I don't care much about what Cybil thinks of me after that.

We stay until the party has died down and the music is off. Jordan and I walk the few blocks to his dorm, talking and laughing. It all feels so easy and fun.

Liam's not here. I didn't see him at the party either, but Jordan doesn't seem concerned, so I don't bring it up.

He flips on the light in his room.

"Do you want a drink or something? I still have some Fireball."

I shake my head, remove my coat, then my boots and socks.

He sits back on his desk, watching me. Reaching behind me, I pull the zipper of my dress down and then let it fall over my shoulders and pool at my waist.

He doesn't move even as I push the material past my hips and to the floor. I take a step closer and unhook my bra. I let the black lace hang from my fingertips before dropping it too to the floor of his room.

His gaze never leaves me. "Damn, you're sexy."

I close the space between us, stepping between his legs. His arms go around me and palm my ass. He hooks a thumb through the string and tugs until it wedges in front, biting into my already aching clit.

My fingers lift the hem of his T-shirt. He takes over, and I work on his jeans. He kisses my shoulder and then threads his fingers through my hair as I squat to free him of his pants and boxers.

I look up with big eyes, and his throat works, Adam's apple bobbing.

Wrapping a hand around his dick, I bring my mouth closer. My breaths come in quick, shallow gulps as I part my lips and take him in an inch, letting my tongue swirl over the head.

His grip tightens in my hair. My free palm rests on his stomach to steady myself, but it's an added bonus that I can feel the effect I have on him—the tightening of muscles, the increased breathing rhythm that matches my own.

I take more of him in each time until my lips wrap around the base, and he tickles the back of my throat. I hollow my cheeks, and he groans a low and deep sound.

"Daisy," he murmurs as I continue, picking up the pace.

He wraps my hair around his hand in a fist. When I look up, his dark eyes are hooded and enthralled. I still, and he takes over. He moves me up and down over his length as we lock eyes.

The ache inside of me is on the verge of painful. I move the hand at his stomach and put it between my legs. His gaze moves to watch me touch myself. I'm too turned on, too desperate with need. He isn't even touching me except the fist in my hair, and I feel him everywhere.

He lets out a guttural growl and pulls me to my feet. He smashes his mouth to mine, pushes my panties down, and then twirls me around and bends me over his desk.

I hear the rip of the foil packet, and then he's finally there, pushing inside, blurring the pain with white-hot pleasure.

My head swims with it all. The corner of the desk bites into my hip bones as he fucks me at a hard and unrelenting pace. This is Jordan, unrestrained and no longer holding back for me. And he's beautiful.

I cry out as my orgasm splinters through me. My pussy clenches around him, and Jordan pushes against me harder until his body trembles around mine.

Our breaths are the only sound as he leans over me and places a kiss on my shoulder.

After he disposes of the condom, he picks me up and carries me to his bed. And that's where I stay.

Me, in Jordan Thatcher's bed, defying all logic and probably physics too.

Chapter TWENTY-SIX

Jordan

CLASSES START BACK, AND I SPEND MOST EVENINGS with Daisy studying—for real studying. If last semester taught me anything, it's that a little studying makes a big difference. I've never seen so many A's before.

It's been raining for the better part of three days, keeping us inside instead of the tree house. Our books and laptops are spread out across the kitchen table.

"Daisy," Violet says as she walks in. Her gaze finds me, and her smile falls. "Oh, you're here."

"Vi, be nice," Daisy chides.

Violet faces me with no remorse on her face. "Hi."

"Hey, Violet."

I don't actually think Violet dislikes me. She's just worried about her friend. I get it, but Daisy's the last person I'd ever want to hurt.

"Sorry," Vi says. "But I thought we were working on the playlist for the ball."

"Oh, right." Daisy looks at me.

"I need to get to bowling anyway." I gather my stuff and come around the table to kiss Daisy before I go. "I'll text you later."

"Okay." She grabs my hand and holds my fingers until I'm out of reach. I wink at her and then head to the bowling alley.

"He's alive," Gavin jokes when he sees me. He stands and pulls me into a side hug. "I came by the dorm twice this week, and you were MIA both times."

"He's spending all his time with Daisy," Liam chirps from his chair. He juts his chin in greeting.

"Really?" Gavin asks. "So you two..." He trails off and looks at Liam.

My roommate waves him off. "It was nothing. She's perfect for him. She has him studying like every night."

"No shit." Gavin drops down in his seat and pours me a beer from the pitcher.

"We aren't just studying," I say, and the memory of last night going down on her while she tried to finish an assignment makes me smile.

"Congratulations," Gavin says. "I'm happy for you."

"Thanks."

"You're smiling like a dopey idiot, but good for you. Are you still going to make it to my party this weekend?"

"Is that this weekend?"

Liam grins. "Told you, spends so much time with her he doesn't even know what week it is."

Gavin chuckles. "Yes, Saturday night. Two kegs, and so much liquor I'm tripping over it in the kitchen. Be there."

"I wouldn't miss it. Welcome to the twenty-one club. Now you can start getting the pitchers."

"Who says I didn't buy this one?" he asks as he refills his glass.

"I do." Liam holds up a hand.

I take a sip of my beer and then get to my feet and rub my hands together. "All right. New season, another chance to win."

"If we're serious about winning, we might want to finally open it up to more players. There are at least two weeks where none of us are in town on league night," Jenkins says.

"I could ask Daisy," I say.

They all go quiet at once and then start laughing.

"Ah, so eager," Gavin says through a chuckle. "Invite your girl, man. If nothing else, I want to see you in all your boyfriend glory."

I flip him off as I get my ball from the rack. "She isn't my girlfriend. We're just talking." I bob my head from side to side. "Exclusively."

"And how is that different from having a girlfriend?" Liam asks with a smug grin.

I think for a second. "Fuck, I don't know."

They laugh at me again.

I lift a shoulder and let it fall, but then I think back to our conversation in the tree house. She said she knows I don't do the girlfriend thing, but that isn't strictly true. I have had a girlfriend, and I told her that. Is the real reason she didn't ask me to be her boyfriend because she still sees me as the fun player only good for hooking up?

I sit with it all night, and after bowling, I FaceTime her.

"What's the difference between having a girlfriend or boyfriend and what we're doing?" I ask as I settle onto my bed.

"Uh, is this the start of a joke?"

"No." My chest shakes with silent laughter that loosens some of my nerves. "I'm serious. My buddies pointed out that not hooking up with other people is basically the same thing."

"I don't know. I guess besides not hooking up with other

people, it's all the stuff in between. Spending time together and being there for each other, *fully clothed*, for all the little moments—good and bad."

"And you're sure that has to be done fully clothed?" I joke.

She rolls her eyes and smiles. "I guess I think of a boyfriend as someone who just wants to be with me, regardless of what we're doing."

It's on the tip of my tongue to ask her to be my girlfriend. What she just described is what I want. Daisy—all day, every day. Preferably naked, but I think there's some wiggle room on that fully clothed thing. But before I can ask, she changes the subject.

"The playlist for the ball is done! I even used some of your angry music."

"Yeah?"

She nods. "Yep. It's the perfect party mix. I can't believe how it's coming together. And you should see all the stuff piled up in Violet's room. She's going to be walking through a candle maze until we set up on Friday."

I crook an arm behind my head. "Oh right, that's this weekend."

"Mhmm. I was wondering if you wanted to come with me. Violet finished altering the yellow dress tonight, and you can finally see me in it."

"It's Saturday?"

She nods eagerly.

"Gavin's party is Saturday night. Big twenty-first birthday bash." The image of Daisy in that yellow dress and then me peeling her out of it is a real welcome sight.

"Right. Of course. It's fine." She shakes her head. "No worries. I figured you might not want to come."

"Slow your roll. Of course, I want to come. I just might be a little late."

"You will?"

"Definitely. I just need to stop by Gavin's party first and have a drink with him. Then, I'm all yours."

She smiles so big you'd think I'd agreed to something really terrible.

"I wouldn't miss it," I say.

What better night to ask her to be my girlfriend and show her how epic of a boyfriend I can be?

Chapter TWENTY-SEVEN

Daisy

I HOLD AN UMBRELLA OVER MY HEAD AS I WATCH JORDAN and Liam unload the flower archway from the back of Liam's truck. They're soaked, and the flowers are looking a little rough. I'm glad Violet isn't here to see it. I don't know how, but I will make it look fabulous before she gets here.

The guys bring it into the banquet room and set it in the spot Violet marked for it. She was very meticulous in her instructions.

"Thank you. You guys are the best."

Water drips off the bill of Liam's hat. "I'm gonna grab the box of extra flowers."

"Thank you," I call to his back as he jogs out of the room.

Jordan scans the space and smiles. "It's going to look amazing."

"I can't take any credit. This is all Violet."

He pushes his hoodie down and then takes off his hat and runs a hand through his hair before returning it backward on his head. "What time do you think you'll be done setting up tonight? Wanna come over later?"

"I can't." I press into him. "I promised Violet I'd help her, and I know we'll be here all night getting it just how she imagined."

"Then I guess I'll see you tomorrow."

I push up on my toes and kiss him. "Can't wait."

Liam reappears with the box of extra flowers. "Where do you want them?"

"Set them on that table for now." I point. "Thank you."

"Need anything else?" Jordan offers.

"Not unless you can make the rain stop, so I don't have to trek in and out of it all night."

He takes the hat from his head and puts it on mine. He steps to me and kisses me. "Stay dry, sweet Daisy."

Violet, Jane, Dahlia, and I sit in our living room after a long night of setting up for the ball. I'm exhausted, but it was worth it. The room looks so good. I have to hand it to Vi, she had a vision, and it really came together.

"How many people RSVP'd?" Dahlia asks.

"Sixty-three," Violet says. "But we have enough seats for a few extras in case people decide at the last minute."

"There isn't going to be much else to do tomorrow." Jane pulls the curtain to look out into the rainy night. Water streaks the windowpane, and flashes of lightning appear off in the distance.

I sit with my feet pulled up underneath me on one end of the couch. Jordan's hat sits in my lap, and I run a finger along the brim.

Dahlia sits next to me and knocks her knee against mine. Her gaze darts to the hat and then up at me. "He's coming, right? I'm excited to hang out with him. The only times I've met him, I couldn't say more than 'hi.' Now that he's taken, I think I'll be able to form complete sentences."

I smile as I think about him. "He's coming, but I'm not sure what time. It might be late."

"He's coming late? Why?" Vi asks from across the room in our worn, plaid chair.

"Gavin's twenty-first birthday party is tomorrow night."

"So?"

I look around the room at the rest of my friends. "It isn't a big deal. He's going to stop by for a drink and then come to the ball."

"Figures."

Dahlia breaks the tension by redirecting me back to the second part of her question. "What's he like?"

"Yeah, spill all the details," Jane adds.

"Well, he's fun and easygoing, but also really perceptive and unexpectedly sweet."

I think about the candy he bought me because I said I never had it. And the time I got drunk and he stayed with me, which led to the white cotton panty fiasco. Speaking of, I think he actually took those with him.

"You're blushing," Jane says.

I cover my face with both hands.

Dahlia pries my hands away. "You really like him. There's no reason to be embarrassed. It sounds like he really likes you too."

Violet is quiet. Too quiet. I look over at her. She's staring down at her hands.

"Vi?"

I need her to say it or at least say something. Her continued disapproval is wearing on me. She barely speaks to him when he's over and when she does, it isn't all that nice. She plays it off like playful banter, but I know there's real pain and worry behind it.

"I just want you to be with someone who deserves you," she says. "You are the best person I know."

"He does," I say.

She smiles, but I'm not sure she truly believes me.

When it's time for bed, I change and then go to the bathroom where Violet is brushing her teeth. I lean on the door. "I really am happy. I know that you don't like him, but he isn't what you think."

She raises both brows but doesn't speak.

"Okay, yes, he's a total party guy. He drinks too much, and he slacks off with school assignments, and he's hooked up with a lot of people. I don't care about any of that. At his core, he's a decent guy. The best, actually."

I want to tell her about all the good I see in him—the way he's always there for his friends, how he'll hold a piece of Mark with him forever, and a million other things. But I think, for now, all I can hope is that Violet will give him a chance.

She rinses out her mouth and places her toothbrush in the holder. "I like him fine. I just don't trust him yet."

"Give him a chance?"

She nods. "Yeah, I can do that."

The next morning, I wake to Violet's voice shouting downstairs. I rub my eyes and get out of bed.

I pad down the stairs quietly.

"I understand," she says in a tone that does not back up her words. "But there has to be something you can do."

She's silent, listening to whoever is on the other line. Her mouth pulls into a tight smile when she sees me.

I finish my descent and sit on the couch while she paces the length of the living room. Dahlia and Jane shoot me tense looks, but neither dares to say anything.

"Thank you," Violet grits out between clenched teeth and holds the phone in one hand like she's thinking about launching it. "The ballroom flooded."

Jane gasps.

"How bad?" I ask tentatively.

"It's on the dance floor, so it didn't ruin the decorations, but we have nowhere to put them. Everything else is either rented or also filled with water."

My brain races with possibilities. Dahlia and Jane fire out options, and one by one, Violet dismisses them. She plops down in the chair, all the fight leaving her. "Those places are all booked up."

Jane's phone alarm goes off.

"Our mani and pedi appointments are in twenty minutes."

"Go." I stand. "I have an idea."

"What?" Vi asks with a tinge of hope in her voice.

"I don't want to say until I know for sure it'll work. You three go, and I'll catch up with you before our hair appointments."

Dahlia and Jane wait for Violet's approval. Tonight is her baby, and I want it to happen just like she envisioned.

"Okay," she says finally. "But no to any dorm lounge or pizza place."

She shudders.

"I promise. No dorms and no greasy food places." With a smile, I race upstairs. I have a Wallflower Ball to save.

Chapter TWENTY-EIGHT

Daisy

IT TAKES ALL MORNING TO MOVE THE PARTY FROM THE banquet room on campus to the gym of The White House. It's located on the second floor, so we'll be at Gavin's party but in our own area where Violet won't have to worry about mingling.

Gavin even agreed to block off the stairs so people don't wander up to see what's going on. It isn't perfect, but it stays within Violet's constraints of not being a pizza place or dorm lounge.

A smile tugs at his lips, and his brown eyes crinkle at the corners as he looks around his transformed basketball court. "This is epic. We should throw more parties in here."

"Thank you for letting us use the space."

"Yeah, of course."

"Oh, and happy twenty-first!"

His smile lifts. "Thanks. Speaking of, I better go drink some more water and Gatorade. It's going to be a long night."

"Yeah, it is," Jordan says, coming up behind me. "Twenty-one shots with your name on them."

Gavin groans, but his smile pops right back up. "Catch you guys later."

"Do you have to go get ready now?" Jordan asks when he's gone. He faces me and runs his hands down my arms. I don't know how I would have pulled this off without him. When I told him my plan, he rounded up guys and made it happen.

"Yeah, I already missed our nail, hair, and makeup appointments."

"Whoa, that's a lot of appointments."

"Tonight is a big night," I say, and nuzzle into his chest. "I'm so glad you're coming."

"And miss seeing you in that yellow dress?"

My smile widens as I look up at him. "You're pretty wonderful."

"Me?" His laughter vibrates in his chest. I like the way it feels against mine.

"Yep."

"I think you have me confused."

"I don't." I wrap my arms around his back and place my head over his heart. It thumps quietly in a steady rhythm that somehow makes mine beat faster.

He kisses the top of my head and then fists my hair, tugging it gently until I look up at him. "I might have my moments, but right now, it's purely selfish. I get hard every time I think about you playing dress up in those big, poofy dresses. The number of times I've looked at the pic of you in the red dress basically makes it porn." He sucks on my bottom lip.

Butterflies swoop low in my belly. "You kept it?"

"Fuck yeah, I did. I think I wanted you long before I was willing to admit it."

"Same."

He kisses me again, and I'm perfectly content to stay here, but he pulls back, and I know I need to head home.

"Go get ready," he says. "Violet's probably in a fit that you're still gone, and I have a bottle of Jager to buy."

"Okay." I start to go, and he grabs my hand and flings me back to him for one more kiss.

"Okay, seriously, now." He steps back and shoves his hands in his pocket. "Save me the first slow dance."

At seven-forty-five, four wallflowers are dressed and ready for the ball. We look pretty amazing, if I do say so myself. And I do. Violet is so freaking talented. We're all wearing her creations. And Dahlia made us all masks to match our dresses.

"You missed all the pampering," Jane says with a pout. She wiggles her fingers in front of me, showing off her manicure.

"Oooh, pretty."

"I think you look gorgeous, and you didn't have to spend three hours sitting still while people poked and prodded at you." Dahlia touches a curl hanging over my shoulder.

Her hair is sleek and straight, and her eye makeup is thick and black. She looks beautiful, but I can tell she's far less comfortable with all of it than Jane and Violet.

"Thanks. I'm sad I didn't get to spend the day with you all, but everything is set for tonight." I check the time. "We should go."

"How are we going to let everyone know the new location?" Violet asks. I still haven't told her where we're going, and now that the party is minutes away, I'm nervous.

"I thought of that," I say. "Dahlia and I will go to the original location. I hired a bus that will bring everyone. You and Jane will be there putting any of your last-minute touches on it."

"Bring them where?" Violet whines through an excited smile. "Where are we going?"

"You're just about to see." We walk outside, and I take off down the sidewalk.

They follow, but Vi asks, "Why are we walking? Are we meeting an Uber or something?"

I walk to the front of The White House, where a path to their front door splits off from the sidewalk. I stare back at my friends.

My pulse bounces and my hands shake as I wave toward the big party house next to ours. "Ta-da!"

Violet's smile falls instantly.

"I thought Gavin's twenty-first party was here later tonight," Jane says as she glances at the quiet house.

"It is, but upstairs they have a big, open space that we can use. It's totally separate, and Gavin promised he'd keep people out."

"Right, like he keeps people from parking in our driveway." Vi cocks a brow.

Dahlia and Jane don't look convinced either.

"It looks amazing," I press. "The guys helped me move everything here. We have even more space than we did in the banquet room." I sway my hips. "Bigger dance floor."

My pep can only take so much silence.

"I don't think so." Violet turns like she's going home.

I look to Dahlia and Jane for help.

"I worked really hard on this for you," I say to her back. "I promise it looks just like you imagined. At least come inside and see it."

Violet pauses, her shoulders stiffen, and she cuts me with a glare over her shoulder. "No, you *think* you did this for me, but you did it for you."

"What?" My cheeks heat even in the cool night breeze.

"Tonight was supposed to be about us."

"It is!"

"No. Jordan blew you off for his friends, and you saw this as a perfect opportunity to force your world into his. He isn't different. He's exactly the same as the rest of them. He won't bend for you, so you will until you break." She spits the words, and each one slices through me.

Violet's hate for anyone associated with the basketball team is well established, but I don't understand why she clings to it. Or why she wants to drag Jordan into it. He's done nothing to deserve it.

"You're mad. I'm sorry. I didn't think it was that big of a deal. I promise you won't have to see Gavin. I will stand guard at the door myself. Please just come inside and see it."

"You think I could go in there and enjoy myself knowing he's downstairs with all his awesome friends? In *his* house? Seriously, did you for one second think about how I would feel taking charity from him?"

My throat tightens.

"He destroyed me," she yells, and for an instant, I can read every emotion on her face—pain, betrayal, humiliation. She steels her expression and repeats it. "He destroyed me. Just like Jordan is going to do to you."

Any remorse I was feeling is wiped away with anger. "You're wrong about him."

"I guess we'll see," she says, and it feels like a curse.

Someone clears their throat, and we all look over to find Gavin standing on the stairs. His eyes are wide, and his hands are shoved in his pockets.

"Perfect." Vi throws her hands up in the air. She heads back to our house, pulling pins from her hair as she goes. The long, dark strands shine and bounce in the moonlight. Jane offers me a sad smile and then follows her.

"Go," I say quietly to Dahlia. "Make sure she's okay, and I'll take care of the party."

She nods and gives me the same sad smile as Jane.

I take an Uber to the banquet room. The bus driver is waiting. Inside, a small line of people has gathered, waiting for the doors to open. Moving to the front, I let everyone know about the location change and that the bus is waiting to take us.

As more people arrive looking happy and excited, it hits me just how many people are looking forward to tonight. It might have started as Violet's need to create something that rivaled the big parties on campus, but she instilled a hope in our classmates and friends that had been waiting for a chance just like this to dress up and dance with their friends.

Vi did this. She created something just for us—the wallflowers, the non-Greek, the unpopular, the whatever you want to call us. And now she isn't even going to see it.

Chapter TWENTY-NINE

Jordan

I TAKE THE STEPS UP TO THE SECOND FLOOR, TWO AT A TIME. A daisy in one hand, I open the door to the court with the other.

She stands in the middle of the room with her back to me in her light-yellow dress, blonde hair falling in waves past her shoulders. My chest tightens, and my limbs feel heavy and somehow weak at the same time. I am so fucked.

I've heard guys talk about falling for a girl like being checked hard into the boards, but I always assumed they were exaggerating.

I roll the stem of the flower in between my thumb and middle finger.

Dahlia and Jane see me first. Daisy turns to face me, dress twirling with the movement. She steps away from her friends.

I go to her and hold out the daisy.

"Thank you." Her voice is quiet and unsteady, transporting

me back to those first days in physics where she couldn't talk to Liam or me without blushing. She stares down at it. Her red lips curve up in the smallest of smiles.

"This is pretty killer." My gaze scans the court that's been transformed. The flower archway is at one end near the DJ booth. People stand all around dressed up in formal attire. Some dance, others chat with friends in small circles.

"Yeah," she says, and her voice breaks. Her lashes are coated in a dark black that makes her eyes look twice as big, and they water with emotion that makes me want to murder someone.

"What's wrong?"

She starts to speak, and the tears well until one dares to fall down her face. I wipe it away.

"I messed up," she finally croaks. Her body shakes as she cries.

I run a hand along the back of her hair and cradle her to my chest. "I doubt that."

"I did." She tilts her head up to look at me with black smudges under her eyes. Her gaze falls to my shirt and tie. "You look so nice, and I just cried all over you. You even shaved." She brings a hand to my cheek and lets her nails lightly scrape across my jaw.

"Tell me what happened, baby?"

"I should have talked to Violet before moving everything here. She wouldn't come."

"Why?"

"Because of Gavin. I should have asked her before I did anything."

"You were trying to save the ball."

She nods. "Still. He hurt her. I knew that, and I blew it off and assumed it wouldn't matter. I let her down, and now she won't even see all her hard work."

"If you'd done nothing, she wouldn't have either."

"Except in that case, my best friend wouldn't hate me."

"I doubt she hates you."

"She said some awful things. She yelled them, actually."

"She yelled at you?" The thought of anyone yelling at Daisy makes adrenaline boil under my skin. "You didn't deserve that."

She takes a deep breath and steps back, scanning the room. Sadness tinged with disappointment lingers in her expression.

I hold out a hand toward her. "Dance with me?"

She tilts her head to the side, considering it. She steps into me and rests her head on my shoulder as we move to the beat.

"Thank you. For today. For this. Just… thank you," she says.

"Anything. Always."

I don't know how long we hold on to one another before the song changes and the heavy bass of the music outside starts up.

"Gavin's party," she says. "You better go make sure the birthday boy has a good time."

"Come with me."

"I'm not sure I'll be very much fun tonight. Plus, I'm wearing this." She lifts up the skirt of her dress with two hands.

"You look gorgeous."

"I'm way overdressed."

I adjust my tie. "No, you're perfect. They're underdressed."

"I should stay." She chews on her bottom lip. "Or go talk to Violet."

"Okay. Well, in that case, I'll be back as soon as I can. Stick with the girls, okay?"

She nods. "Sorry to be a major bummer."

"Never. I'll be back before you know it."

"You don't have to rush. I know what your friends mean to you."

"You're my friend, remember?" I wink and drag the pad of my thumb along her bottom lip until she frees it from her teeth. She's so much more than that. I forced my way into her life for all the wrong reasons, but somehow she's become the most important thing.

I leave her with Dahlia and Jane and go downstairs to find Gavin. He's easy to spot in the back yard. A circle of people are gathered around him cheering him on as he takes a shot of something that makes his lips curl and his eyes squeeze shut.

Liam's among the guys watching on.

"Hey," I say as I step up beside him.

He grins at my outfit. "You look nice."

"Thanks." I jut my chin toward Gavin. "How many shots is he in?"

He holds up his phone and swipes through his photos showing me the evidence of each of the four shots Gavin's taken already.

"How's the party upstairs?"

I shake my head. The noise around us gets louder as someone else thrusts a shot in Gavin's hand. "I'll tell you about it later."

After his fifth shot, we take the birthday boy away from the liquor. At this rate he's going to be passed out before midnight. We play washers and beer pong. His teammates throw him in the pool. It's a good time, but I'm struggling to enjoy it, knowing Daisy is upset.

I'm in the kitchen nursing a beer when Gavin comes back downstairs in dry clothes. I pull out the bottle of Jägermeister I bought him from the freezer, a big red bow on top. "Happy twenty-first, man."

"Pour it up," he says as he runs a hand through his wet hair and takes a seat on one of the stools at the big ass island in the middle of the room.

I do and slide one his way. I hold up my glass. "Happy birthday."

He clinks the bottom of his shot to mine and tosses it back before saying, "I really screwed up, huh?"

"What do you mean?"

"Violet." He pours another shot and swallows it.

I shrug. "She doesn't like you. That's for sure. Though she doesn't like me all that much either."

"She's worried about you hurting her friend. That's different. You're paying for my sins. I'm sorry about that."

I'd rather gnaw off my own arm than hurt Daisy, and I tell him that because I can't tell Violet. Not that she'd believe me.

"Go check on your girl, Thatch. If Violet's upset with her, then she's probably a mess too."

"Shut the fuck up. It's not even ten o'clock. I'm not leaving your twenty-first birthday party before you're good and drunk."

"You are." He stands. "I'm kicking you out."

He comes around, and we slap hands, and he pulls me into a side hug.

"It's about to get ugly, anyway." He blows a breath that puffs out his cheeks, and a half-smile pulls at the left-side of his mouth. "I'll catch you this week."

Daisy isn't upstairs. Dahlia and Jane tell me she went home, but where I find her is in the tree house looking over at Gavin's party.

"Hey." I sit beside her.

She rests her head on my shoulder. "Hi."

"Talk to Violet?"

"She doesn't want to talk to me."

"You're freezing," I say as I run my hands up and down her arms.

"I can't go inside."

"Come to my place. You can work things out with Violet tomorrow after you've both slept."

She comes without protest.

I kick off my shoes and loosen my tie as Daisy climbs into bed, still in her dress. It billows around her small frame, taking up half the mattress.

I sit against the headboard, and she lies down with her head against my chest. She looks up at me. "She said things about you. About us."

I'm not shocked by that, but it picks at something that's been on my mind all day.

Daisy sits up. "I'm sorry that she hasn't been fair to you. You have been amazing to me, and I know you don't like when I say nice things about you, but truly, you are wonderful." Her eyes fall to her lap. "When we first met, I judged you too. I did. And I'm sorry."

With a finger under her chin, I lift her face to look at me. "That's human nature."

"I still feel bad about it."

"You don't owe me any apologies." My stomach rolls. "While we're admitting our sins, I have something to confess about when we first met too."

"What?" Her lips part into a hesitant smile.

"When we first met and you were into Liam, I made it my mission to get in the way of you two any chance I could. He was struggling with hockey, and you came along. A sweet little distraction." I place a kiss on her lips.

"I was hardly a distraction. He barely noticed me."

"Not true. He was going to ask you out, but I told him not to."

"You did what?" Her voice lifts. She doesn't wait for me to answer. "Why would you do that?"

"I thought if the two of you started dating, he'd lose his head. He was already having a hard time."

"But..." she starts, brows pulling together. "You told me to ask him out. 'He won't say no', remember? Why would you tell me to do that if you wanted to keep me from him?"

"That was my attempt at doing the right thing, I guess. But I couldn't even do that. I stopped you before you could. I, uh, didn't really need a tutor, but it seemed like you were going to finally ask him out, and I thought as long as you were busy with me, it would keep you away from Liam." My palms sweat. "It was dumb, I know."

"I'm confused. You wanted to keep Liam and me apart, not because you liked me but because you were afraid that it would hurt his game?"

A lump lodges in my throat, so I nod.

"That's insane."

"Not my brightest idea, but it did bring us together."

"You mean while you were pretending to need my help with school? Who does that?"

Up until this very second, I assumed, or maybe hoped, that she'd find it funny. I can see now how stupid that was. Panic surges through me, but I truly don't know what to say.

"So all this time that we've been hanging out it was just to keep me from him?" Her eyes widen and a pretty flush creeps up her face.

"No, of course not."

She scrambles off the bed. "What was the plan? To string me along until after the season? To make me fall for you instead? Was any of it real for you?" Her body is shaking now. "Or are you still pretending to like me just to keep me from Liam?"

Fuck, fuck, fuck. "All of it was real. I'm crazy about you. I told you that I fell for you long before I realized it, and I meant it."

"Then why would you keep something like this from me until now?"

"I tried to tell you once. The night in the tree house. You said whatever happened in the past didn't matter."

"I thought you were talking about hooking up with other girls." She throws her hands in the air, then puts on her shoes and grabs her purse.

"What? I haven't hooked up with anyone since you and I started hanging out."

She isn't even listening to me. I can practically see her thoughts spinning around in her head. "I can't believe this. Violet was right."

I don't know what Violet said about me, and I'm not sure I want to know.

"Don't go." I get up and take her by the arm before she can flee. "Everything happened so fast. One minute we were emailing about physics and hockey, and the next I couldn't get enough of you. I didn't tell you sooner because I think deep down, I was always doing it for me, not him."

"Then tell me one thing."

"Anything."

"If Liam had never wanted to ask me out and I hadn't shown interest in him, would you have ever looked twice at me?" Her voice is steel, and her eyes brim with unshed tears.

"I don't know."

She smiles sadly and nods, then heads toward the door.

"Don't go. Please?"

She doesn't stop.

"Daisy, wait," I say. "I love you." The words are out before I can process them, but I know they're true instantly.

Her body stills. I hold my breath and wait for her reaction.

"You don't love me," she says.

"I do," I insist. "Maybe it started for all the wrong reasons, but I love you."

"No. This isn't love. It can't be. I could never love someone that could do something so cruel."

My heart cracks wide open as she slams my bedroom door. I rush after her, reaching her as she's about to give the hallway door the same treatment. With a hand, I stop the door. "I'm so sorry. I should have told you sooner."

"Yes, you should have. Or maybe just left me the hell alone in the first place."

"Please don't go. I need you."

"No. You don't. You were pretending to need me, remember?"

Liam's coming up the stairs. He looks wide-eyed between us and raises a hand in a tentative greeting. "Hey."

Daisy swipes tears from her cheeks before she faces him. "Can you give me a ride home?"

I start to move in front of her. "Daisy, plea—"

"No," she says, refusing to look at me. "I don't want to hear anymore. I just want to go home."

"Let me take you."

"Still trying to keep me from him?" She laughs softly. "Don't worry, after tonight I don't ever want to see either of you again."

Liam glances at me, and I nod. He goes out the door first, and she finally looks at me. "She said you would destroy me."

Violet's words tear through me, and I want to refute them a thousand times over, but the words sound weak now, all things considered.

She whispers four final words, ripping my heart from my chest. "And she was right."

Chapter THIRTY

Daisy

By Wednesday, all evidence of the rain and gloomy weather is gone, and in its place, the sun shines bright and taunting. I pull the pillow over my head. I'm all out of tears which is too bad because for once, I'd like to wail and scream instead of being shy, quiet Daisy.

The house is still. I haven't seen or spoken to Violet since Saturday night. Jane and Dahlia check on me at least once a day, but the only time I've left my room is to go to campus. Violet's either in her room with the door closed or not home. It hurts to fight with her like this, but after everything that went down Saturday night, I don't have the energy to hear her say, 'I told you so.'

I haven't spoken to Jordan either, though he's texted and must have come by the house because I found a box of candy on the doorstep when I got back from class yesterday. No note (I guess he figured the dozen of *I'm sorry* texts were enough), just the entire candy aisle of the gas station up the street. The box is now shoved under my bed with all the other things I don't know what to do with. Like my heart.

I meet Dahlia downstairs to walk to campus. We have a psychology class together this semester.

"Hi," she greets me with the same tone you might use when approaching a wounded animal.

"Hey." We start down the sidewalk. "Thanks for sending your notes from Monday. Mine were a mess." *Like me.*

"You're welcome. How are you doing?" She's the only one who knows about Jordan. I ran into her when I came home Saturday night and broke down the second I saw her. I needed to tell someone so I could stop hoping it was only a bad dream.

"Okay. Terrible. Depends on the minute."

The hockey team is out of town for an away game, but it doesn't stop me from imagining him around every corner as we get to the heart of campus. Every dark head of hair and backward hat makes my pulse spike and my stomach twist. He's everywhere and nowhere, and I can't decide which is more devastating.

"Have you talked to Violet yet?"

I don't answer, but the cutting look I shoot her is all she needs.

"She's hurting too. You should talk to her."

"And hear her tell me how she was right? No thanks."

"Come on. Vi wouldn't do that."

I'm not so sure. Not even sure I don't deserve it. I thought what I had with Jordan was *so* different than whatever she'd had with Gavin. Untouchable even. That's the problem with falling in love. It makes you feel invincible. Or maybe that's just the problem with falling for someone like Jordan.

When class is over, I linger on campus, avoiding home. I go to the bookstore and look around, but the Valley Hockey merch reminds me of him. From there, I go to the art lab and pull out my sketchbook, but after forty-five minutes of holding my pencil to the pad, I haven't summoned the desire to draw anything. My creative muse is drowning her sorrows in a bottle of Fireball.

With no sanctuary in sight, I go back home. Sitting on the floor next to my bed, I reach under and carefully pull out the box of candy. I don't open it, just stare at it, trying to picture Jordan tossing things inside.

I miss him, and I really, really hate that I do.

He knew I liked Liam and he deliberately kept us apart. I'm used to being overlooked or dismissed, and that hurts in its own kind of way. But being seen and not being good enough—that's brutal.

I don't even wish that Liam had asked me out, not anymore, but I hate that Jordan took that from me. It wasn't his place. He did something he knew would hurt me and then he knowingly deceived me by throwing himself in front of Liam and pretending to need my help.

All those nights getting to know him that I've held so close to my heart. I can't help but look back at every encounter and second-guess the things he said and did. How could he do that? How could he kiss me and say such sweet things without telling me?

I'm mad at him, but I'm mad at myself too. I ignored all thoughts that we didn't make sense together. Did I really think the hottest player on campus was spending all that time with me because he genuinely liked me? The ache in my chest gives me my answer.

Leaving the box untouched, I go downstairs and out into the back yard. The music is going next door, and voices carry over the fence. It's early, and the party isn't at full volume, but it drowns out my footsteps as I cross the yard to the tree house. My favorite place is ruined with memories that make me feel like a fool.

My chest lifts and falls as my breaths quicken. My steps are slow and measured, my body trembling. *I hate him. I hate him. I hate him.*

I love him.

My fingers wrap around the ladder. I squeeze the wood and pull, wishing I could tear the whole thing down with my bare hands. It doesn't budge.

This close to the fence, I can hear the party more clearly—the laughter, the happy chatter, and drunken squeals of delight.

I grip the ladder until my knuckles turn white and my palms sting. And then I open my mouth, and I scream.

I scream until my throat is raw and no sound is left.

I scream until I'm me again. Quiet Daisy.

Chapter THIRTY-ONE

Jordan

WE GET BACK TO VALLEY LATE WEDNESDAY NIGHT, and Coach gives us Thursday off practice to rest.

Rest, get blackout drunk, tomato tomahto.

Power hour is followed by a trip to the bar, and then we head to McCallum's apartment. I haven't found the point of drunkenness that makes me forget about Daisy and the gaping hole where my heart is supposed to be, but I have found the point that makes it a dull, blurry ache.

I'm not really in the mood for cards or video games or even talking, so I head outside to the back deck. Someone brought the speaker out here, and girls are dancing in a big group.

"Yo," Dallas says as I fall into the chair next to him. He eyes the bottle of Fireball in my hand. "Can I get a shot of that?"

"This one is all mine," I say, and lift it to my lips. The cinnamon whiskey slides down my throat. It's the same bottle Daisy and I shared, and I'm going to drink every drop myself unless it's her asking to have a drink.

I let my head fall back, and I stare up into the clear night sky. The stars are visible, the moon shining bright. Is she in her tree house looking up right now too? Maybe plotting my death or wishing on a shooting star she'd never met me.

Long hair falls into my face, and for a couple of glorious seconds, I think it's her.

"Thatcher!" Cybil's voice rings out, and then she tucks her hair behind her ears, so her face is visible. I sit up, and she comes around in front of me.

"Hey, handsome. Wanna dance?" She tugs at my hand.

"No thanks."

"Come on." She pouts.

"Busy drinking," I say, and then bring the bottle up to take another drink. The last drops trickle onto my tongue, and it feels like the end of so much more than a fucking bottle of whiskey.

"Looks like you aren't busy anymore."

I let her pull me to my feet, but I hold on to my bottle. I sway, and the world spins.

"Nope," I say before dropping back into the chair.

"Fine. You sit, and I'll dance."

I don't understand at first, but then she takes a step closer until she's standing between my legs. She moves slowly to the beat. Cybil's gorgeous and fun, but she isn't Daisy.

I'm about to move when Liam walks up next to her and steps between us.

"What the hell?" he grits out.

"It wasn't what it looks like," I start, but my tongue feels funny, and the words come out jumbled.

"Sorry, Cybil," he says. "I need to get him home."

"I'm not ready to go home yet." I pull my arm away when he grips my elbow. "Grab me a beer, will you?"

"I got it," Cybil offers.

"No." Liam's tone is hard as he snaps at her, and I can see the regret immediately as she looks at him in shock. His voice softens. "Can you give us a minute?"

She nods and turns toward the door.

"I've never heard you be such an ass before," I note when she's gone.

"Yeah, well, I've never wanted to kick someone's ass as much as I do right now."

"Cybil? She's harmless."

"I'm talking about you. What the fuck are you doing here, wasted off your ass?"

"I think you just answered your own question." I hold up the bottle then remember it's empty. "Why are you here anyway? Weren't you going out with..." I wave my hand in the air. I still haven't met or even learned the name of the guy he's dating.

"I had a bad feeling when you bailed on your classes today, and you haven't answered any of my texts."

"Sucks to be ignored, doesn't it?" I've sent Daisy like twenty texts, and every single one has gone unanswered. I even dropped by her house earlier this week, hoping she'd let me in so we could talk in person. No answer there either. She's made it clear that she wants nothing to do with me.

"Up." Something in his tone gets me to my feet. He wraps an arm around me like he's going to carry me out.

"I can walk," I insist. I don't bother fighting him on leaving. I'm tired anyway.

He motions for me to go ahead of him, and I lead us through the party and out the front door.

"What time is it?" I ask as he opens the passenger side door for me. The parking lot is dark and quiet.

"You have about four hours until our morning workout."

Damn. Where did the day go? I groan as I heave myself up into the truck.

He shuts me in and jogs around the front. I close my eyes on the short drive back to campus. A week of shitty sleep and an entire day of drinking has caught up with me.

Liam wakes me when we're back at the dorm. My head swims with the alcohol and fragmented memories of Daisy. Her smile, her laugh, the blush she gets high on her cheeks when she's embarrassed or turned on. Fuck, I miss her.

I stumble into my buddy as we walk through the front door of the dorm. "This is all your fault."

Liam grunts and steadies me. "How do you figure?"

I let my full weight lean against him, and he shuffles us up the stairs.

"She wanted you. You two make sense. Me and her..." I shake my head side to side. "I don't know what the hell I was thinking. Daisy is so... well, you know. And I'm, well..."

"Drunk?"

"Yeah, that too." Damn, am I tired.

He lets me ramble more nonsense as he helps me into our room. He grabs a water and thrusts it at me. "Drink this."

"You're fucking bossy tonight."

"I'm tired, and we have a quiz in the morning."

"Fuck that. I'm not going."

He growls and musses his perfect hair. "You know what was really great about you the past couple of months?"

My brain works slowly. I can think of a lot of really great things from the past two months, but none of them are me.

"You actually applied yourself."

"I was keeping her from you." Saying the words out loud are like a punch to the gut.

"No." A muscle in his jaw ticks. "Maybe that's how it started, but you were different."

I don't know anymore. Not even sure it matters since either way, she's not here.

He keeps going. "She made you want to be better. You've been skirting by, drinking too much, barely studying."

"We're not all dean's list material."

"Fuck that. You're smarter than me. Always have been, but after Mark died, you stopped giving a shit about everything but partying and hockey."

I narrow my gaze at him in warning. "No, I just let go of the bullshit, like perfect grades. As long as I keep my GPA high enough to play hockey, that's all that matters. And I always do, Captain."

"Yeah, yeah, I know. Nothing matters because if it did, you might have to risk caring about something else and it not working out. Failing, losing people—it sucks."

"You don't know what you're talking about."

"Fine, but what I do know is that since you started hanging out with Daisy, you quit the constant partying, you went to class, and you found other things to fill your time without being wasted or on the ice. And you were fucking happy."

Ignoring him, I uncap the water and chug all of it.

The asshole won't let it alone. "You love her. Tell me I'm wrong?"

"Love is bullshit. I wish I'd never met her."

Liam curses under his breath, pins me up against the wall with a forearm, brings his other hand up to my face, and smacks me. Hard.

The sting radiates down my cheek, and I work my jaw back and forth. I'm stunned.

"What the fuck was that for?"

"For saying dumb shit that you don't mean." He pushes off me. "You love her, and tomorrow you're going to remember spewing nonsense and wish you'd have done it yourself."

"So I should thank you?" I rub my fingers over my cheek. "Damn, that really hurt. Are you gonna punch me next?"

The motherfucker grins. "Don't tempt me. Go to bed, Thatch. Then wake up and use that big brain of yours to figure out how you're going to get her back because you're a miserable son of a bitch without her."

I make it through Friday on Tums and energy drinks. I crash after my last class and wake up to voices on the other side of the wall in the common area.

Pulling a T-shirt over my head, I walk out of my room to find Liam and a guy I don't recognize. They're playing video games, two pizzas stacked in front of them on the coffee table.

"Hey," I say as I linger in the doorway.

They both glance quickly from the TV screen to say hello and continue with the game.

"This is Cole," Liam says with another sideways glimpse in my direction, but this time his eyes widen a fraction.

It takes me a second to realize this is the guy Liam's been seeing. My brows lift, and my mouth makes an O.

I catch myself before Cole looks up and smiles.

"Jordan," I introduce myself.

"I know. I mean, I've heard a lot about you. It's nice to meet you." He has a slight drawl that makes his words slow and smooth, friendly even.

"Yeah, same."

"We have pizza." Liam nods his head toward the boxes.

"No thanks. I—" I can't think of an excuse quick enough.

Liam grabs the bottom pizza and holds it out to me. "Cheese."

I still don't move, and he shakes it. "Soak up whatever alcohol is still in your system. Captain's orders."

We have a home game tomorrow against our rival ASU. They're undefeated, and we would love nothing more than to destroy their perfect record.

Cole scoots closer to Liam, and they both look at me expectantly.

"All right." I take a seat, and Liam passes me the box over Cole's head, grinning like a fool.

"How's the cheek?" Cole asks, biting back a smile.

I bring a hand up to rub my face. "Fine. No thanks to this fucker."

We laugh, and the sound dregs up emotions I've tried to keep at bay.

"No offense, but it sounds like you deserved it."

I flip him off, and Cole just laughs at me.

That's how I find myself spending a Friday night hanging with Liam and Cole. We play video games and eat pizza.

I learn that Cole is from Texas, majoring in exercise science, and totally gone for Liam. He doesn't say the latter, but he gets this look on his face—pure adoration—anytime the two of them are talking. I like him, and I like how happy Liam looks.

Eventually, they go to Liam's room, and I shut myself back in mine. Over the last week, I've perfected my playlist of sappy songs that say all the things I feel and can't say to Daisy. Staring up at the ceiling in the dark, listening to other people's confessions of the heart, I compose a thousand texts that I won't allow myself to send (twenty unanswered texts is a line even my pathetic ass won't cross).

I vacillate between frustration and self-loathing. That's to say nothing of the sadness that lingers like a second skin.

I miss her.

Fuck, do I miss her.

Liam lifts a fist as I pass him in the line down the tunnel for the final period of the game.

I tap it, and he falls in beside me. He has a pep in his step as we make our way to the ice. The crowd is on their feet, and the nearly packed arena is electric.

I don't dare look at the student section for Daisy. I know she isn't here. I can feel it—the distance between us.

I let it fuel me for the next twenty minutes of play. Hockey is the perfect distraction. I dig deep, tapping into the anger and frustration, even the sadness. Aggressive on the verge of reckless. Only Liam understands the real reason. The rest of the team eggs me on, mistaking my hustle for my determination to beat ASU.

And we do.

But I still miss her, and when the game is over, I'm back to needing a distraction.

"You want to go to The Hideout?" Dallas asks me as we're changing in the locker room.

"Yeah, I'm in."

Liam stops me before I can go, stepping in front of my path to the door. "Did you hear anything I said the other night?"

"Yeah, I heard you."

He cocks a brow.

"I heard you." I sidestep him. "I just don't think there's any getting her back."

Chapter THIRTY-TWO

Daisy

I WENT TO BED EARLY AGAIN. NOW IT'S TWO IN THE morning, and I'm wide awake, and my stomach is grumbling. I skipped dinner because I could hear Violet downstairs. We still haven't spoken, and it's reached the awkward point where I'm tiptoeing around waiting for her to leave before I come out of my room.

But now the house is dark and quiet. I pad softly out of my room and downstairs to the kitchen.

Violet's sitting at the kitchen table with her tablet in front of her. The only light comes from its screen as she hunches over, drawing on it with the stylus.

Momentum propels me forward when I'd really like to backtrack. She looks up as I'm trying to decide how to flee without being seen.

"I thought you were asleep," I blurt out.

"No. Not yet." She blinks a few times. Her eyes are heavy with the hour. She hasn't been to bed.

Since I've already intruded on her, I go to the fridge and open it. It's as empty as I feared, and the only thing in the pantry cabinet is a sleeve of Saltine crackers.

I turn on my heel, prepared to go, when she pushes the bag of pretzels on the table an inch in my direction. She doesn't say a word, but the invitation is there.

Violet and I have never had a fight like this. I've never had a fight with anyone like this. Now I'm not talking to two people that mean everything to me. It's been a rough week.

I pull out a chair and sit on the very edge where I can make a fast getaway if needed. The pretzels soothe the hunger pains, but that only makes me more aware of the pain everywhere else. Obviously, I've never minded the quiet, but this type of heavy silence is unbearable.

Grabbing the biggest handful I can manage, I murmur my thanks, stand, and start back to my room.

"I'm sorry." The words are spoken quietly. So quietly that I'm not sure she really said them.

I glance over my shoulder and find her watching me. She repeats it. "I'm sorry."

We talk all night, sitting at the kitchen table while we finish off the pretzels and then the crackers.

"I can't believe you've been going through this all week, and I wasn't there for you. I selfishly assumed you were upset about us."

"I was. I am. You're my best friend, Vi. I hate fighting with you."

"I want to murder him for doing that to you. All those nights, he was over pretending to need help with school stuff."

My throat tightens. "I didn't really want to talk about it anyway. I'm such an idiot. I'm sorry I didn't listen to you."

"You're not an idiot." She reaches across the table and takes my hands.

I drop my forehead to the cool wood.

"Come on," she says. "It's late."

I follow her upstairs, and she climbs into bed next to me, where we sleep until noon the next day.

When I open my eyes, she's sitting up, looking at her phone. "Jane poked her head in a few minutes ago. She and Dahlia are going over to the rec center for yoga. Do you want to go?"

"Yeah." I stretch. "Maybe it'll help me find my center, or whatever."

There's still a lingering awkwardness between us. We talked about me and Jordan, even a little about us, but there's one topic we steered far clear of last night.

She starts to get up, and I stop her.

"Wait, one more thing." I sit up. "I'm sorry about Gavin."

Her mouth opens like she might interrupt.

I keep going. "I didn't realize how much he hurt you, and I should have. It's just that you always seem so strong. I admire that about you so much."

"You didn't know because I didn't tell you." She wraps a finger around a piece of hair and twirls it. "I… I slept with him. I'd held out all of high school, waiting for the perfect guy. Then a month into the school year, I thought I'd found him. Two days later, I woke up to him in bed with Bailey."

"You were a virgin?"

She laughs. "Is that so hard to believe?"

"Well, yeah. Even I gave it up before college."

Smiling, she says, "I had opportunities. I just wanted it to mean something."

"And then he screwed your roommate."

"And then he screwed my roommate," she confirms. "We weren't a couple or anything."

But she wanted them to be.

"Do you want to egg his house?"

She laughs. "Maybe later."

I spend the whole day with the girls. I think we all needed it, Vi and me especially. Jane treats us to brunch after yoga, and then when we get back to the house, all four of us stay downstairs.

Jane doesn't run off to her room, Dahlia doesn't even mention practice or workouts, and we just sit and talk all afternoon. It's so much fun hanging with my friends that for minutes at a time, I forget Jordan and how much I miss him. It hits me randomly, stealing my breath and making my stomach dip.

As the day fades into night, we break out the alcohol, and Violet and Dahlia bring out new pieces they've been working on. It's almost like being transported back in time. Like nothing has changed.

But, when Violet pulls out the infamous red dress, my heart stops. Everyone's too busy to notice as I slip away into the kitchen. I grab a glass of water and go over to where my phone is charging on the counter.

Jordan hasn't sent any more texts since Tuesday. His sudden silence is as annoying as the candy bomb he dropped on me. It isn't like I expected him to keep apologizing forever, but now it really feels over.

"Are you okay?" Jane steps into the kitchen in a green dress that makes her eyes pop. She's pulled her hair up into a high ponytail, and it sways from side to side as she walks. She looks like a movie star.

"Yeah. Fine. I just needed a drink."

She grabs a glass, fills it, and stands next to me. "You miss him?"

I nod, and then because I don't want to talk about it, I motion toward her dress. "That fits you perfectly."

She stares down at the emerald material. "It really does. I wish I had somewhere else to wear it. Do you think my professors would mind if I wore it to class?"

We laugh, but then I think, why do we need to wait for a special occasion? So, I say, "We should throw a party."

"What?"

"Yeah. Right here with all our friends."

"A ball do-over?"

"Something like that, but less pressure. I can't ask Vi to do all that again."

"And I already sent all the centerpieces back. Plus, the flowers are gone."

"We don't need that stuff," I say. "The four of us are fabulous enough on our own." I look at her dress again. "But you should definitely wear that."

Her lips curve up into a smile. "Let's do it."

Chapter THIRTY-THREE

Jordan

MONDAY MORNING I'M DRAGGING, BUT I MANAGE TO make it (and stay awake) for my first class. After, I text Liam to see if he wants to meet up at University Hall. We have an hour before our analytical mechanics class, and I need caffeine and something made of sugar.

He shows up a few minutes later with Cole.

"Hey." I push off the wall outside when I see them. Cole has become a constant presence. I like him, and I like him for Liam. I was so worried about how dating Daisy would impact his game, but I guess the joke is on me because ever since Liam and Cole worked things out, he's on fire. Relationship Liam is focused and playing the best hockey I've ever seen out of him.

"Made it to class this morning, eh?" Liam grins.

"Barely." I didn't want to if I'm honest, but a weekend of drinking hard didn't help me forget about Daisy, so I guess that just means it's time to get back to normal life. Whatever that is. Hard to imagine my days without knowing I'm going to see her later to study together and make out until her lips are red and puffy.

But she hasn't texted, and I respect her too damn much to force my way into her life again. Or maybe I am just too chicken shit to put myself out there a second time. Liam was right about one thing (okay, fine, he was right about everything), losing people sucks.

Cole holds the door open, and Liam steps through.

"Thanks," I say to Cole as he continues to hold it for me to go before him.

Liam stops abruptly, and I run into the back of him.

"Dude," I start and step around him. There's no one in front of him, so I look around to see what his deal is. Then I come up short too.

"Daisy," I say her name out loud. She hasn't seen us, and the shock when she looks up mirrors my reaction.

I step out of the doorway, Liam and Cole behind me.

"Hi," Daisy finally speaks. She briefly glances at Liam and Cole and nods, but her gaze is drawn back to me.

"How've you been?" I ask as I catalog everything about her. The pink of her cheeks, the tremble of her bottom lip, the way she clutches her sketchbook to her chest.

The dress she's wearing is new, or not one I've seen before, and for some reason this makes me angry. I want to be someone that knows everything about her. Even something as stupid as every item in her closet. One of my favorite things used to be looking forward to seeing what little dress or shirt she'd picked out for the day. I bet I know her closet as well as I know my own. Except, maybe not anymore.

She removes one hand from her sketchbook and tucks her blonde hair behind an ear. "Okay. How are you?"

I consider lying, but since that got me into this mess, I just nod and redirect. "It's good to see you. Can I buy you a coffee or pastry?"

"I have to get to class," she says.

"Ceramics?"

She inclines her head like she can't believe I remembered. I remember everything.

University Hall is busy this time of day, and people are funneling around us. Someone bumps her as they cut around her, and she steps closer to me. I place a hand on her elbow. Daisy flushes under my touch, and her chest rises and falls with quick breaths.

"I better go," she says.

Reluctantly, I drop my hand and step out of the way. She heads out, looking back at me once she's outside, then turns and power walks away.

Liam cuffs me on the shoulder. "That looked painful."

I forgot he was standing there. I blink at him.

"Are you okay?" His brows pull together.

"Yeah."

"Are you sure? You look weird."

"I forgot you were there. She barely looked at you."

"Yeah." He gives me a face that says, *so?*

A small grin pulls at my lips. I backhand him softly in the chest. "She didn't look at you. She was looking at me."

"O-kay. She was talking to you, not me."

"Exactly!"

"You're talking in riddles."

"Her face was flushed, and her voice was trembling. She was nervous."

"And you look so excited about that because?" Cole asks.

"That's how she used to look at him." I motion with a head to Liam.

They still don't seem to be following my twisted logic.

"She likes me," I explain. "She still likes me."

I take off for the coffee line with a bounce to my step, brain spinning with this new knowledge.

"Of course, she didn't look at me. I'm in a relationship," Liam says with a hint of defensiveness as he gets in line behind me.

"Yeah, but she doesn't know that."

We order and take it to a table in the back of University Hall.

"Now what?" Liam asks.

"I don't know. I guess I figure out how to get her back."

"Don't ask me," Liam says. "I'm old hat. She barely looked at me."

Cole bites back a laugh. "It's okay, babe. I still want to look at you."

Liam grumbles under his breath, but he smiles ever so slightly as Cole squeezes the back of his neck.

I spend the next hour brainstorming and bouncing ideas off Liam and Cole.

Knowing that she still likes me is awesome, but I don't know how I'm going to make up for lying and breaking her heart.

Later that afternoon, I'm sitting in front of my laptop with a blank sheet of copy paper in front of me, following some YouTube guy who boasted he could teach anyone to draw. Anyone but me, apparently.

Liam is playing video games on the couch next to me. He glances over and narrows his gaze. "What is that thing sticking out on the side of your leg?"

Yes, I've attempted to draw myself.

"It's a daisy."

"Why do you have a daisy sticking out of your thigh?"

"I'm holding it in my hand. See?" I put the pencil on the spot. "It's like I'm offering her the daisy."

"Yyyyeah. I think real daisies might get that across clearer."

"I want to give her this *with* the daisies. Drawing is something that's important to her."

"Maybe not when it's done like that." He cracks a grin. "It's sweet."

I sit back and look at it with fresh eyes. Yeah, it's terrible. I scribble along the top, *I miss you. P.S. Maybe you could tutor me in drawing? x, Jordan*

"Are you going to take it by her house?"

"No, I thought I'd have the florist drop it with the flowers. She'll probably be happier if it comes from someone else."

"Sounds promising."

I ignore him. "Besides, this is just the first of many gifts. I need to show her I was paying attention. That it wasn't all a lie."

Liam chuckles. "Oh, this is going to be fun. What do you have planned next?"

The next night I recruit Gavin's help.

"Hey." He opens the front door and eyes the boxes of lights in my hands. "You were serious? I thought when you asked me to help you with a lighting project, you meant get high and stare up at the stars."

I breeze past him to the kitchen, where I set the lights down on the island. "They're for Daisy."

Gavin pulls two beers from the fridge and offers me one. "I take it she still isn't talking to you then?"

"I ran into her at University Hall yesterday. She said hello, but no. Nothing after I sent the flowers."

He scans the boxes of twinkling lights in front of him and picks up one. "Okay then, what are we doing with these?"

Out in the back yard, we stare over the fence to Daisy's house, looking for movement inside. The lights are on, but we haven't seen anyone in the five minutes we've been watching.

"Give me a boost over," I say.

He links his hands together and holds them out for me to step on. Then he helps me over. I land on the other side with a thud. I hunch down by the tree house to make sure no one heard me, then Gavin hands over the lights.

"Oh shit. How are you going to get over?" I ask.

He grins. "Stand back."

He walks backward and then gets a running start before placing his hands on the top of the fence and leaping over it.

"Nice hops."

We hurry up into the tree house. My heart is racing being back here. Gavin hunches over in the small space. He hands me lights, and I hang them along the ceiling.

"You really like this chick, huh?" Gavin drops to a sitting position as I wrap the lights down the ladder.

"What gave me away?"

He laughs. "This is cool. I'd forgive you."

I glance up to find him staring at the house. I look over my shoulder and through the kitchen window. The top of Violet's head is visible in the living room.

"Do you ever think about doing something big to apologize to Violet?"

"I don't think there are enough lights in the world for that."

"I'm serious. What the hell really happened with you two?"

"Eh." He lifts the hat on his head and runs his hand through his black hair. "I fucked up. We had this really amazing night together. Ya know, those nights where you feel like the world has stopped, and it's just the two of you?"

He's staring at her and not me, but it doesn't matter. My thoughts are on Daisy anyway. "Yeah."

I swallow down a lump in my throat. Every day was like that up here in this tree house with Daisy.

"Anyway." He drops his gaze to the wood floor. "A few days later I got roped into this date auction thing with her roommate."

"And Violet assumed you were blowing her off for her roommate?"

He rubs his jaw. "Little worse than that."

"You slept with her roommate?"

The pained expression on his face tells me more than he does. "I was so drunk. I don't even remember it, but I woke up naked with her roommate, so yeah, I guess I did."

"Damn."

"Yeah. There's no walking back from that. I've apologized a million times. She hates me. Almost as much as I hate myself for it."

I finish hanging the last strand, and Gavin jumps down from the tree house.

"Where are we going to plug in the extension cord?" he asks, holding it up.

I motion toward his house.

"I should have known," he says dryly. He hops back over the fence, dragging the cord with him.

"Here we go," he says. "One, two, lights."

Chapter THIRTY-FOUR

Daisy

I was nervous about asking Violet to help throw a party when we were just coming off the failed Wallflower Ball that she put her heart and soul into, but she was completely on board.

It isn't like we've never had people over before, but I want to invite everyone—a real blow out party like the ones I watched from the tree house. I'm through wishing and waiting for my life to happen.

Over the next week, we transform our house together. Maybe other people can just invite people over and call it good, but not us. The four of us spend all our time working on it, from what alcohol to buy, to the playlist, and if we should clear out the living room for dancing. It feels good to have a hand in the creation of it instead of letting Violet do it all on her own. It feels more like something that belongs to all of us.

Tonight we're hanging lights from the living room ceiling like a canopy. We got the idea from Jordan and the lights he strung in the tree house.

I haven't had the heart to go up inside of it yet, but last night it looked beautiful from the window all lit up.

"Are we going to wear our dresses again?" Dahlia asks as she stands on a ladder waiting for me to hand her another strand of lights.

"No dress code," Violet says. "Come as you are."

"I'm wearing my dress," Jane says. "I got three numbers that night."

"What about the green one?" I ask.

She thinks for a minute. "Maybe I'll do a wardrobe change halfway through."

Vi smiles. "I'm wearing my dress, too, but I don't want people to feel like they need to dress up."

"Thank god," Dahlia says, and we all laugh.

"What did Jordan send today?" Jane asks as we finish and sit in the living room to admire our work.

"Nothing," Violet answers for me.

"Nothing?" Dahlia asks, a stunned expression on her face.

I'm a little surprised, too, but trying not to show it. Ever since I ran into him at University Hall, the gifts have come daily. Monday was a drawing with daisies, Tuesday was the tree lights, and last night a playlist he made just for me.

I've started to look forward to them. Not the gifts so much as knowing I'll have some interaction with him, even if it isn't directly. As much as I'd like to hold on to the anger and betrayal I felt when I realized he deceived me, I can't deny how good it feels to hear from him every day. I've missed him.

I can't decide if that means I should forgive him and let him back into my life or if this sudden resurgence of apology gestures are just to assuage his guilt for breaking my heart. I'm sure he could see it all over my face Monday—the heartbreak that lingers since I walked out of his dorm.

Honking outside tears me from my thoughts. It's continuous and impossible to ignore.

Violet groans. "What the hell are they up to now?"

She moves to look out the curtains toward The White House.

The honking continues, as well as music blaring.

"Uh, Daisy." She jogs to the front door and pulls it open.

The music and honking get louder. Dahlia and Jane rush to join her. I'm slower to my feet.

"Oh. My. Gosh." Jane punches each word and smiles as she looks back at me. "If you don't forgive him, you're crazy."

I finally get to the doorway, where I can see the parade of vehicles slowly rolling down our street. Their windows are down, and they drop daisies onto the sidewalk in front of the house. The music is coming from the back of the line, which I can't quite see, but the Shawn Mendes song gets louder with every passing vehicle.

"Is that the entire hockey team?" Jane asks.

I can only nod. Jordan's vehicle isn't among them, but I can see the last truck now—Liam's. I walk outside to the curb as he gets in front of the house. But it isn't Jordan in the passenger seat. It's some guy I don't recognize holding a handful of daisies.

Liam stops and turns down the music. The passenger hands me the flowers.

"You must be Daisy," he says.

"Where is he?" I ask.

"He isn't here," Liam says, and pulls a folded piece of paper from the dash. "He asked me to give you this."

I take it, and he rolls forward slowly.

"For what it's worth," he says, "I think you two are great together. Maybe not what either of you expected, but that's how it goes sometimes." He gives the guy in the passenger seat the briefest of glances and then nods to me. "Just thought you should know."

"Thanks, Liam." I step back, holding the paper in front of me.

The girls join me in the yard.

"What did he say?" Jane asks.

"He gave me this." I hold up the note and then unfold it slowly. Jordan's small handwriting greets me.

Daisy,

I'm so sorry. I know I don't deserve a second chance, but I'm hoping you'll give me one anyway. I wasn't lying when I said I love you.

x,

Jordan

"That's it?" Jane asks when I show them.

"I don't understand. Why didn't he come with them?" Dahlia looks to me for an answer.

Violet crosses her arms over her chest and stares at the ground.

My friends might not understand, but I do.

He's giving me room to decide what I want.

No gifts come Friday evening, but I don't have a chance to worry about it. Well, not much time anyway.

The party is tonight. There's a chance of rain again all week-end, so we focused our efforts inside. We moved all the furniture upstairs, all by ourselves, thank you very much, and the living room is our dance floor and mingle area.

In the kitchen, we set up a serve-yourself station with cases of champagne that Jane bought for the event.

I'm looking forward to it, but admittedly, I can't completely shake the memory of dancing with Jordan in my yellow dress. But I'm determined to have a good time tonight with my friends.

The four of us gather in the kitchen for a drink before everyone arrives.

"I have a little surprise," Dahlia says. She grabs a bag from the counter and pulls what looks like four small notebooks from it.

She hands one to each of us. The booklet is small with only a few pages and has a small golf pencil attached.

"What is it for?" Jane asks.

I flip open my booklet, and the giggle erupts as I read the first page. *Dances,* it says in a pretty, bold font, and then there are six numbered lines. "It's a dance card."

"Just like Elizabeth Bennett," Dahlia says proudly. "I don't really expect you to use them. I just thought they were fun."

"I'm totally using mine," Jane says. "It'll be a good place to get numbers."

Violet lifts her plastic champagne flute with a laugh (Jane also bought boxes of those—the heavy plastic kind that almost looks real). "To Elizabeth Bennett."

By midnight, our house is filled with classmates and friends, and friends of friends. Some dressed up, others are casual, but everyone is having a good time.

Jane has her dance card tucked into the cleavage of her dress, and as promised she's taking down numbers in it.

Dahlia is wearing one of her own creations. A baggy sweatshirt in a light gray with a black pleated skirt. She hangs off to the side of the dance floor, but she's smiling.

Violet steals the room in a black lacy dress that hits above her knee and bright purple heels. She and Jane are currently in the kitchen drinking champagne and talking to two guys that are friends with Eric.

And me, well, I'm watching it all with a bittersweet happiness stirring inside of me. I sit on a stair halfway up to give me a nice bird's-eye view, sipping champagne and sketching in my dance card. I glance up from time to time to make sure I'm getting the details just right. I don't want to forget this moment or the looks on my friend's faces.

Violet appears at the side of the staircase with a tipsy smile. "Daisy, there you are! Come dance with us."

She gives me a playful, pouty face, and then Jane joins in.

I tuck my dance card away and let them pull me to the center of the dance floor. Dahlia comes, too, and we form a circle, linking arms and belting out the lyrics to three or four songs in a row.

"I need a drink." I hold a hand to my dry throat. In the kitchen, I refill my flute and sip, letting the sweet bubbles dance on my tongue.

"This was perfect," Violet says, leaning her back against the counter and sighing. "Thank you for doing this."

"We all did it. Together."

"Yes, I know, but after the way things went down the last time, you had little reason to want to go through it all again."

"It wasn't the best night of my life," I admit. "But it made me realize how much we all needed it. You said it earlier this week, come as you are. And people did."

"Yeah," she says the word softly.

I bump my hip against hers. "Are you okay?"

"Yeah. Tonight has been a blast. I'm going to remember this forever, but I hate seeing you like this."

"I'm fine," I insist. "Or I will be."

"You didn't tell me that he said he loved you."

"He said a lot of things. Who knows how much of it was true?"

She nods. "Come with me."

She goes to the back door. The rain held off, but the temperature has dropped, and the wind has picked up.

I haven't gone out there since the night I screamed until I lost my voice, but I go with her now. She steps outside, and I follow, clutching my bare arms to my stomach as the breeze nips at my skin.

The tree house is lit up like it has been every night since Jordan strung the lights, but tonight lanterns pave a path from where we stand to the ladder. My heart squeezes in my chest. I can't see inside of the tree house, but I know he's there the same way I know my name.

"I don't know if he was telling the truth or not when he said that he loved you, but if he doesn't, then he's really committed to the lie." A small smile tugs at the corners of her mouth.

"But what about jocks being evil and all that?"

She laughs outright. "You know I don't really believe that. It's just easier to hate a collective group than letting one person have so much power over your emotions."

I get that.

Violet squeezes my arm. "No matter what, you always have me."

"And us," Dahlia says. I look back to see her and Jane in the doorway.

"You guys all knew about this?"

Vi shrugs. "I called him."

My eyes widen.

"If you really don't want to see him, I'll go tell him to leave, but if you're only staying away because of the things I said..." She looks down. "It wasn't fair of me to judge him because of something someone else did."

"He screwed up all on his own," I say.

"I know, and I've got one eye on him." Violet grins. "But you were happy. And that's all I want."

"All that *we* want for you," Dahlia says.

"I know a guy who knows a guy who has a cousin that works as a hitman," Jane says it loud enough that I'm sure Jordan can hear. "Just in case."

"I love you guys."

The three of them crowd around and hug me.

I let out a breath. "Now what?"

"Go hear him out," Dahlia encourages.

Jane squeezes my arm. "Good luck."

Chapter THIRTY-FIVE

Jordan

Her steps are light on the ladder. So quiet I almost miss the sound (it could also be that my heart is pounding so hard it's drowning out all other noise).

I go to the ledge and offer my hand. She slips her fingers into my palm, and my pulse jumps.

"Hey," I say in a rough scrape of my voice.

"Hi." Her blue eyes bore into mine, pupils wide. Her gaze flickers to the lights strung up from the ceiling before coming back to me.

"You look beautiful." I don't drop her hand. I glide my thumb along her finger, and she stares at our joined hands. "Sorry for showing up like this. It looks like some party in there."

She says nothing. I never felt like I needed to fill the silence between us before, but right now, I need something before I lose my mind.

My voice cracks as I continue. "I had to come see you in person and apologize again, and tell you something I should have said weeks ago. I want to be the guy that shows up for you. Tonight. Tomorrow. Every day. I want to be your person that's there for the good and bad, for all the fully clothed things. I've played it in my mind a million times. What if this or that, but I refuse to believe that there's any scenario that wouldn't have led me here. I love you, Daisy. In a sexy red dress, in white cotton panties, and everything in between. And I'm sorry that I wasn't honest with you, but I wouldn't wish it away either. Spending those nights studying with you changed my life." I take a breath. "That's it. That's my big speech."

I force myself to stop rambling and give her a chance to speak. It felt longer in my head, but now I worry it isn't enough. That I'm not enough.

Her bottom lip trembles. I resist the urge to lift the pad of my thumb to it. I'm perfectly still and waiting.

She's quiet for so long, I think, well, there's my answer. My heart drops. I knew there was a chance she didn't feel the same or couldn't forgive me, but I climbed up this tree, refusing to accept it. Swallowing thickly, I loosen my grip on her fingers and let my hand fall.

I didn't plan for this. Climbing down this ladder with a boner was more comfortable than standing here while she figures out how to tell me to fuck off.

I start to move my hands to my pockets at the same time she launches herself at me. Arms around my neck, Daisy crushes her body against mine, throwing me off balance and into the wall where she continues to press into me.

"Thank you for coming," she breathes the words against my jaw.

A whoosh of air leaves my lungs. "I thought you were about to kick me out of your favorite spot."

"It isn't my favorite spot anymore without you."

"I've missed you so much. I was trying to give you space, but—"

She shakes her head. "I like my space better with you in it."

"Oh, thank fuck."

A small lift of one corner of her mouth loosens the giant lump in my throat. She glances up to the ceiling. "The lights are beautiful."

"So are you."

A bigger smile spreads across her lips and she twirls her hips to make the red fabric swish around her. "I hoped wearing this dress would bring me luck again."

"Luck?" My brows pull together in confusion. "I thought you were mortified you sent those pictures."

"I was," she admits. "But it changed things between us. You saw me differently. Without it and without everything else, then maybe nothing would have happened between us. And as mad as I was, I wouldn't wish it away either. I love you too."

Her words hit me right in the chest, and I let out a long breath. Circling my arms around her waist, I lift her and spin around like I'm a kid on a sugar high. I am. On my sweet Daisy. When I put her down, she tilts her face up and I bring my mouth to hers.

I can't get close enough or kiss her deeply enough. I missed her so damn much. Tangling my hands in her hair, I groan as she sucks on my tongue and claws at my back like she's struggling with the inability to meld our bodies any tighter, too.

"This dress is too big," she complains. "I can't get any closer."

I glance down to the lacy layers bunched up between us. "In my fantasies, it was much easier to get under the skirt and still kiss you."

She laughs. Damn, it's the best sound.

"Be my date?" She inclines her head to the house.

"I left my suit and tie at home."

Her gaze sweeps over my jeans and tee, backward hat. With a smile, she says, "You'll do."

The rain starts as we are running inside—a hard downpour that soaks through my shirt. She pulls me through the kitchen and into the living room where people are standing around in groups, others dancing.

Her friends are in the middle and that's where she leads us. They scream and hug her when they see our linked hands. Then Daisy pulls me closer. She rests her hands on my shoulders and I wrap my arms around her waist. She lifts the hat on my head and sets it on hers.

"My hats always look better on you," I say. "Even when it says, 'I heart MILFs.'"

"What?" She takes it off and reads the front.

"You still have my other one," I say by way of explanation.

She shakes her head. "I love you, but I'm going to burn this hat."

But for tonight, she wears it. We dance, we kiss, she introduces me to some of her friends I haven't met yet, and it's perfect.

Later that night, Daisy is naked on top of me, a pile of red lace beside us. The rain stopped almost as soon as it started, but the cold front it brought with it makes the tree house chilly and breezy. The clouds block out the moon and stars, but the lights in the tree house shine down on us.

"We should go in before you fall asleep," I say, and pull the blanket up around her shoulders.

"Just a few more minutes." Her eyes are heavy and voice thick and quiet. "I missed this place. And you."

"All right." I let my eyes fall shut and I take a deep breath, breathing her in and relaxing. "Just for a few more minutes."

Or as long as she wants, whichever comes first.

Chapter THIRTY-SIX

Daisy

"Wow." Jane's eyes are wide with excitement as the final buzzer sounds. "That was amazing. And they won!"

"Have you never been to a sporting event?" Violet asks her.

Jane shakes her head, making her platinum blonde hair move around her shoulders.

"Not even in high school?" Dahlia asks.

"Hellooo," she says. "Fellow wallflower here."

Jane pulls a mini bottle of vodka from her bra to pour into her drink and then passes it to Violet.

"If you two get me kicked out of my boyfriend's game, I'll kill you." I shoot a glare at them and return my attention to where Jordan is celebrating with the rest of his team.

"Ooooh. Your *boyfriend*," Dahlia teases.

It never gets old. Who knew a silly label like boyfriend could feel so awesome?

"The game is over anyway." Jane stands. "And you're going to want us tipsy if we're going to the hockey party."

"I don't know," Vi says. "The more I drink, the less I filter what comes out of my mouth."

I take the cup from her and chug half of it. My throat burns, and I cough as I hand it back to her. "There."

Am I nervous that my friends are coming with me to a party at McCallum's apartment? Yes, yes, I am. But they're doing their best to be supportive, and I can't think of anything better than spending a Friday night with all my favorite people.

By the time we make it to the party, Jane has produced a bigger bottle from her purse, which she also shoves in her bra. She and Violet are giggling as I push open the door of the hockey guys' apartment. The same couple that was making out behind the door the last time I was here is at it again.

"Sorry," I say as the door nearly hits the guy in the back of the head. He doesn't so much as look up. That's real dedication.

We get a few looks from girls sitting in the living room. I recognize some of them. They don't look any friendlier than last time, but I care a lot less with my squad behind me.

"Wow," Jane says for at least the hundredth time tonight. "I'm at a college hockey party." She has no chill. I don't know if it's a super-rich person thing or what, but she walks into the apartment and squeals like she doesn't care that anyone can see how excited she is.

Jordan lifts a hand from the dining room table. His mouth pulls into a smile, and my stomach flips. I start in his direction.

He's on his feet and coming toward me in quick steps that mirror my excitement. Scooping me into his arms, he kisses me hard. I melt into him. I didn't know I could feel like this about someone. When he's around, I just can't stop smiling or feeling like my heart might burst.

Jane clears her throat behind us, and Jordan sets me down.

"Hey, ladies," he says. "Booze is in the kitchen."

"Then that's where we'll be," Violet says.

Jordan returns his attention to me. His eyes twinkle with excitement, and his smile is all charm. "Fuck the Dealer?"

"I was thinking power hour and maybe some dancing."

His brows raise. "Are you going to need me to carry you out of here tonight, sweet Daisy?"

"Who says I needed it last time? Maybe it was all a ploy to get you back to my room." I flutter my lashes.

He tips his head back and laughs. "The white cotton panty seductress."

My face heats.

With a wink, he juts his chin to my friends in the kitchen. "It doesn't look like your friends need any more liquid courage."

Jane pulls the bottle stashed in her bra and starts filling shot glasses. Dallas walks into the kitchen for a beer and lingers until they offer him one. In seconds, five more guys are crowding around.

Jordan leads me to the dining room table. Liam smiles as Jordan pulls a chair out across from him and guides me down on his lap.

"Hi." I wave to Liam. The guy next to him I recognize from the parade of trucks last week. He was the passenger in Liam's truck.

"Daisy, this is Cole." Liam rests an arm around the back of the guy's chair.

Cole leans forward and adjusts the ball cap on his head. "Nice to meet you. I've heard lots about you."

I stare at them a beat. "You too."

"Doubtful," he says with a grin he tosses at Liam.

Liam brings the hand resting behind him up to his neck. His fingers tenderly ruffle the reddish ends curled around his hat. It's a simple gesture, quick, but unmistakable and intimate.

"I meant it was nice to meet you."

Cole nods and sits back. Liam's arm goes around the back of the chair again.

Jordan circles my waist and places a kiss on my neck. "So, I figured out why Liam was so distracted at the beginning of the season."

I turn in his arms.

He offers me a sheepish grin.

"He was seeing Cole this whole time?"

Nodding, Jordan stares at me like he's waiting for me to be disappointed. I steal another glance at Liam. He looks happy. I hope he is. I am.

"You went to all the trouble to keep us apart for nothing."

"Nah. Not for nothing."

His mouth descends on mine, and he kisses me like he can't get enough. I guess that makes two of us.

"I love you," I say as I bring my hand up to his face and trace my thumb along his lower lip.

His mouth stretches into a big smile aimed right at me. "That's my line."

Chapter THIRTY-SEVEN

Daisy

About two months later

"ARE YOU SURE IT'S OKAY THAT I'M COMING?" VIOLET asks as Jordan drives us up the winding road.

It's a rare weekend he has off from practice and games, and we're camping on top of Mount Loken. Liam and Cole are meeting us there. Jenkins, too, with a girl he just started dating, Taylor. I haven't met her, but Jordan says she's nice and that I'll like her.

"Yes," I say for at least the third time since we left.

"I feel like I'm intruding on a couple's getaway."

"It's going to be a blast," I promise.

Jordan looks at her in the rearview mirror. "Jenkins has an extra tent."

"Good because, no offense, but I don't want to hear you banging my cousin."

"None taken." He looks back out to the road. "I plan to bang her a lot. Loudly."

Vi scrunches up her nose, and I give Jordan a playful smack on the arm.

Our friends were all busy this weekend. Dahlia had a golf tournament and Jane flew home to visit family. Violet decided camping was a better option than staying at home by herself. But just barely.

We're the first to arrive at the campsite. Jordan pitches our tent while Violet and I unload the rest of the stuff.

Liam and Cole show up next, and then Jenkins arrives. From the passenger side, a girl who I assume must be Taylor gets out, and then the back door opens. I yelp.

"What?" Violet asks.

I stare at Gavin unfolding himself from the small car and stretching. He scans the campsite and spots us.

I can't make words come out of my mouth, but when he waves, I lift my hand to reciprocate.

Violet swivels around, and I watch her expression slowly morph from confusion to shock to anger.

"What the hell is he doing here?"

"I don't know," I say quickly. "I promise. I had no idea he was coming. Jordan said he had a date or something."

Her eyes blaze with uncontained frustration. "Lucky girl. She dodged a bullet."

"Do you want to go? I can ask Jordan to take us back, or maybe Uber comes up here."

She shoots me a doubtful look. We're more than thirty minutes from Valley, and reception is sketchy.

"It's fine," she says, and goes back to moving stuff out of Jordan's SUV. "He isn't running me off. I was here first. I'll just avoid him for the next forty-eight hours."

When camp is set up, Jordan, Vi, and I go for a hike. Violet is taking pictures with her phone from the overlook. Jordan and I walk farther down the trail, where it narrows and drops. A big rock perches next to us, but it's too steep for me to climb.

"I think I'm good here." I stop, and he takes a step, tugging me behind him closer to the dropoff.

"I won't let anything happen to you."

He grabs me by the waist and lifts me onto the rock. His hand goes to my ass, steadying me while I crawl to the middle and sit. He's right behind me and sits beside me. Valley is off in the horizon.

"I feel so insignificant up here."

"Not to me." He bumps his shoulder against mine and takes off the backpack he was wearing.

He hands me his water bottle and then unzips the backpack.

"Got anything good in there?" I ask. All the hiking made me hungry.

He pulls out chips, beef jerky, and then with a grin, a candy necklace.

I take it from him and put it on. His eyes flash with desire as I nibble on a candy bead.

"I brought this too." He hands me my sketchbook and pencils.

I flip it open eagerly. When I packed it for the weekend, I imagined getting up early and sketching while he was still sleeping or maybe when he was off doing stuff with the guys. "What about you?"

"Oh, don't worry about me. I know how to keep myself occupied." He moves my hair away from my neck and places a kiss just above my new candy accessory. His teeth wrap around my necklace, and goosebumps dot my arms.

I don't get very much sketching done.

Later at camp, we grill burgers and hot dogs, and then gather around a small fire. Jenkins brought a speaker and plays music while the eight of us share stories and roast marshmallows.

Violet sits next to me with her knees pulled up to her chest. She's managed to mostly avoid Gavin today, but I can tell she's still feeling his presence. He's quieter than normal, too, drinking from a bottle of Jager that never leaves his hand.

"We should play cards or something," Liam says.

"I think I'm gonna go to bed," Vi says.

"Your bag is still in the SUV," Jordan says, and tosses her the keys.

"Thanks." She lets her head fall on my shoulder. "See you in the morning."

"Night."

She retrieves her bag from Jordan's vehicle, then takes it with her to the bathrooms not far off on the main grounds.

Liam grabs a deck of cards from his tent, and we move our chairs closer together.

"Don't deal me in on this one," Gavin says. "I'm going for a walk."

He stands with his bottle dangling from his fingers.

"Are you good?" Jenkins asks him. "Want some company?"

He gives his head a shake. "All good. Probably heading to bed after. Which tent is mine?"

I nuzzle closer to Jordan as Jenkins gets Gavin squared away on the sleeping arrangements.

"I think I might be ready for bed too," Jordan whispers in my ear and hooks a finger around my necklace.

He's been nibbling on it all day. Slowly, and a little bit torturous.

He kisses my neck, leaving a trail of warm kisses along my skin. He slides a hand under the bottom of my sweatshirt, and his cold fingers travel up until he finds the hook of my bra. It gives under his touch, and he brings a palm around to cover my breast.

"Jordan?" Liam's voice interrupts our makeout sesh like it isn't the first time he's said his name.

My boyfriend doesn't move his hand but looks up. "Yeah?"

Liam chuckles. "Are you two playing?"

Jordan deflects the question to me with a glance.

"One game."

We settle on Fuck the Dealer with a minimum ten-second drink wager. Jordan has the deck, and Liam is up. I'm nuzzled into my boyfriend's side, giving me a view of the cards as he places them on the table. Liam gets the first two wrong. He glances at me before he decides on his final card. It's a nine, and the last card was an eight, and I can see the hesitation on his face. Moving my other hand just above the table, I point my thumb up.

"Higher," he says.

Jordan flips the card with a groan, and Liam grins as we count to ten while Jordan drinks. Cole goes next, and I do the same thing, forcing Jordan to drink for ten more seconds. Taylor isn't playing, but Jenkins guesses the right suit on the very first card, no cheating needed.

"Fuck." Jordan finishes off his beer with another long chug.

"The dealer," I say with a smirk. "My turn."

Jordan angles his body to keep me from seeing the cards. Liam gets up to get another beer as Jordan shuffles and lays out three for me. I do not have the same good luck as Jenkins, but when Jordan flips over the third card, a five, Liam lifts both arms like he's stretching and gives me a thumbs down with his right hand.

Jordan catches me looking at Liam and follows my gaze. Liam doesn't drop his hand fast enough. He tries to play it off, but that nice guy smile turns into a devious smirk.

"You," Jordan says, tossing the cards down. He stands and looks at me, jaw dropped. "And you. My own girlfriend. You're totally going to pay for that." He grabs me around the waist and lifts me over his shoulder.

"Nice playing with you," he says dryly before hustling off toward our tent.

"Sorry, man," Liam calls after him. "Don't go. We'll play nice."

Jordan smacks my ass before setting me on our blankets inside the tent.

"I can't believe you, sweet Daisy." He pulls his sweatshirt over his head.

"I'm sorry. We can go back, and I promise I won't cheat."

"Oh, please cheat, baby. It'll make it sweeter when I torture you until you scream my name so loud the entire campsite hears you."

He crawls on top of me, sliding one hand back under my sweatshirt and my still unhooked bra. The material bunches up around my chest, and he pushes it higher, forcing me to raise my arms. He leaves me tangled in my sweatshirt and bra with my hands above my head.

He goes to work removing my jeans while I try to wriggle the rest of the way out of my sweatshirt and bra. I'm not as successful as him, and when his mouth covers my pussy, I stop caring that my arms are restrained.

I arch into him, and he brings me to the brink of orgasm, body trembling. A scream outside stops us both.

"Was that Violet?" I ask, scrambling on my hands and knees to unzip the tent.

My heart is racing as I stick my head out to check on my friend. She's two tents down, hair piled into a bun on top of her head and in sleep shorts and a tank top yelling at a shirtless Gavin.

"What the hell?" she screeches. "This is my tent."

"No, this is *my* tent," he replies.

The rest of our camp has gathered to see what the yelling is about.

Violet and Gavin both look to Jenkins. He rubs at his jaw and fights a smile. "Yeah, sorry, I forgot."

"You forgot?!" Violet's eyes are wild as she narrows them at him. "Forgot what?"

"I promised you the tent before I knew that Gavin was coming, but it's actually his tent."

"See?" Gavin says, and pushes past her back inside the tent.

"Oh no, get out of there." Her voice trails off as she follows him.

Jordan chuckles and kisses my shoulder. "Well, that's going to be interesting."

"I should probably go check on her."

"In a minute," he says. "You haven't finished fucking the dealer."

Epilogue

Jordan

HERE'S THE THING ABOUT LOVING SOMEONE LIKE Daisy. She makes me want to be a better person. That's it. That's the thing. Sounds like a cheesy slogan, I know. But it isn't just about being a better human. It's in the details.

I work harder at everything—not just the things that used to matter to me like friendship, partying, and hockey. I've become a badass in the kitchen (I grill a mean steak and my spaghetti sauce is chef's kiss perfection), I'm the fixer of things around the house, the killer of spiders (I let them free outside, shhh), the loud and sometimes crazy, but above all, I'm whatever she needs.

I think that's the most important thing I've learned. People need different things at different times in their life. But what hasn't changed in the five years since I met Daisy is my need for her. And my desire to give her everything she needs.

Every day, she amazes me, teaches me something, and loves

me harder than I ever thought someone could. And man, do we have fun.

Case in point, today. We're having a huge party at our house. It's the off-season, and I'm enjoying a couple of months at home with my wife. Yep, that's right. You may now refer to Daisy as Mrs. Thatcher. I'm not sure she knows what she got herself into. Or maybe she does. She's way smarter than me.

Some of my teammates are here, along with our friends. The weather is perfect, the pool is ready, and the beer is ice cold. As soon as I find my gorgeous wife, I have a long afternoon of nothing but fun and sun planned.

"Daisy!" I yell as I enter the house through the back deck. The downstairs is quiet, so I head up the steps.

"Baby?" I check all the rooms as I make my way down the hall to our master bedroom. "I need your ass in that pool, sweet Daisy."

The en suite bathroom light is on, door open.

"Are you in here?" I ask without going in.

"Y-yeah." Her quiet voice transports me back in time. These days, she's not so timid—at least not around me.

"Is everything okay?" I peer in carefully to find her sitting on the edge of the bathtub in her cute little yellow bikini.

"I'm fine. I'll be down in a minute." The corners of her mouth lift, but I know a bullshit smile when I see one from my girl.

"You're not fine. What's wrong?"

She stands and tries to pass off another fake smile. "Everyone is downstairs. Go." She shoos me. "I'll be down in five."

"Nice try." I pull her into my arms and lock my hands behind her back so she can't get free. "What's up, baby?"

Her stubborn little mouth pulls into a thin line like she thinks she's going to get away without telling me.

"We have a house full of people," she says.

"Ask me if I care?" I brush my lips against hers. "Everyone is having a blast. Everyone but you. So tell me, what's up? Let me fix it, and then we can have a blast too." I focus on her boobs which are bursting out of the little, tiny top. Damn. I bring my face down and bury it in her cleavage. "This bikini should be illegal."

I move my head to lightly bite a nipple, and she jumps back and cups her boobs. "Ouch."

"Oh shit, I'm sorry."

"It isn't your fault," she says quickly. "I mean it is. I'm... I'm pregnant."

"Say what now?" My gaze goes from her face to her tits, which I can't stop staring at. Did they get bigger, or is that bikini just some sort of magical push-up wonder?

"I'm pregnant," she says again, and this time it sinks in. *Pregnant. Baby. Holy shit.*

"We're having a baby?"

She nods, that unsure smile still plastered on her face. "I know we were going to wait. I don't know how it happened. I'm still on the pill, and I take it every day at the exact same time. Always right after we have morning sex. Every day, the same time."

Happy laughter spills out of me. Yeah, sex every morning and most nights too might be the problem. I got an A in statistics and probability, after all. "This is amazing."

"It is?"

I hug her to me and spin around. Then it all hits me, I mean *really* hits me, at once, and my stomach gets a little queasy. "Oh shit."

I drop her and stumble back to sit on the side of the bathtub. "I'm going to be a father. I'm going to be responsible for a tiny, helpless human."

"You're going to be an amazing father. Just like you're an amazing husband." She squats down in front of me, and my gaze goes back to her boobs. It's an unfortunate time to be noticing, I realize, but seriously.

"Did your boobs get bigger?"

"Right?" she asks and looks down at her chest. "They're huge and so sensitive. I almost cried getting my sports bra off this morning after yoga. I thought I was dying or something, but apparently, it's normal during pregnancy."

"Pregnant." I rest my hands on her hips and let my thumbs glide over her smooth stomach.

"Yeah. I just took five tests, to be sure. You're not mad?"

"Mad?" I shake my head. "No, sweet Daisy. I'm anything but mad. I'm just stunned. Holy shit, baby, we're having a baby."

She slides onto my lap and hugs me around the neck.

"Are you feeling okay? Do you need anything? Oh man, we need to get stuff and paint the spare room. Oooh, we need a tree house and—"

She kisses me mid-sentence. A real smile finally pulls at her lips. "I'm great, and we have lots of time. How about today we go enjoy the party?"

"I can do that." I stand, carrying her in my arms, out of our bedroom and downstairs.

"Jordan, I can walk," she says as she clings to me.

I don't set her down until we're outside among our friends and my teammates. The music is loud, but I'm louder.

"We're having a baby!" I yell over the noise in our back yard, and then I kiss my girl as everyone cheers and calls out around us.

Excitement and nerves pulse through me, but I'm not worried. With Daisy, I know life is always going to be sweet.

Playlist

- "Meet Me At Our Spot" by The Anxiety, Tyler Cole, and Willow
- "Ghost Town" by Benson Boone
- "Shivers" by Ed Sheeran
- "Don't Be Shy" by Tiësto and Karol G
- "Have Mercy" by Chlöe
- "Hailey" by Wrenn
- "Don't Want My Heart" by Sarah Cothran
- "Life Got Crazy" by Mike.
- "That's What I Want" by Lil Nas X
- "Daisy" by Ashnikko
- "Hero" by Faouzia
- "What A Shame" by Leyla Blue
- "Love Story" by Sarah Cothran
- "abcdefu" by Gayle
- "Treat You Better" by Shawn Mendes
- "Bad Chick" by Liv Grace Blue
- "It'll Be Okay" by Shawn Mendes
- "Crazy in Love" by Beyoncé
- "Candy" by Machine Gun Kelly feat. Trippie Redd

Also by
REBECCA JENSHAK

Campus Nights Series

Secret Puck

Bad Crush

Broken Hearts

Wild Love

Smart Jocks Series

The Assist

The Fadeaway

The Tip-Off

The Fake

The Pass

Wildcat Hockey Series

Wildcat

Wild about You

Standalone Novels

Sweet Spot

Electric Blue Love

About the AUTHOR

Rebecca Jenshak is a *USA Today* bestselling author of new adult and sports romance. She lives in Arizona with her family. When she isn't writing, you can find her attending local sporting events, hanging out with family and friends, or with her nose buried in a book.

Sign up for her newsletter for book sales and release news.

WWW.REBECCAJENSHAK.COM

Made in the USA
Monee, IL
30 April 2022